IT WAS THE ONE THING THE MOUNTAIN MEN FEARED MOST . . . DEATH BY FIRE . . .

Fanning out on the open ground and driven by the wind was a wall of flame perhaps a quarter of a mile wide and growing. Kit kept his shivering mount clamped tightly between his legs. The horse smelled the fire, too, the scent of death on racing tongues of flame.

Suddenly the animal reared, whinnying in fright. Kit tugged at the halter rope and looked around to see what had frightened the horse. What he saw made his blood run cold.

The fire was less than ten miles away. A herd of buffalo was on this side of the wall of flame. In the dull glow, Kit could pick out dozens of the black, humped beasts moving now like thundering mountains toward the stream where his men were camped.

"Stampede!" he roared. Wheeling his horse, Kit raced flat out toward the campsite.

"Buffalo stampede!" His men looked up in alarm at their leader, barely understanding the sense of his words. All further commands were lost, as the earth shook with a sudden roar. A blinding flash struck the tree nearest Kit, and he was thrown to the ground ten feet away. The cottonwood trembled as a great cracking sound was heard. The tree split in two, falling away from its own center as cleanly as if a giant axe had been swung through it. . . .

KIT CARSON
TRAPPER KING

KIT CARSON
TRAPPER KING

Laura Parker

A Dell/Banbury Book

Published by
Banbury Books, Inc.
37 West Avenue
Wayne, Pennsylvania 19087

Dell ® TM 681510, Dell Publishing Co., Inc.

ISBN: 0-440-04584-3

Printed in the United States of America
First printing—May 1982
Second printing—November 1982

FOR ROSE.
THANKS.

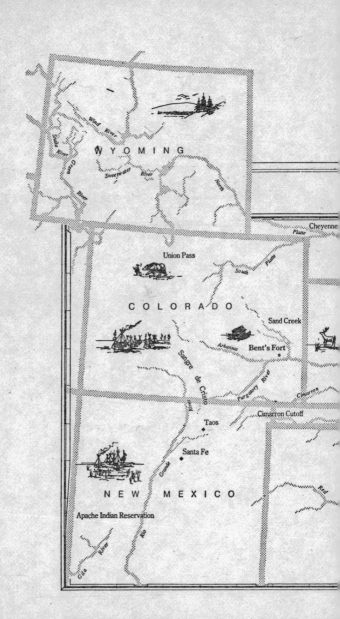

WYOMING

Wind River

Snake River

Green River

Sweetwater River

Cheyenne

Platte

Union Pass

South Platte

COLORADO

Sand Creek

Arkansas

Bent's Fort

Sangre de Cristo

Purgatory River

Cimarron

Cimarron Cutoff

Taos

Santa Fe

Rio Grande

NEW MEXICO

Red

Apache Indian Reservation

Gila River

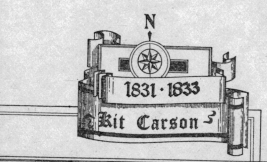

N

1831 · 1833

Kit Carson

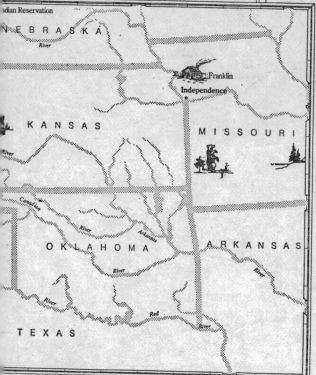

Indian Reservation

NEBRASKA

River

Franklin

Independence

KANSAS

MISSOURI

River

Canadian

River

Arkansas

OKLAHOMA

ARKANSAS

River

River

River

Red

TEXAS

River

Chapter 1

The pink-stuccoed walls of San Fernandez de Taos gleamed like a beacon across the broad valley in the late afternoon sun. The young man drew a weary breath of relief. He was going home. After months of wandering as far south as Chihuahua, after working the stinking hot copper mines of the Gila River as a teamster, he finally was going home.

"Damn stupid greenhorn!" he chided himself. "That's what you are, Christopher Carson, letting the lure of euchre take your last peso. Now your belly's grumblin' and you ain't got a thing to fill it with."

Earlier in the week he had crossed the bald humps of the orange-pink hills just north of Santa Fe. They were studded with pinyon trees; his mouth watered at the thought of the many tasty dishes the half-breed women of the territory could prepare from the roasted nuts of those trees. Hunger leaped in him again at the thought of beef and potatoes served up with a black bottle of *aguardiente*. That had always been a favorite meal at Ewing Young's American House in Taos.

The youngster chuckled. Hell, he should know about such meals. For one long winter a year back he had been cook and bottle-washer for Young. He had learned to turn buffalo, antelope, mountain goat, bear and even panther meat into succulent stew that Americans and many a ranchero had found too tempting to pass up.

As a trickle of sweat traced a path along his dusty cheek, the boy squinted against the brittle sunlight. Three years had passed since he had left his home in Franklin, Missouri. He had had hopes of becoming a frontiersman like Andrew Jackson, or perhaps like his own personal hero, Daniel Boone. He could almost laugh at himself now. Almost.

Jerking impatiently on the reins of the burro he straddled, he urged her forward with Spanish words. At eighteen years of age, it was tough to face up to defeat. But he couldn't kid himself. The half-empty pouch hanging around his neck revealed the fact that he was no richer than he had been the day he ran away. Money never had a habit of finding its way into his pockets. There were always food, shelter and liquor to be had, and women to be pacified.

At the thought of women, he felt a rush of heat spin through him. Eighteen certainly was not a great age of experience where the ladies were concerned. But there had been that sloe-eyed señorita from Santa Fe the winter he had been a cook. Not only had she taught him Spanish, but also a new kind of hunger, the kind that made a man yearn for a woman. The mysteries she had revealed stayed with him long after she had given up interest in him.

Just thinking about the Spanish girl kept the youngster occupied as his mount covered the plains that led into town. Once there, the sight of his adopted home made him forget everything else.

Taos fit in perfectly with his notion of what a frontier town should be. He loved the adobe houses. Some had walls so bright they hurt the eye; others were crumbling into ruin and had canvas flung over their flat roofs to keep out the wind and rain. Narrow, unpaved streets wound through the tightly-packed houses, leading eventually to the plaza where he was headed.

He ignored the catcalls of the bold women who lounged in the shade of their doorways. Sultry and eager they were, but as dangerous as the climate in which they thrived, Carson thought.

"Hey! Gringo!" a woman hailed as he rode past. Her dark-brown eyes looked seductive as she gazed at him invitingly. Carson hid his blush in the shade of his flat-brimmed hat.

A skinny dog darted out of a doorway as the boy kicked his burro into a trot and clattered past; it seemed to bark more out of habit than real desire for a chase. The air held the heat of a midsummer sun that was disappearing behind the hills and slanting long shadows across the land. The accumulation of refuse in the streets lent its unmistakable odor to the thin wind that girded the high valley. To the boy, all of this meant home. He wanted to find work here. If he couldn't, then he would have to head back to Missouri.

Pulling up short, he dismounted in front of one of the larger adobe buildings that flanked the square. From the doorway, set back so far in the thick wall that it seemed to be a tunnel, he heard laughter and raised voices—American voices. Quickly he swung off his mount, hitched up his trousers and swung his father's old flintlock onto his shoulder before marching in.

The room was large. A rough-hewn wooden bar ran the length of one wall. Around the tables that filled the floor were men who held his future in their hands.

He strode right up to the only one he knew, the proprietor of American House, Ewing Young. "Howdy, Cap'n Young," he greeted.

Ewing Young, a large, middle-aged man, was one of the few enterprising Americans with enough cunning to make illegal trapping in New Mexico profitable. Ewing raised his head and looked into the eyes of the short, stocky youngster with the shadow of whiskers beginning to tickle his chin. "Why hello there, Kit Carson," Young said, a grin spreading in the midst of his thick beard. "Where you been?"

"I come to offer you this here rifle." Kit swung the flintlock from his shoulder and laid it quietly on the table in front of his former boss. "It ought to buy a meal or two."

Young sized up the situation instantly. He had seen that gaunt look in faces like Kit's many times before. It was because of his experience with young men like Carson that he had opened up American House. Another reason for starting his program here was the cover it gave his illegal trapping arrangements. American House kept him one step ahead of the Mexican authorities. They had little sympathy for gringos who trapped in their territory without license or taxation.

"Well, son," Young began, "you sure look whiskey-dry and spindly. Take a chair. Jasper?" Young addressed the skinny young boy behind the counter. "Get this here boy a plate of grub. Won't have it said Ewing Young don't have enough hospitality to go 'round."

A minute later a tin plate of fried potatoes, dried jerky and fresh white bread was set before Kit, and he dug in with his fork. Slowly, the hot food and the bottle of Spanish rum jolted him back from the fog of near starvation and thirst.

"Now, son," Young said gently after Kit had pushed his plate back. "Keep your mouth shut and hear good what I got to say."

Young's eyes surveyed the rest of the men in the room. They had become unusually quiet since Carson's entrance. "Now, listen you fellas. You know why I called you here."

Grunts of agreement rumbled through the group of men, and Kit looked around more carefully. They were trappers, this motley bunch. He studied the long, fringed buckskins and Hawken rifles. The guns were tucked casually under the trappers' arms, even as they ate in the relative safety of the cool, dark room. Mountain men. How he envied them and longed to be one himself. That was why he'd come West—to be the best, richest trapper the territory had ever seen. All he needed was the chance.

The humiliation of defeat still gnawed at him. For a moment, he imagined that every man present had to know how miserably he had failed. What a pitiable sight he must be. He'd told himself that the failure was not completely his fault. How could he trap successfully without equipment and experience? And he had gotten neither. No one had risked time or money on such an unlikely candidate as Kit Carson.

At five feet six inches and one hundred twenty pounds, Kit knew he did not fit the image of the typical mountain man. But he could be as good as any one of them. He knew he could.

". . . got to be done!" The final words of Young's speech rang out and swept Kit's attention back to what was being discussed.

"Make 'em come, that's what this child says!" the lanky Kentucky man named Gibbon roared from his place at the bar. "Owe 'em one on account of Tim. Mighty fine child, he was. Reckon he deserved more than bein' shot full of arrows."

"Damn Apaches!" muttered his partner. "If we don't teach 'em no different, there won't be none of us left!"

Young heaved his full-bellied frame from the chair. "Like Gibbon says, if we don't retaliate against the Apache raid on our last brigade last month, them red devils will think they've scared us off for good." He looked slowly around the room, judging the number of men listening to him to be about forty. "There's a good-sized posse here," he said finally. "How many are for ridin' up to the Gila at next light to teach the Apaches what's what?"

The frustrated mutterings that had underscored all the remarks spoken until then exploded into war whoops and shouts of delight.

"That's for showin' 'em!"

"This here boy knows what's what!"

"Apache hair'll set up right fine on my new leggings!" Gibbon joined in. He spat a stream of tobacco juice that cleared three feet before ringing the spittoon at the end of the bar. "Here's for dead Indians!"

Kit's face fell. He realized what a slim chance he had of joining the fight. He was not one of Young's trappers, and Young had never indicated that he was either old or strong enough to be included in any special plans. Tonight, Young would be the last to think that Kit was experienced enough to ride square into battle with the fiercest warriors in the Southwest.

"It's the only way to do it, Cap'n," exclaimed a wolfish trapper who came up and slapped Young on the back. "Nothin' them darned Spaniards are gonna take care of. Too busy shinin' their silver spurs to care how many of our boys go under. Got to treat them red devils like they deserve. Aim to throw not a few of them plumb center with Bess here." He patted the butt of his buffalo gun affectionately.

When the trapper moved back to the bar, Young turned to Kit. He saw the glimmer of excitement in the boy's eyes. And Kit's clenched jaw could not mask the sullen expression that meant he was broke again, half-starved and without prospects.

Young could not help but smile at Kit. The boy had guts. For nearly three years he had watched him tackle jobs that his own trappers thought were beneath them.

Kit had cleaned hides, mended saddles and wagons, rustled up grub, and done everything he could just so he could stay out on the frontier. Young's eyes searched the young, freckled face. The boy was still just a child at heart behind those ruddy features. But those callused hands of his were as strong and as steady as those of any other man present. "You once told me you could pick a fly off a wall with that there rusty ol' museum piece you call a rifle, Kit," Young said, a new idea perking. "You still know how?"

Kit met the man's inquiry with a quick shrug. "You want to hire me to keep flies off your meat, Cap'n Young?"

"Maybe." Young allowed a moment to lapse. "Actually, I was of a mind to hire that there gun o' yours for huntin' a different kind o' varmint."

"What do you have in mind, Cap'n," Kit asked, scarcely daring to breathe.

"Well," Young said, trying to contain his amusement, "you been thinkin' about headin' back for Missouri, ain't you? It'd be an almighty shame you leavin' just when I can use all the good men I can find. If you came along with me and the boys, you might find you'd take a shine to fightin' Indian-style."

Young beckoned to Kit, and the boy leaned over the table. "Just between you and me," Young whispered, "Apaches ain't all we're after. The Mexican authorities don't like me trappin' in their territory. Revoked my license long ago. Fighting Apaches is a fine excuse to ride out of Taos with all my men and full gear without rousin' the soldiers. First we hunt Apache, then we go for beaver."

Young chuckled to himself as Kit struggled to maintain the calm exterior expected of a frontiersman. "Well," he began slowly, fearing that his voice would crack in his delight, "reckon I ain't got my heart set that hard on Missouri just yet, at least not if you really need an extra man." Suddenly his face turned grim. How could he pay for his food and equipment without shaming himself by asking for money?

"If it's pay you're wonderin' about," Young said smoothly, "you ought to know I'm a hard boss. You'll be expected to up out of your wages at the end of the season for the supplies I'm providing you at the start. Sign your name to an IOU, same as the others."

"For truth?"

The guileless question set Young's belly to shaking with laughter. "For truth, son. Maybe you'll add a notch or two to your rifle butt before this wrangle is over."

"Yes, sir!" Kit replied smartly. He was already dreaming of the glory of the battle to come.

By dawn the party of volunteers had gathered together under the portal of American House. Rifles had been newly oiled and wiped clean. Pack mules were securely loaded with possibles, powder and shot. Beneath these, illegal beaver traps were hidden.

Kit took his cue from the men around him. He went about the business of loading his new pack mule with calm assurance. Still, he could not completely shake his nervousness. Each glance in the direction of the Mexican soldiers who had been consistently watching Ewing Young's place started him quaking.

"Just keep 'hellfiring' and 'goddamning' the Apaches till we get them Spaniards off our tails," Young had admonished his men. "And, remember. Them Apaches is camped near the Cimarron—United States territory."

The trappers had listened well. Kit saw a few of

them go so far as to offer some of the soldiers a swig from their cups. Geniality, indeed, from a mountain man.

"Saddle up!" Young roared from the doorway of American House as the sun began to rise over the hills. The expedition had begun.

They traveled quickly the first two days, covering more than fifty miles in the hills northeast of Taos. Kit rode his mount in relative comfort, having drawn a place near the head of the caravan. From time to time he looked back to check on the two platoons of Mexican soldiers that were following them. "Think they're ever gonna get enough of our dust and droppings, Cap'n?" he asked Young, riding beside him on the third morning.

Young's grin cracked the mask of dust that covered his face. "It takes them sons o' bitches some time to get goin'. Once they start up, it's like herdin' buffalo to get them reined in again. Patience, son. There's nothin' worse gonna happen than us gettin' a few extra guns in the battle on our side. Course, they'll like turn tail soon enough, if it comes to a real fight."

On the morning of the fourth day, dawn broke to the sounds of sharp Spanish commands, coupled with rattling reins and snorting horses. In the same instant, Kit opened his eyes and drew his brand new Green River skinning knife. But it was not an emergency that called the men to mount. The Mexican platoons were pulling out, leaving the taciturn mountain men to fight their war with the Indians.

"Well, that takes care of that," Young exclaimed in broad satisfaction. He watched the soldiers in the blue coats disappear over the rise to the south.

"That mean we ain't for Indians after all?" one of his men inquired.

"Sure thing," Young shot back. "Never take a lickin' from no Indians if you ever expect to set foot in their territory again. We got business up north just like I said."

The next two days of hard riding, along with Young swearing at his men and pack mules alike, were evidence of the tough stand Young took as brigade leader. The hills of Sangre de Cristo gave way to broad, grassy plains. Then, on the fifth day, they reached the sandy stretch of the Cimarron Desert that loomed before them.

Buffalo had been spotted on the plains a day earlier, and none of Young's men were surprised when, not long after dawn, they crossed paths with a mob of men and burros scurrying across the open ground. Kit raised himself in his stirrups for a better look. He had encountered these Mexican buffalo hunters many times before, but never before had he seen them in such an uproar. "Lord! They're churnin' up the plains fit to be a twister!" Kit said as he watched the stampeding caravan. "What you figure they're runnin' from, Cap'n?"

Young called a halt to his own brigade and sent three of his scouts out to intercept the hunters before replying to Kit's question. "Got to be Indian trouble. Only thing that can scatter a caravan that size."

Within an hour, Young's words were confirmed by the buffalo hunters themselves. The two brigades had drawn up to share counsel.

Though he often had passed them on the plains, this meeting offered Kit his first real opportunity to study these adventurers. The first thing that impressed him was their clothes. Each man of the hundred or so who had joined them wore a leather jacket and tight trousers that were unbuttoned halfway up the side of each leg to allow for freer movement. Flat-brimmed straw hats or glazed sombreros were the headgear that shielded swarthy faces. The men wore heavy mustaches. Their weapons were muskets, which were wide-barreled and plugged with wads of straw to keep out the prairie dust. In Kit's view, the flamboyance of their costumes rivaled even the Indians' ceremonial clothing.

"Thousands, señor! The hills are crawling with Apaches!" the hunters' spokesman declared. "*Los Americanos*, they will never make it to safety. Huge heavy wagons, slow oxen, like lambs for the slaughter."

This news, the first to be gleaned from the more than thirty minutes of garbled conversation, caused Young to lift a silencing hand. "Americans? Gringos? Where?"

"Behind us," answered the hunter, pointing northeast. "The Apaches, they await the sign from the spirit, and then. . . ." Suddenly he slammed his palms together with a loud smack. "Los gringos, they are no more."

"Must be Will Bent and his brother Charles," Young murmured offhandedly. "That'd be just like them two, settin' out across Mexican territory without the American army at their backs." Young cursed under his breath, then broke into deep laughter. "That kind of guts shouldn't go unappreciated. No, sir! Saddle up! *Levez! Levez!*" he roared and came to his feet.

"Por favor, what will you do, Señor Young?" the spokesman asked in alarm.

"I'm just goin' to help out an old competitor. The Bent brothers are of a mind to set up permanent American trade down Santa Fe way. I wouldn't want it said that I just sat back scratchin' while them Apaches picked 'em off. I can beat the competition fair and square. If you men knew what was good for you, you'd climb into your saddles and stick with us a while."

"Señor, we are not the army," the spokesman protested.

Young gave the young man a long look, then shrugged. "Fine. Do what you like. But to be fair to yourselves, you'd best think on what them Apaches are liable to do once we run 'em off. Once they smear on war paint, they ain't gonna wipe it off till they got something to celebrate. If it ain't gringos they scalp, Spaniards' hair will look just as good on their leggings."

Kit had gone immediately to his own mount. No one was more surprised than he when, a few minutes later, the buffalo hunters were back on their own horses, plodding along behind. For the rest of the day, he threw sidelong glances of admiration at his boss. Young had a way with men. That was obvious. He didn't yell or threaten. He merely spoke calmly, then let a man decide for himself.

Kit sucked in a quick breath. A thousand Apaches. Well, an arrow in the back was as ugly as a bullet. He hoped the hunters appreciated the odds. Their fusees would help even them.

Dark set in before the Bent caravan was observed along the horizon. Young kept the men in their saddles. "Our only chance," he told Kit, "is to surprise them under cover of night. The Apaches won't attack in the dark. We sure have to be careful 'round here. There's little room to hide ourselves."

Kit's eyes, long accustomed to broad vistas, were the first to pick out movement in the distant camp. "Leastways, they're alive," he told Young.

Young's more experienced eyes told him that while Kit's observation was true, the ragged defense line of the wagons indicated the plight of the Americans. "Wouldn't have lasted another day," Young said to his men. "We make camp here. Yes, damnit!" he swore before there were any protests. "In the open! If we was to ride in there now, them Bent folk would fill us full of lead before they knew we was the rescuers. Now camp!"

The men began to settle down for an uneasy night. "Come the first glimmer of dawn," Young lectured, "we send a man up to Bent's caravan. A couple more we send to scout out the area. The Apaches will know that Bent is about to collapse. They'll figure to wait till the sun is high overhead before they attack again. And what we've got to find out, meantime, is where they are. Once we know, we'll beat them Indians at their own game."

At dark, Kit wrapped himself in his Navaho blanket for the night. But, on the hard ground, without even the meager comfort of a campfire, he couldn't sleep. At least, he wasn't afraid of dying. Like he had once heard a grizzled old trapper boast, "You kin only go under once. Besides, hell's bound t' be full of Indians!" No, he would not have come West had he feared for his life. It was his honor that would be at stake at dawn. He had been hired to fight Indians, something he had never done before. He had never killed a man. Would he be proud of himself when the day was over?

An hour before sunrise, the Young camp bristled with activity. There was no need this day for the familiar wake-up command of, "Levez! Levez!" The awareness that there was a village of one thousand Apaches camped within an hour or two's ride had kept most of the men awake all night. And the few men brave enough to doze had dreamed vividly of past close calls.

Though most of the men preferred to sit crosslegged on the ground until Young's call to battle sent them hopping for their saddles, Kit paced and stared at his companions. Most of the men were Americans, clad in buckskin like himself. Some, though, were Frenchmen wearing plaid wool shirts and leather trousers with Indian capotes and knit hats to see them through the worst weather. Others undoubtedly were born and bred on the frontier. Kit stared unabashedly as one walked past him. The man, gaunt and dark as mahogany from the sun, was nearly naked. Around his waist he had tied the leather whangs that held his breechcloth and a small pouch. He also wore the thick leggings that had protected him this past week from the wear and tear of the brush through which they had ridden. The man did not speak and Kit did not dare to begin a conversation, but the two exchanged a quick glance. At least he had done that much, Kit thought, feeling more at ease.

Young's call, when it came, was surprisingly subdued, but it still carried well. "Joe, here—he's found 'em," he announced to the men who quickly surround-

ed him. "Them Apaches is close all right, camped not
two miles from here at the nearest water hole. It's up
to us to make 'em come where we want 'em. They're
five, maybe six hundred warriors to our forty."

"What about Bent's men?" someone asked.

Young shook his head. "Sent a man up there.
They ain't got no fight left in 'em. And them Mexicans
won't be much help. But we'll use 'em somehow. A
show of force is what's needed. Got to hit hard and
fast, make the Indians think there's a thousand of us.
Here's what we'll do. . . ."

An hour later, Kit was in the saddle along with
three-fourths of the men in Young's brigade. He did
not like the idea of leaving Young and a few of the
other men the responsibility of fending off the brunt of
the Apaches' attack. The plan had as many holes in it
as Swiss cheese, as far as he was concerned. Still, nobody had asked for his opinion. He pulled out to the
rear of the camp with some Mexicans. Then, when
they were out of sight over a rise, the party divided.
They were to circle around to ride flank for Young's
small band, while at the same time keeping a ridge between themselves and the camp in the shallow valley
below.

Kit's hands stiffened as he rode, one closed tightly
on his reins, the other clutching his flintlock. If they
had been stalking in the mountains, it would have been
possible to approach the village protected by woods
and long river grasses. Here they had only the meager
shield of buffalo grass.

Just as Young expected, his small party didn't
have long to wait before they spotted an Apache scout
on the ridge in front of them. Young saddled up his

men. He sounded a contrived cry of alarm, and they started after the scout. The group had reached the rise when they heard hoofbeats thundering toward them. The men looked down into the next broad valley. A huge party of warriors were riding in their direction. On command, the trappers fell back as if in frightened retreat. Then they swung their mounts around toward the valley where the Bent camp was.

As blood-chilling whoops from the Apaches spiked the still air, Kit's mule sidestepped nervously, whinnying in protest. Kit yanked it back in line.

"You stupid son of a bitch!" the man nearest him complained as Kit's mule rammed into his. "Look where you're goin'. Tarnation, you're gonna kill us all!"

Other tempers flared, but the men in Kit's group did not ride out. They had been ordered to remain where they were until the first rifle shot had been fired by Young's group.

"Them Apaches are circlin' the Bent caravan," the lookout in Kit's party called back over his shoulder. "Seems like they aim to take their leisure before they attack. Cap'n Young's boys done made it safe into the Bent camp, leastways. Ho! By damn, that's it. Saddle up! The cap'n done fired a shot!"

His heart pounding, Kit kicked his mount into full gallop. This is it! he thought with nearly unbearable excitement. This was his chance to win a place in Young's brigade permanently. Over the crest they rode, the trappers setting the air vibrating with their own brand of war whoops, French howls and Spanish hollers. They roiled thick clouds of valley dust as they rode, jamming their rifles against their shoulders in anticipation of firing.

As they topped the ridge, Kit could scarcely register the spectacle he saw below. The Apaches had encircled the Bent caravan. They were showing off—wheeling and rearing their mounts, not to mention displaying their lances and bows in the traditional prelude to warfare.

At first, the Indians did not see the two platoons of white men riding down to them from opposite directions. When they finally did, the cry for blood soared up within their midst and their warriors charged.

That move was all Young had been waiting for. "All right, boys!" he cried to the men with him behind the Bent barricade. "Let loose with your fire!"

As planned, the Apaches were caught in the crossfire between the caravan and the horsemen. Warriors and animals squealed in pain and fright as the trappers' superb marksmanship found many an Apache horse and rider.

Kit heard an arrow wing past his left ear, so close it stirred his hair. Then he saw a warrior riding fast, straight at him. One moment he was staring at a naked brown chest topped with shoulder-length black hair and a cloth headband. The next, he fired and felt the familiar kick in his father's gun. For a brief time, smoke eclipsed his view. Then he heard a cry as he passed the Indian at full gallop, and Kit's mule stumbled.

Kit never knew what was directly responsible for his mule's death—the tumble, or the lance that had fallen from the sky to skewer it—but suddenly he was on the ground, dust filling his mouth and nostrils. He panicked. Blinded by fear, he felt the ground for his rifle, expecting to feel an arrow spear his back at any moment.

By the time Kit grabbed up his weapon, staggered to his feet and turned to look for another enemy, the sound of the battle was already diminishing. In the midst of the heavy, dusty haze, he tried to get his bearings. The ground around him was littered with bodies. Some writhed in agony; others were still, no longer in need of help. Blood had been splattered on the grass at his feet. Sounds of retreat and pursuit filtered back to him, and he knew that the Apaches were heading back to their camp.

Feelings of joy and misery mingled in Kit as he headed toward the caravan. He had lived through his first battle.

After taking no more than ten steps, he found himself staring down into the face of one of the fallen warriors. The Apache was still, and he was so perfectly stretched out that he looked ready for a ceremonial funeral. But that was not why Kit felt the salty sting of tears start in his eyes. The warrior was only a boy, the same age as Kit or perhaps even younger. And on his serene face, there was no longer even a hint of aggression or savagery. This was the young warrior Kit had killed. He knew it—especially when he noticed the small hole his flintlock had made in the Indian's chest.

Kit looked up. The sky was yellow-grey. The first of the buzzards soared about lazily, waiting for a turn at the kill.

Kit had done it—he had killed his first man. But he didn't feel good about it.

"Whoopee! Ain't that just fine. Throwed your first Indian!"

Kit turned around in fear, but it was only Gibbon at his back. "That's mighty pretty work, son," Gibbon continued. "Just one more thing you ain't done, though."

Swift as lightning, the man bent down, his Green River knife flashing in his hand. Kit looked away as Gibbon grabbed the Indian's hair. A moment later, he stood and turned back to Kit. "This is yours, son. You've earned it fair and square."

Numbly, Kit held out his hand and took the bloody scalp.

"You been hurt, boy?" the trapper asked. "You look worse than a gun-shot polecat."

Kit shook his head dumbly, and Gibbon slapped him on the back. "Your first, huh? Well, don't worry. It gets easier, boy. Just you wait."

"Maybe," Kit muttered after Gibbon had run off to claim a scalp of his own. "Maybe the fighting and killing does get easier. But, by damn! I'll know the anger of the next man whose life I claim!"

"So proud of you fellas," Young told his men that night around the campfire. "We done just what we aimed to. Them Apaches will think a spell before they attack another American caravan. And you, William Bent, what you got to say to your saviors?"

Kit was content by the time the speechmaking began. He had had his tin filled repeatedly with whiskey and his stomach bulged with a large portion of the fresh buffalo meat begrudgingly shared by the hunters. But he did look up at the mention of William Bent's name. He wanted to see for himself the man who'd been fool enough to bring a caravan of merchants into Apache territory without enough riflemen to protect them. Kit could barely contain a sputter of surprise when Bent stepped forward.

He was short, as short as Kit, broad-bellied, and he wore a dark suit and moccasins. His black hair and neatly trimmed mustache had been oiled and combed. Kit noticed the mark of a black eye swelling the man's upper cheek, and he flinched. If Bent was ever to tell Young about the story behind that black eye, Kit's days as a trapper might be over before they had properly begun.

"Served him right," Kit said defensively under his breath.

The two men had met before. Bent had been standing at the entry to his caravan's barricade when Kit had plodded in without his mule. The merchant had taken exception to Kit's brushing roughly past him. Angry, tired, and more than a little sick of the battle, Kit had swung the scalp he had been holding and smacked the stranger in the face with it. Cursing, Bent had tried to retaliate, but Kit was ready and landed a punch that had sent the man sprawling. "Damn Yankee!" he'd shouted. "Ain't got no proper appreciation for them that's saved you."

Now he backed away from the revealing campfire light, hoping his absence would prevent Bent from relating the incident to Ewing Young.

When Young came to seek him out an hour later, Kit learned that he had been told the story. But instead of criticism, Young offered praise.

"You fought well, Kit," Young said, patting the

boy on the back. "You've all the makings of a first-rate frontiersman."

"That mean you've hired me on for certain?" Kit asked.

"Yep," Young replied heartily. "Providing, of course . . ."

Kit interrupted, "I guess Mr. Bent told you what happened."

Young chuckled. "Son, you've got good instincts. "You're more than a fair shot. You're able and willing. But you've got to get a handle on that temper of yours. A man can't afford too many of the wrong kind of enemies out here. Just livin' is hard enough. You don't need to aspire to trouble of any other sort. Recklessness has lost me more good men than Indians and grizzlies combined. A man can't afford too many mistakes." Then he winked. "But I guess one a year ain't so awful much."

"You just give me another chance, Cap'n Young, and I'm gonna show you what first-rate trappin' is. Gonna be the best trapper this territory ever had. You just watch me!"

Chapter 2

It was dusk when William Bent and his new partner,
Céran St. Vrain, climbed the southeast tower of their
newly completed fort. From this vantage point, which
rose eighteen feet above the valley floor of southeastern
Colorado, the entire plain lay open to their view. Bent
smiled as his eyes searched the lines of the complex.
One hundred and seventy-eight feet by one hundred
and thirty-seven feet. The rectangular walls of the fort
rose fourteen feet high and were more than three feet
thick. An identical tower rose at the northwest corner
of the fort, enabling those inside to view the surrounding terrain from all sides. There could be no attack
without warning. On this stretch of soil bordering the
Mexican border and the territories of at least a half
dozen Indian tribes, security was second in importance
only to the trade business he planned to establish.

For that reason, a sentry was stationed at all times

at his post above the main gate. Through the gate passed incoming caravans from the east. Flanking it were the blacksmith's shop and two huge warehouses.

Along the north, west, and south walls ran the other rooms of the square that comprised the fort. In each was a door facing the center courtyard, the fort having been built in the Spanish style like the houses Bent had seen in Santa Fe and Taos.

"Isn't it a beauty?" Bent prompted.

"If one is enamored of Spanish design," St. Vrain conceded with a shrug.

The inner courtyard was not the only symbol of Spanish architecture William Bent and his brothers Charles, George, and Robert had incorporated into the fort's design. The use of brick had been William's idea, and he thought it would prove its worth in the long run. He scratched his cheek gently, the skin of his face still tender from the dreaded infection of smallpox. Charles had been right in his accusations that William's idea had nearly cost all of them their lives.

The thought of disease had never crossed William's mind when he and St. Vrain had gone south to recruit one hundred and fifty Mexican laborers to make and lay the adobe brick for the walls of the fort. He had thought only that the brick would provide more security against the scourge that every wooden building faced—fire. From experience he knew that the whitewashed walls provided more warmth in winter and less heat in summer. Practical, he had called his idea. The brick would be easier to maintain.

The project had required the skill of artisans from the Mexican territory. He and St. Vrain had offered them ten dollars a month to be paid for in food and goods. Wagonloads of Mexican wool had been brought up from Taos and tons of mud had been hauled in from the river to make the thousands of bricks that were needed.

The recruits had worked diligently. Then smallpox struck. It had passed through like wildfire, first consuming the laborers' camps and then the Americans themselves.

William began to sweat when he thought of how his good friends, the Cheyennes, had suffered. He had sent runners to warn the Indians camping near the fort, and they had fled north. After a few weeks, the disease had run its course, leaving some dead and many disfigured.

William touched his cheek again, thinking that perhaps he would grow back the beard he had shaved off while suffering from the disease. A beard would hide the few remaining scars.

The interruption had been months ago. Since that time, the walls had begun to rise steadily again as the population recovered enough to resume work. Now, at last, everyone was ready to begin the business for which the fort had been planned.

William had not allowed the near disaster of two years earlier to run him out of the territory, but his brush with the Apaches had taught him the folly of betting his entire livelihood on the luck of caravans getting through. The United States Army had no authority beyond the Arkansas River. Those traveling by caravan from Independence, Missouri, were already exhausted even before they reached the most dangerous leg of the journey.

Because of this reality, the idea had come to

William of building a permanent trading post just north of Mexico, a place where caravans could be provided with fresh stock and men. As the only link with trade back East, William felt he would have the enviable job of trading on the plains with all the other frontiersmen, while at the same time maintaining the maximum security possible. It was a shrewd gamble that might one day make him one of the richest men west of the Mississippi.

Bent stared out over the countryside. To the south, across the Arkansas, lay the low sandhills of the Mexican territory. Closer in, on the American side, grasses were being grown to feed the fort's livestock. The fort itself stood on a gravel bench above the flood line. To the southwest, the distant Spanish Peaks gleamed copper-red in the sunset. To the north and west, dim in the distance, were the Rockies. To the east and north the countryside rolled in waves of untamed prairie. It was harsh country they had chosen. Shallow prairie sod, spike-studded yucca and needle-sharp cacti provided little welcome. If trade were to be wrested from the wilderness that surrounded them, the men would need to muster infinite amounts of determination and skill.

William turned back to the fort. They would also need the good will of the Indians. If Chief Yellow Wolf and his people, the Hairy Rope Cheyennes, did not return—and soon—he and St. Vrain would have problems they would likely not be able to handle.

"So, we are ready for business," St. Vrain mused when their survey was complete. "I have with me the United States license for trade with the Cheyennes, Arapahos, and all other Indian tribes who inhabit these lands east of the Rockies. The question remains," he continued, stroking a thickly-whiskered chin, "where are our customers? Must our livelihood depend forever on . . . on . . ." St. Vrain paused, reaching for the appropriate English phrase. Suddenly he smiled. "A roll of the dice?"

William smiled. It was not often the American-reared Frenchman was at a loss for words. He had to be genuinely concerned. "I don't quite see our future riding on a pair of dice, as you so colorfully call it, Céran. We got the fort erected by going out and finding the men to do it. One thing we both should have learned by now is that in this wilderness you have to make your own way."

The Frenchman shrugged, a reluctant smile dragging at the corners of his mouth.

"Same thing with the business," William continued. "If business doesn't find *us*, we find *it*!"

"We had business," Céran reminded him drily. "The Cheyennes. You sent them away."

William hunched his burly shoulders. "Sent you away too, come to think of it. And I'd do it again in a minute if I needed to. One epidemic of the pox in the Rockies, and we'd all be out of business. Old Yellow Wolf is just waiting for my word. The Indians will return."

"Such confidence," Céran murmured, faintly amused. "If you're really sure of yourself, why have you not gone to fetch them?"

"Well, if I'd known you were in such a hurry, we could have ridden out yesterday. As is, we ride at first light," William replied.

"If one is allowed to ask, how in the hell you plan on scarin' up the Hairy Rope Indian?"

William laughed. Céran spoke the western dialect as well as the next man when in good temper. William pointed to the sky where the first night star was visible. "I've been reading the sign. Sign tells me Yellow Wolf has taken his people north to their favorite horse-running spot. It's a little place near the head of Sand Creek, directly north of here."

Céran frowned at his partner's flippant tone. "You are certain they had not been frightened all the way back to the Dakotas?"

"Sure as hell hope not," William admitted. "Of course, you come with me and you'll get to find out firsthand."

It wasn't until several days later that William could draw in a true sigh of relief. The time for it came when he and Céran spotted the buffalo-hide tepees of the Southern Cheyennes on the banks of Sand Creek.

Nightfall found them seated inside the chiefs' lodge, sharing buffalo stew and pemmican.

When the meal was over, the chiefs brought out the sacred pipe. William's gaze wandered about the interior of the tepee as the ceremony began. He and Céran were in the council lodge, the largest tepee in the camp, and one guarded by two sentries who stood just outside the door. While the meal was being served, women had been permitted inside, but now there were no women, only the two of them and the four chiefs. Little Wolf was the tallest and youngest member. Wolf Chief, Little Wolf's father, White Thunder, the tribal priest and keeper of the sacred Medicine Arrows, and

Yellow Wolf made up the group. Dressed in buckskin shirts that had been decorated with elk teeth, beads, and paint, their forelocks were adorned impressively with eagle feathers and beaten silver Spanish coins. William interpreted the signs of wealth they displayed as proof of well-being among the people. This time, William was confident the Cheyenne had been spared smallpox.

When the pipe had been passed around twice, Yellow Wolf broke the silence. "Enough, this puffing of smoke. Our spirits know we honor them. The business of men awaits."

Inwardly, both trappers thanked the small, wiry Cheyenne chief for not standing on ceremony. William took his words as a cue to begin.

Reaching into his possible sack, he drew out a pouch of coffee beans. To William's way of thinking, the gifts that were offered were designed to open the hearts of the chiefs to the white man's words. "In appreciation of Wise One Above for keeping my favorite people free from the putrefying disease that visited us last winter, we offer you, the representatives of the Hairy Rope People, this small gift."

The elaborate words spoken in meticulous Cheyenne impressed William's hosts, as it was meant to, and William saw their pleasure increase when they opened the pouch. Immediately, he added a second pouch containing white powder. "This is to make the black soup lie sweet and good upon the tongue," he explained as each, in turn, tasted the sweet sugar.

The next half hour was spent exchanging additional gifts and brewing the coffee. Bent and St. Vrain were patient. Their trading experience had taught them that patience was probably their best ally when dealing with would-be customers.

At last, a tin cup of sweetened coffee was passed around for the hosts to taste, and William spoke again. "Seven moons have ripened and withered since my friends, the Cheyennes, left the Arkansas River. We grieve that you have not returned, and we come to tell you that all danger has passed. The fort which we have built is ready and waits with open gates for your return."

Yellow Wolf nodded his approval, but the other chiefs were curiously silent. William and Céran traded worried glances. Yellow Wolf was the strongest of the council chiefs; his reputation as the best horse thief of the plains was well-known, and he was feared even by the warrior Comanches he stole from on a regular basis. But Yellow Wolf's status would not help the trading if he split from the others and brought only a portion of this vast village to the fort.

Resorting to sign language, Bent asked what disturbed the great council. The chiefs conferred in hushed voices for some moments before Yellow Wolf lifted his head and spoke. "The signs are not good for our people. Troubles follow in the shadow of the Hairy Rope. Have you not yet learned the way of the Wise One Above?"

"What did he say?" Céran whispered, his command of Indian tongues limited to the Sioux language.

William silenced him with a hand. "The sign you speak of—the dreaded disease—is gone. I speak the truth."

Wolf Chief shook his head sharply, setting the eagle feathers in his scalp lock swinging. "We see the signs, bad signs. Last season we lost many Dog Soldiers to the Pawnees. White Thunder, keeper of the Sacred Arrows, holds great ceremony to help us in our revenge. The Wise One Above does not hear us. In the battle with the Pawnees we lost the Medicine Arrows."

The news upset William nearly as much as he knew it must have upset the Indians in front of him. The Medicine Arrows were the heart and spirit of the Southern Cheyennes. Moses could not have revered the Ark of the Covenant more piously. The loss could mean great trouble, if only because the Cheyennes themselves thought their power diminished by it.

"Have there been no other signs?" William asked, though he knew the question was irrelevant. Unexpectedly, there was a ready answer.

"The winter signs promise starvation. The pelts on the beavers in the lake grow heavy. The flight of the birds begins two weeks early. We have no protection. We will perish in the snow."

"Not so!" William responded, to Céran's astonishment. "Perhaps we are a sign from the Wise One Above. We come to offer you the protection of our great new fort in exchange for the right to trade with you for the beautiful buffalo robes made by your women. Trade us your robes for food and both of us will prosper."

Yellow Wolf did not wait for doubt to set in amongst his fellow council members. "Yes. This is good. We must take the way offered to us. We must return to the river near the Big Timber."

"How can we know that the Wise One Above will aid the white man?" Little Wolf broke in. "How can we bind our fate to those who are not Cheyenne?"

William did not direct his answer to the young man who had asked the question. Yellow Wolf was the man he had to appease. "You ask how you may know that our destinies are one. Have I not always regarded the Cheyennes—your people, Yellow Wolf—as my friends? Did I not protect two of your brothers when the Comanches rode into our camp two summers ago demanding their scalps as payment for crossing their land? Show me what more proof you need and, if humanly possible, I will get it."

William Bent had surprised even himself when these words came tumbling from his lips. Until this moment, when all that he had worked for seemed to hang by the thickness of a beaver's hair, he had not realized how deeply committed he was to the success of the fort on the Arkansas. Only the good Lord knew how he could ever keep the promise he'd just made. But he meant what he had said—and the determination shined in his dark eyes.

William's vow was one Yellow Wolf had hoped for, and he responded eagerly. "You speak wisely," he told the trappers. "The Hairy Rope People believe. These white men have never broken their word," he added to the council. "We will provide as many buffalo robes as they have goods to trade for them. To seal the bargain and bind it with the one we call Little White Man, it is we, now, who must offer a gift."

The four chiefs conferred again, giving William a moment to mull over what had just been said. At last White Thunder, his wrinkled face daubed with the sacred red paint that was the emblem of his status as priest, spoke. "Little White Man speaks powerful words that gladden the hearts of the Cheyenne people.

We make you a gift in return for your generosity." The old man clapped his hands.

Neither William nor Céran had seen anyone come in or leave the tepee during their conversation, and they wondered how a message had been carried out. But soon the tepee flap was thrown back and two young girls entered, their faces lowered in respect for their elders.

Yellow Wolf smiled when he saw William staring at the girls. He had paid special attention to the older one. In his wisdom, the Cheyenne chief saw that it was not only the white men who would benefit from the trade between their two nations. The fort he had seen being built up from the banks of the Arkansas would mean protection from the Comanches and Pawnees, the Cheyennes' enemies. "You take one squaw, maybe two," he said.

William swallowed and turned to meet Céran's glance. The Frenchman shrugged and turned his smiling face away. William considered his situation carefully. He knew the chiefs thought of their gift as testimony to the esteem in which they held him. He, in turn, would be expected to offer the older girl's father several horses to prove his own worthiness. "You wish me to marry?" he ventured.

The four council chiefs nodded in agreement. Little Wolf's face was the only one which held a trace of reservation. "You take two wives?" Wolf Chief suggested with a smile.

"I . . . I can afford only one," William murmured, his attention fastened on the two girls.

Well, hadn't he promised to do anything to win over the Cheyennes?

"You take one now. Take second woman along. Maybe take her as wife later," Yellow Wolf instructed matter-of-factly. "Two women, both untried." He reached out and swiftly lifted the hems of both girls' leather shirts to reveal their sturdy brown legs. A length of rope had been wrapped around their waists, then tied to each thigh. "You see? Rope not cut."

William stared openly at the curious chastity belts. He had heard of them but never before seen them. He knew the Cheyennes and their cousins, the Arapahos, were not like the other much-praised, licentious Plains tribes whose women were often loaned out for the evening to any man who had a bead necklace or fine-meshed cloth handy to trade. The older girl raised her head. The moment William Bent looked up into her face, he knew his fate was sealed.

"You like Owl Woman. That is clear," her father, White Thunder, stated approvingly. "Good. She will bear you many strong children. And she is beautiful. She has large breasts to supply good milk for your sons. You take her. Yellow Woman will be companion to her sister until you decide if you want her, too."

Later in the evening, when Céran found a moment to speak to William privately, he said, "You could learn something, my friend, from your new in-laws. You may have gained a trading agreement, but you have also gained a thousand hungry relations. How will you feed them all?"

William shook his head wearily. "Hell! How do you think? Going to have to hire myself a whole party of hunters to work at the fort. When you get back home to Taos, you tell any Americans you meet that I'm hiring. Lord, Céran, have you looked at her? She's just about the loveliest thing these eyes have ever seen."

"Lucky for you." Céran chuckled. "When that shriveled up old man offered you one of his daughters, I expected a toothless hag. *Mon Dieu*! The old man has powerful medicine hidden in his breechcloth!"

Chapter 3

"Damn! This one's got his guts filled with stuff. 'Nough to last a lifetime!"

The gruff, whiskey-blurred voice rumbled across the confines of the adobe room.

The youngest man in the room, lying on his bedroll, lifted his flat-crowned hat from his eyes to peer at the malcontent who was disturbing his siesta.

"Foofaraw, that's what this galoot says. Ain't a man livin' in this pigpen fit to scrape my mule's droppings," the drunk man claimed. Got to find me some real beaver to skin!" The burly American trapper reeled past the younger man's view, but not before he had been identified.

O'Nery. Drunk as a skunk again, Kit Carson thought. He dropped his hat back over his eyes in disgust.

As the hat fell once again into place, Kit's sur-

roundings seemed to fall away. Once more he was at
the rim of the broadest canyon on the continent. The
sight of the narrow trickle of water far below was, in
his mind's eye, as clearly breathtaking as it had been
the first time he had seen it a year earlier. At that time,
his dreams had been realized. He was, at last, a beaver
trapper. Well, the truth was that he had spent most of
the first year following the more experienced men. For
two years they had trapped the Gila and Colorado,
even the San Pedro, each man earning enough in beaver and other fine furs to trade them in Santa Fe for
Spanish silver. Finally, he had ridden back into San
Fernandez de Taos on a red California mule, sporting
new buckskins—all quilled and beaded—and perched
atop a brand new silver-mounted saddle.

That was over four months ago. And four months
turned out to be more than enough time to see the
dream of permanent wealth dwindle faster than the
silver in his possibles. It was all gone. Taos Lightning
and gambling and women—the lure had been irresistible. Now what was he going to do?

Kit mumbled a curse. Ewing Young was not hunting this fall. There had been a near miss in California,
when they had come within hours of losing the expedition's entire catch to the Mexican authorities. The adventure had dampened Young's enthusiasm.

The aspens to the north were turning gold under
the breath of autumn. The distant Sangre de Cristo
peaks lay dusted with the first snow. And here he sat,
broke and out of work.

"If I ever get another chance, I swear I'll never
squander everything again," Kit vowed silently.
"Never! Only, I got to get another chance."

The hat disappeared from his face, snatched back by a callused hand. "Well, you comin' or ain't you, sonny?"

Kit opened his eyes. "Coming where? Ain't got two pesos to rub together, and you know it, O'Nery."

The big man's jaw worked the wad of jerky tucked into his cheek. A thread of spittle hung in the tangled wire of beard that protruded from his chin and furred the upper portion of his leather shirt.

Runt of the litter. That was O'Nery's opinion of American House's youngest trapper. Even though the boy's blue eyes were set in the permanent squint that was the mark of every veteran of the Santa Fe Trail, he was still a boy—underneath those whiskers, his skin was still as smooth as a babe's.

"Ain't got no need for silver this time, son," O'Nery said when he'd finished chewing. "We's goin' out to the edge of town. Arapahos is camped just outside the city walls. Talk is, there's soup doin's tonight."

"Soup doin's?" Kit snatched back his hat, careful that the act was deemed friendly by punctuating it with a smile. "Gut-sore for buffalo grease, I am. Soup ain't gonna shine beside that."

O'Nery let loose with a string of oaths that drew the attention of the few other men in the room. "Soup doin's? Hell! We're goin' dancin', son. Nicest little dance you ever saw. Plenty little squaws, plump and tender as prairie chicken and just as ready for the pluckin'." That said, O'Nery clumped out, shoulders stooped and heavy under his sweat-blackened buckskins. He looked more like a buffalo carrying his hump than a man.

"Appears you ain't much acquainted with the

Arapaho," someone drawled from the corner just behind Kit's head.

Kit rose from his seat, his skinning knife drawn almost without conscious will. "Think you got something to teach me?" he asked, challenging the person who had spoken to him.

The stranger lounged against one sand-brown wall of the room, a long and lanky figure of a man. His hat was pulled low over his brow. His body was wrapped in Mexican plaid. He certainly did not fit the description of anyone Kit knew.

The stranger's hand moved with deliberate speed to indicate the knife in Kit's hand. "You go in much for that kind of fun, son?"

"Name's Carson," Kit shot back, disliking the tall man for no particular reason except that he had been restless for too long. Backing a greenhorn down was just about what he needed to settle his dinner. "You got something to say, you spit it out."

The man shrugged. "I'm new in Taos. Lookin' for a *compadre* for the evening. Of course, if you're not interested," the deep voice finished on a questioning note.

Kit relaxed his grip on the Green River knife. "You're a mite friendly to a man you ain't met."

The stranger leaned forward, pulling himself away from the wall, and pushed the hat back from his face. In the dusty light pouring in from the single narrow porthole in the room, Kit watched a dark, thick beard emerge, then craggy, sunburned features and friendly eyes. "Name's Brant. Royce Brant."

"Been in Taos long?" Kit asked, ignoring the man as he stuck his hand out. He put his knife away.

"About a week," the stranger replied, withdrawing his hand. "In from St. Louis. Been trappin' the Mississippi the last two years. Aim to try my luck a bit farther west this season."

"Who'd you kill?" Kit inquired boldly, raising his eyes in time to see the bigger man start.

"Did I say I was runnin'?"

Kit burst out laughing. "Touchy, ain't you?" he asked, teasing. "Folks in these parts only move about on account of empty traps or trouble."

Kit's glance stopped on the expensive new buckskins the man wore. He frowned. A year of trapping and they would have been black with blood, grease and sweat. Either the man had enjoyed a prosperous year or he was new to the business—or he was lying.

Then Kit noticed the long, appraising look the man was giving him in return. "You see something humorous?" Kit queried, pulling himself up to a height that came almost near the man's chin.

Royce Brant decided not to provoke the youngster with a smile. He couldn't fault the boy for what conclusions he might draw. Besides, fighting was not among his favorite pastimes. "I was just thinkin'," he answered easily, "how I'd purely love a tinful of Taos Lightning. I'd even buy a cup for a *compadre* if I knew his name."

"Carson. Folks call me Kit." Brant took the hand that was extended, and didn't flinch when Kit's fingers closed over his like a bear trap. "Arapaho camp?"

"Why not?" Kit shrugged. "Sure beats the hell out of an evenin' swattin' flies and smokin' corn shucks."

"That broke, huh?" Royce turned away before Kit could reply. He had suddenly decided to leave. He

reached the doorway in three strides, cursing when he
bashed his head against the top of the door frame.
"What the hell kind of folks built this place? Any man
with more than six years of growth'll kill himself if he
doesn't duck low!"

Kit did not bother to follow the man right when
he left. Instead, he headed for his possibles to dig out
his last silver coin. The gleaming silver circle looked
lonely and small in his palm. His only thought upon arriving back in Taos had been to wring from his share
of the hunt all the joy and pleasure that could be had.
He had drunk more whiskey and fought more contests
in the last four months than ever before, yet when it
came to the señoritas. . . .

Kit spat on the earthen floor. It was not that he
didn't know what to do with a woman or did not enjoy
them—there had been more than a few times in the
last months when he had paid for their company, but
not one of them had held his interest for long. And
they, for their part, had lost interest, too, when his
pockets stopped jingling.

The trouble, Kit thought to himself, was that he
was not like the other trappers, content on just being
satisfied, even when the woman was reluctant. There
had been times when he had seen fear start in some
women who had been caught up in an embrace they
did not desire. Not that it was his business, of course.
In Taos, a man kept his own counsel unless he was
willing to risk a bullet for his advice. Whiskey, now
that was a different matter.

Kit moved out into the dusty lane, scattering a
brood of scrawny chickens that had gathered in front
of a nearby doorway. He was going to the Arapaho

camp, north of the Mexican settlement. Sometimes a small village of one of the great tribes that roamed the plains above the Arkansas River would cross down into New Mexico to trade for the turquoise they prized. This was particularly true of the Southern Arapahos. "Soup doin's," Kit murmured under his breath as he started off on foot toward the origins of the tom-toms. "What the devil is that?"

The unmarried Arapaho girls had formed a line to one side of the open ground where Royce Brant stood. Brant's stare ran appreciatively over their bare, smooth limbs gracefully exposed by sleeveless rawhide tunics. The torch poles glowed and warmed their red-brown complexions to burnt gold. Brant quivered in response to the enticing sight before him.

He smiled. It had been quite some time since he had held a woman hard against him. But he meant to change that soon, and not with some sweet savage. If only Renata would keep her promise. . . .

The sudden activity at the edge of the women's line drew his attention. From a cluster of tepees came six women, walking in pairs, each carrying a kettle of bubbling stew. They passed in front of the girls' line and set the pots on the ground. Immediately a group of young braves lined up opposite the girls.

"Soup doin's! Didn't I tell you? Yes, sir. I'm ready for a fandango!"

The rough voice was O'Nery's. Royce spotted him standing with the other trappers who had gathered around a whiskey wagon. The wagon had been brought up from town. Kit was there, too. He acknowledged Royce with a slow nod, but before Royce could cross the distance that separated them, the Arapaho musicians at the far end of the two lines struck up a tempo. Flutes and whistles were added to the tom-toms, and a lively, erratic melody rose into the night.

Royce smiled as the first girl moved forward and dipped her spoon into a stew pot. Moving forward in time to the beat, she approached a young brave wrapped in his blanket, the polished-horn spoon extended to him.

A ripple of laughter shook the brave's line, then a whispered dare sent the chosen young man forward to meet the girl. The girl had nearly touched her spoon to the brave's lips when she began retreating from him, in rhythmic step. The brave pursued, matching his steps with hers until she was once more in line with the other women. Then, immediately, he began backing away, suffering stoically from the gibes of his fellow braves.

Royce's face wore a wry expression. He, too, had suffered the embarrassment of a flirt.

The next girl moved into place quickly. There was no question which brave she preferred. She danced over to face the brave who had been spurned a moment before and eagerly permitted him to drink from her spoon. When the stew had been tasted, the girl dropped her spoon with a mock shriek of fright and ran from the dance grounds. Urged on by his friends, the brave was soon after her.

The girl ran neither very far nor very fast. Giggles and squeals erupted in the camp as the boy swooped down on her and wrapped her in his blanket. The two did not move away entirely from the other villagers— that would not have been permitted—and Royce decided that what could be accomplished standing wrapped in a blanket was not enough for him. He glanced at the sky, his trapper's eye gauging the hour. Then he sighed. He would have to wait. Renata would not come before midnight.

Eager for another tin of whiskey to console himself, Royce strode across the clearing to the wagon. He had almost reached it when a wild Indian war whoop split the silence of the night. The musicians faltered, their music dwindling to silence. The women scattered silently as their warriors pushed them away and headed in the direction of the sound. Royce reached for his Green River, noting that his action was repeated by those trappers who did not already have their Hawken rifles gripped in the crooks of their arms.

Strangers materialized out of the night. There were not many of them—ten maybe—and they were not armed. But the hackles rose on Royce's neck. He knew there was trouble. He could smell it a mile away.

"Lord! Knew I heard Indians makin' whoop." The speaker was clad in greasy buckskins. A salt and red-pepper beard flowed from his chin to his chest.

"Didn't I tell you boys there'd be plenty of fun in Taos?" he continued, lifting an arm to wave in the direction of the Arapaho warriors who had formed a barrier between the strangers and their village. "Evenin'. Howdy!" Smiling broadly, the intruder tapped the center of his chest with his fingertips, the Indian sign for Arapaho. "You old goats know me, by damn. All the Arapahos know Old Bill Williams."

The chief studied the lean, sinewy man with the squeaky voice and permanent slump. Then he made the sign for friend and moved aside.

Royce let his knife slide back into place. Only then did he notice that Kit had come to stand by his side. Their eyes met briefly, but they did not speak to each other.

Kit moved away and did not look back. He was not quite certain what had put him by the man's side in the moment between he had sensed danger and was then facing it. He scratched his chin. One of the newcomers intrigued him, and he stared at the stranger.

Kit had known many large men in his time but this one dwarfed them all. He was at least six and a half feet tall. His shoulders strained the seams of his homespun shirt, which hung open to expose a massive, muscular chest. Two hundred fifty, maybe two hundred seventy pounds, Kit estimated.

The man stood still, his eyes concentrating on the line of Arapaho maidens who had again begun dancing. He was hatless, his shoulder-length hair so matted with grease that it barely stirred in the wind coming in from the mesa. His puffy, flat face held the cunning of an animal that feared nothing.

Half-breed, Kit decided. He shot a glance at the rest of the proceedings, then his gaze returned to the gigantic man. For the first time, he noticed the bandanna tied loosely around the stranger's neck. Red silk—the designation of a voyageur, a French-Canadian fur trader. That could mean a new trapping brigade had arrived, and in turn a chance for work.

The stranger was staring at the women. His ham-sized fists closed hard as Kit imagined the lust that had to be surging through that meaty carcass.

"Ain't you gonna let some of us have a turn?" a trapper called from the side. "We're here for dancin', same as the others. Come on, boys, let's show them little gals how Americans go about 'spoonin'!"

A few other trappers joined the speaker, clapping their hands and stomping their feet in time to the music. One man pulled a harmonica from his pocket and added the bars of a Cajun folk song to the Indian tune.

"Get along, little gal," one trapper beckoned to the line of dancers. "We're fixin' to show you folks how it's done."

One girl came forward, giggling self-consciously. Filling her spoon, she offered it to the man and then withdrew sharply when he leaned forward, his tongue wagging for a taste. Laughter exploded in the camp.

"Looks like you ain't welcome to share no blanket tonight," O'Nery heckled.

"He's too old for that little gal, anyway," another man cried out. "Where's the boy? Where's Carson?"

Kit flinched at the sound of his name. He knew he'd had too much whiskey to join in the revelry. Whiskey made him moody and sour-faced, and he sure as hell didn't want woman troubles on top of that.

Looking up, he was just in time to see another trapper make a grab for the girl. She spilled the soup, but the trapper didn't seem to mind. He caught her up by the waist and planted a wet kiss on her astonished lips before letting her go. The action brought cheers from his companions, but Kit could almost feel the wave of dissent traveling amongst the braves.

To guard against any trouble, Kit strode forward boldly. "Can't any man here see the right way to go about this?" he bellowed. "Move aside. Let a body that's got some grace get in them doin's."

With inward reluctance, he positioned himself in front of the line of women. Almost at once, he noticed the girl who faced him. She was tiny, a foot shorter than even Carson.

Just a babe, he thought in relief. She wouldn't stir the desire of these men. Kit swept his hand toward the soup pots, nodded his head, then waited.

The young girl came forward slowly to fill her spoon. Her feet barely kept up with the beat of the tom-toms as she crossed to the sandy-haired American.

Kit smiled as he watched her, knowing how afraid she must be. Yet the girl seemed determined not to show her fear. When she stopped in front of him, she raised her spoon in offering, neither dropping it nor flinging its contents in his face as he almost expected she would. When the spoon was just short of his lips, it came no closer.

Kit raised a questioning brow, and for the first time he looked closely at the girl's face. Why, she's downright pretty, he thought. The high cheekbones, full lips and enormous black eyes made a most appealing picture. Intending, before, to do no more than turn away when the Indian moved back from him, he changed his mind and followed her. It was a shame the girl wasn't a year or two older, he thought.

"That's doin' us proud, son," a man called after him.

"Get after her!" cried another.

"Go on! Get yerself a handful of woman!"

Kit had advanced halfway to the women's line when he was shouldered aside roughly. Even as he saved himself from stumbling, he heard the young girl shriek. In an instant, the sound she'd made became a wail of terror, and she flung the contents of her spoon in the face of the huge white man who had lifted her into a smothering embrace. When the attacker did not release her, the Indian girl cracked him sharply on the side of the head with her spoon. With a guttural oath, the French Canadian knocked the spoon away and lowered his head to grind his mouth against her lips.

Amid the laughter and cheers of the trappers, Kit also heard the angry grumblings of the Arapaho warriors. Suddenly he saw a silvery flash as a steel blade caught the torchlight.

The big man had pulled out his knife and was trying to subdue the young girl, who had been thrashing and biting him to protect herself.

Kit reacted instinctively and grabbed a lodgepole. He swung it low and hard. As the pole met the back of the big man's knees, he fell like an axed tree and released the girl. She scrambled up and ran behind the line of women.

Kit's attention did not waver from the raging man, for he had regained his footing almost at once. He gripped his long skinning knife in his huge fist and, looking like a monstrous bear, fell into a crouch.

Kit knew the stranger was deadly. His hand flew to his own Green River at his waist, but a split-second thought made him hesitate. He knew that if there were a fight, the whole camp of trappers would find a way to join in. Perhaps there was still a way to prevent that kind of bloodshed.

A smile stretched slowly across his lips as he bent to pick up the Arapaho girl's spoon. "You new here, hombre? Ain't got the hang of things?" he asked. He backed up a step until his moccasin touched the soup pot just behind him. Without taking his gaze off the swaying man, he dipped the spoon into the pot. Then, in a perfect parody of the Arapaho girl's dance, he stepped forward to offer the spoon to the man. His eyes never left the voyageur as he approached, but from the corner of his eye Kit saw the bows and rifles in open display. One wrong move and all hell would break loose.

Eyes twinkling in pure mischief, Kit waved the spoonful of stew under the man's nose. *"Voulez vous, monsieur?"* he asked in a thin, girlish voice.

Surprise registered on the man's face at hearing his own native language spoken by the small American, but he did not reply. Kit stiffened. In another minute, someone's taut temper would snap.

"Don't seem to be your day, son," Royce Brant yelled out, his bass voice breaking the stillness and startling everyone. "First you can't get no woman to share your bedroll. Now you can't even find a trapper for a bedmate. Must be something powerful wrong with you, son. Ain't often a trapper ain't for a kiss and cuddle, howsoever it's offered."

This reference to the unconventional habits of some women-starved mountain men who spent long months alone together set the trappers howling; the tension melted away.

Kit joined in quickly. He was not one to forgo a joke at his own expense, particularly when saving his hide was part of the bargain. The Arapaho warriors must have had someone among them that spoke enough English to translate. Very quickly they were laughing, too, and lowering their weapons.

But the gaiety proved to be too much for the voyageur. His knife made a wicked hiss as it slashed at Kit's middle.

Kit jumped back. Roaring like a wounded grizzly, the big man went for Kit again, but Kit sidestepped smoothly enough to avoid a nasty wound. Kit stuck out a foot to trip the man as he went rushing past. Sprawled in the dust, the troublemaker groaned, began to get up onto his knees, then shook himself like a wet dog before collapsing on his stomach in the dust.

"Taos Lightnin'! Does it every time," Old Bill pronounced after he'd walked over and peered down into the voyageur's face. "Must have drunk two gallons of the stuff before we traipsed up here. If I was you, son," he added, pointing at Kit, "I'd be plenty scared before St. Nair, there, wakes up. Isn't a meaner man alive than that there voyageur when he has a sore head."

Indifferently, Kit shrugged and dropped the spoon. "I'm from Taos, myself," he announced loudly. "Them señoritas know just how to handle a man. Less likely to lose my hair, besides. Give me a willin' woman every time."

He turned and started back to town, hoping the others would follow, but not daring to look back. He had not gone far when he heard conversation close behind him.

"Never seen anything to compare with that! Lil' David and Goliath haven't got anything on our boy, Kit. Reckon that boy knows how to tie knots in foxes' tails, too?"

Smiling, Kit pushed back the hat on his head and, continuing along the trail, struck up a tuneless whistle.

Chapter 4

Grass Singing lay awake long after the white men had abandoned her village and the members of her tribe had retired for the night. She pressed her cheek into the soft leather of her buffalo robe bed, its smoky odor a reminder of the many months it had been used around the campfire. With the next summer she would need to help her mother and sisters cure a new robe for herself. The robe she was sleeping on now would then be turned into leggings for her family. At the moment, she was glad for its warmth. The wind was cold. Soon, the winter would come rushing down upon them from the land of the Shining Ones, the great mountains far, far away.

This reminder of her home in the mountains of northern Colorado made Grass Singing long to be back there. She was not fond of this new place.

An infant's fretful cry broke into the stillness. It

was followed by the sound of her mother, Hawk Woman, moving to calm the hunger of her youngest child. In the darkness Grass Singing heard her mother pick up the baby, who was still tightly strapped to his cradle board, and rock him gently to a whispered song. No Arapaho child was ever allowed to cry. That was good, Grass Singing thought. In another moment the sucking sound of the ravenous infant had replaced the lullaby.

Grass Singing envied her mother. Though only thirteen years old, she already longed for children of her own. Wasn't she the most eager of her sisters to bear her new brother on her back when her mother, Hawk Woman, needed to be free of him? And, though she was younger than Mountain Flower and Evening Star, she wished more than they to wed. That is why this evening had had a special meaning for her.

Never before had she been allowed to participate in the evening dancing. But by promising to dance with only White Eagle, the brave she knew her family hoped would ask for her in three year's time, she had won her father's approval to take part.

A giggle nearly escaped her as she remembered White Eagle's embarrassment at her sister's boldness. She did not mind that Mountain Flower had shared his blanket. In fact, she wished that White Eagle would marry Mountain Flower and leave her to find a husband of her own choosing. She did not think too well of the Arapaho custom that encouraged a warrior who had married one sister of a family with many daughters to wed a second or even a third sister.

"I will never marry with a warrior stupid enough to wed Mountain Flower," Grass Singing promised herself. Mountain Flower was the eldest of their father's children, and vain beyond all understanding. They would fight continually if placed beneath the same roof to share the same man. "Never! I will not marry!"

At least she knew there was every chance she could attract the man of her choice. If her reflection in the creek were not enough evidence, there were the many stares of the young braves who watched as she made her way through the village; their attention told her that she was becoming a woman whom men would want.

The unfamiliar twang of a distant Spanish guitar vibrated in the cool night air. Grass Singing raised her head until she could see out of the door flap of the tepee. Down below their camp lay the white man's village, its fires flickering like fireflies in the autumn breeze. And there was the small white man with hair and beard the color of the ground squirrel—she remembered that his eyes were as blue as the precious turquoise her people prized.

Grass Singing sighed. Her father had not been pleased when the white men joined their dancing. But Chief Soaring Vulture was wise in the ways of the white men. He would not provoke a battle where women and children might be hurt.

If only the ugly one—the huge man—had not touched her, Grass Singing knew she would have been glad the white men were there. She had ceremoniously scrubbed the sour taste of the gigantic stranger's lips from her face with juice from the soap plant. At least the memory of the other smaller white man provided soothing relief. She had liked his smile. And, while natural modesty had kept her from staring directly into

his face, Grass Singing knew his eyes of summer blue
had been as warm in their regard for her as any Arapaho brave's.

Grass Singing's cheeks colored. She wondered
what it would have been like had Turquoise Eyes
pressed his mouth to hers. It was a strange custom—
kissing. The white man seemed to find value in it, but
her people found the tradition crude and distasteful.
Perhaps the small white man would have made her feel
differently.

When Hawk Woman finished nursing her son, she
placed him gently on the ground and reached out to
drop the door flap over the lodge entrance. As she
crept back to the warmth of Soaring Vulture's robes,
she cast a parental eye over her youngest daughter; at
last she was sleeping soundly.

Kit had not joined the other trappers who had
headed for the smoky light of the nearest Taos cantina.
The men's earsplitting yells had been packed with all
the ferocity of a war party as they enveloped the sleeping village, and he'd wanted nothing to do with them.
As Kit passed a row of adobe huts, he heard a child's
wail of fright and cursed under his breath. The liquor-
swollen bravado of the trappers would soon be tamed
in the arms of the local prostitutes. Then the village
could be peaceful once again.

When he heard footsteps behind him, Kit paused.

"Evenin'," Royce Brant's voice sounded softly behind him. Keeping his distance, he asked, "Just what
would you have done if that big voyageur had taken a
shine to young bucks?" The rumble of laughter that

followed the taunt did not help Kit's mood, and he uttered a curse.

Brant didn't look back as he passed by. After a moment Kit sauntered in the same direction he had taken. Something he couldn't hit upon made him want to know more about the hombre who drank his whiskey alone, then offered his friendship to a stranger.

The two men reached American House at the same time. The main room was empty except for the lone *mestizo* woman who kept house for those trappers who could afford the luxury. She smiled when the two men entered, stretching out a withered claw of a hand to each of them in expectation of a coin. Kit shook his head angrily, embarrassed that he had nothing to offer her. Royce did the same, but more gently.

"Gringos sangrientos!" she grumbled under her breath as she left them alone.

"Don't seem to be your night all around," Royce commented. He drew a light for his tobacco from a sputtering oil lamp.

The aroma of fresh tobacco set Kit's nostrils quivering. It had been a month since the smell of authentic, cured tobacco had filled his lungs. But he distracted himself, saying, "You seem mighty preoccupied with my welfare."

Royce squatted down in a corner, resting his back against the adobe wall. "Just friendly interest. You nearly got yourself killed just a while back. Why the hell should you care if some gorilla gets a bulge in his britches for some little squaw? What's the difference? They're just damn redskins."

Kit's eyes narrowed. "You got something against

the Indians, you won't last long for this country, friend. They can smell an Indian-hater a mile off."

Kit didn't get the reaction he expected. "So you got more feelings than you allow. Took a shine to the little gal, did you? You needn't have fretted. The big fella would have got a quiverful of arrows in his lights before he could do more'n drop his britches."

Kit caught the pouch of tobacco Royce pitched at him. "You and me, we're like spark and tinder," he commented as he pulled out a cornhusk to use as a cigarette wrapper. "Thing I didn't get was why the chief didn't call off the dancin' when the Americans came into camp."

Royce knew he was being put to a test. "And have those whiskey-blind trappers turn the night into a blood bath?" He shook his head. "Women and children would have been the ones hurt. What's more, the Arapahos prefer to trade with the Americans. They don't like the Mexican government. Better that a few squaws get squeezed than risk a war in their own front yard."

Kit shot Royce a respectful glance. "You're not too stupid, are you?"

Royce shrugged. "So I've been told. You did some fast thinkin' yourself. Take's a cool head to meet danger the likes of St. Nair with anything other than a loaded Hawken." Royce rose to his feet. "I gotta be goin'."

But Kit was not satisfied with what he'd learned about the mountain man. "Where's your home?" he asked, trying to get Royce to stay and talk. "You've been out here a spell, I'd say."

The animation left Royce's face. "There's no

place I call home," he answered, his lips tightening over the words. Kit could have kicked himself. He needn't have asked such a clumsy question. In the West, no man ever asked another more than he was willing to answer.

"I'm from Missouri," Kit volunteered slowly, shifting briefly to see if Royce was listening. "Been in Spanish territory for five years. Ran away at fifteen, lookin' for adventure."

"You got folks somewhere?" Royce asked.

"Hell, yeah! Got enough brothers and sisters to set up a town of our own. Reckon farmin' don't leave a man near as tuckered out as a body might suppose."

The two men shared their first genuine exchange of laughter. Kit felt as though he had won a small victory.

Royce lingered a moment. Almost as an afterthought, he asked, "You got plans for the fall?"

"Maybe," Kit said noncommittally. "That new brigade of trappers came into town tonight. Could be they'll be signin' on new men."

Royce nodded. "That'd be Fitzpatrick and his Rocky Mountain boys. Met Tom a few weeks back, in Santa Fe. He's headin' for the Rockies come the end of the week. You know somethin' about trappin' beaver, Carson?"

Kit straightened his shoulders. "Course I do. Trapped for Ewing Young all the way to California."

"That so?" Royce said gently. "You know how to handle traps and all, then."

"Surely," Kit boasted. Actually, he knew a little about laying traps, but mostly he had followed the lead of others. "I'm not sayin' I know it all. But I'm a quick learner. You ask anybody who knows me. I don't have to be told nothin' twice."

Royce decided to change the subject. "Why aren't you goin' after that Arapaho gal? It's not polite to keep a woman waitin'."

"Don't want that Arapaho child," Kit growled. "Could get myself a real woman, was I of a mind. But I ain't." A slow, uneasy grin spread across his face. "Learned the hard way a pretty gal is mostly interested in the silver a man's got in his possibles."

"Maybe." Brant threw Kit a salute and started for the door. "See you in the mornin', Carson. Fitzpatrick will be in front of Young's place signing up trappers. If you're lookin' for adventure, you'll sure enough find it with him." He paused, then called over his shoulder, "They're paying four hundred American dollars for the season."

Four hundred dollars! With four hundred dollars, he could see his way clear to working for himself every season after.

"I'll do it!" Kit announced, but Brant was gone.

Renata Lopez gasped when the chair she bumped into in the dark teetered, then fell over. Her family's two-room adobe house was larger than most, but there was only one room for sleeping, and Renata shared it with her mother.

In the living room, her brother Miguel slept near the front door. Renata feared him. He always slept with a knife in one hand. "To protect my family from the Americanos!" he would consistently exclaim, spitting in contempt.

Renata set the chair upright, and Miguel did not

stir. He had been at the neighborhood cantina until after midnight, and she had been certain he was drunk when he came in singing and swearing half an hour earlier. She pulled her rough shawl tightly over her head and shoulders and lifted one slim bare foot after the other over Miguel's sprawled form. The ruffle of her short skirt brushed his face, but Miguel scarcely moved.

Only when Renata had reached the corner at the end of the second street did she draw a deep breath. Immediately her heart began to pound with excitement. There was new fear stirring inside her. Never before had she slipped away to meet a man.

Oh, she had flirted openly from time to time with boys who lived in town. She loved to dance provocatively and remembered appreciative eyes staring at her swaying hips. The sensual strains of the guitar had always shaped an undefinable longing in her. But each time she had danced, she had been under the watchful guard of Miguel.

A shiver of anticipation raced the length of her spine as she moved through the soft night breeze. A week ago she had met and danced with a tall Yankee trapper. Instantly, she knew he could quench the longing in her.

She skirted the center of town where the newest detail of trappers had set up camp for the night, scurrying past the makeshift corral where two dozen pack mules were tethered. Silently she made her way over the dusty road leading north to the Pueblo ruins. Once those adobe walls had housed Jemez and Apaches who had held off the Spanish for more than a hundred years. Now only a few Pueblo Indian families made their homes there.

"Be there, be there," she whispered anxiously as she neared the houses.

Royce saw Renata coming, but did not show himself immediately. Instead, he watched her move toward him, his emotions a mixture of relief and consternation. She was just a child. He had been vividly aware of that when, last week, he'd slid an arm around her waist to twirl her out to dance and she had barely reached his upper chest. He had not been able to tell exactly what she looked like. But halfway through the dance, he had inadvertently stepped on her foot, and two black eyes, wide and furious as a storm, had accosted him.

Now, for a moment, his conscience pricked him. "Conscience be damned," he muttered, thinking how her ivory complexion had made him want to touch her everywhere.

He stepped out to meet her. "Evenin', señorita."

"Señor Brant," Renata replied softly after recovering from the sudden surprise. For a moment her timidity rankled Royce. It was unlike her. Well, he thought philosophically, at least she's here. He swung an arm toward the room behind him. "Come inside, señorita. It's too cool a night for stargazing."

The first stirrings of uncertainty began circling in Renata's mind. Where was the easygoing hombre who had made it his business to speak to her each day when she went to the well in the plaza for water?

Royce turned away. He recognized the fear growing in the girl's expression. Ducking into the room, he held his breath until he heard the soft padding of her footsteps behind him.

"Isn't safe to make a fire," he said in the dark room. "Don't want anybody to come skulkin' up after us. On account of that I brought us some cover against the cold."

Renata could not see what he referred to as she stood inside the doorway, her arms clasping her scarf tightly about her.

Royce racked his brain for something to say to fill the silence. "You don't say much for a little lady who's known how to keep me on your trail all week long." His tone lightened as he added, "You meant any of those scandalous things you said, or did you come up here tonight just to excite me, then leave?"

"Señor?"

"You know what I mean. You've been flirtin' and teasin' enough to inflame a gelding. Now you stand there meek and mild as a saint." Royce moved toward Renata until she was close enough to touch. "What did you come for, señorita?"

Renata licked her lips nervously. What could she say? She was not certain herself why she had come. She had been drawn to the tall, easy-mannered American who had looked down into her face and silently promised her a knowledge of herself as a woman. And yet, she knew that danger and even death might follow. It didn't matter. She could not stay away. "I came because you asked it of me," she said finally.

The honesty of Renata's reply was like a spark on dry brush, igniting the longing Brant had kept in check. "Come," he whispered, reaching out for her. His hands closed gently around hers and he drew her into his arms. They stood quietly for a long moment, their bodies touching while the aroma of Renata's spicy perfume, made heady from the heat of her body, stirred Brant almost to a frenzy. It no longer mattered whether Renata had come to lay with him or just appease her curiosity. She would stay now. He would not let her do otherwise.

When the Yankee's hands smoothed over the ripples and folds of her clothing, Renata was faintly embarrassed by her nakedness under her blouse. Her mother would have wept in horror. But when his strong fingers delved into her bodice to enclose a breast, she surrendered, moaning.

Desire struggled with shame as the Americano drew the blouse over her head and loosened the skirt so that it slid easily to her feet. Renata heard her lover suck his breath in sharply as his hand brushed her thigh. He kissed her long and hard before he undressed.

They lay together and Renata felt the hard, smooth expanse of the Yankee's chest under her cheek. With her fingers, she traced the solid muscles of his back. In a moment he pulled her close. She felt the mixture of the warm fur and the hard, lean heat of his flesh pressing down on her, and she moved eagerly to capture even more.

"Oh, Renata, you feel so good to me," Brant whispered in her ear as his hands spread over her.

Swearing viciously under his breath, Royce reached out to cradle Renata's slight frame, but her shivering and tears would not be stilled.

I've done it again, he thought. Five years was a long time, but some men just don't learn. If she had told him she was a virgin, that would have saved her.

No, that was a lie. He wouldn't have believed her. The look in her eyes had convinced him she was no stranger to a man's embrace.

When Renata pulled out of his arms, he did not reach for her again. A sharp sigh took the edge off his tension. He was not certain he wanted to comfort her anyway. She reminded him too vividly of another woman. His desire for her had brought on a tragedy that had made him leave behind the only life he'd ever wanted.

The woman's name was Patience Swift. She had been as pretty as the first bloom of the Kentucky goldenrod. Every man in the county desired her, but he had loved her most. She'd become his mistress on the little farm his father had willed to him at his death. It was not a grand place, certainly not up to the standards of the Swifts' Blue Grass estate, but he had thought it enough to offer her. And, for a time, it seemed as if Patience had thought the same. They had passed the summer of his twenty-first year enjoying a string of rapturous summer afternoons.

A thousand times afterward, he told himself that he should have been more alert. When they'd been discovered by her brother and three of his friends, Patience's desire for their times together had been destroyed. She had gone sobbing to her father, saying that Brant had forced her to be with him. Afterward, he had gone straight to Blue Grass to ask her father for her hand, but was refused. Then, a few nights later, vigilantes had thundered into his yard, killing his livestock and burning to the ground everything he had ever owned. He remembered grabbing up his rifle and firing a single shot before being ridden down. That shot

had meant death for Hiram Swift, Patience's brother.
Later, he had run—run as far and as fast as his own
wounds would allow. And he had never looked back
... until now.

Renata's weeping drew Royce back from the
memory. "What's wrong?" he asked softly.

Renata, startled by Royce's voice, choked on a
sob. *"Dios mio,"* she murmured. She had not wanted
to shame herself with tears. It was only that her fear
had grown larger than her pleasure when their bodies,
slick with perspiration and the musky essence of lovemaking, had drawn apart. Blindly she put out a hand
to touch him and found her palm sliding over his thigh.
"Forgive me," she whispered faintly. "It is only the sil-
liness of a woman in love."

Renata's words brought Brant unexpected gratifi-
cation. The girl never said quite what he expected.
That was one of the things that drew him to her. Her
honesty came, no doubt, from her inexperience with
men. Royce sighed in frustration. In the future, she
probably would become one of the most accomplished
flirts in the whole damned territory, thanks to him.

"Did I hurt you?" he asked.

"Oh, no!" Renata reached out, seeking his face.
"It was, it was . . . I cannot name it. Too much beauty
and happiness to name."

"Then why the tears?" Royce's hand found her
cheek. Tears moistened his fingertips as he traced a
line from her ear to the corner of her mouth.

"I am afraid." Royce's hand left her face and
Renata brought it back to her lips for a kiss. "Not for
myself," she whispered shyly. "It is my own selfishness
I fear. For my own joy, I risk your life. Do you not un-

derstand? If my brother Miguel learns what has passed between us this night, he will kill us!"

Royce snorted. He seemed to have a penchant for repeating his mistakes. Did every woman alive have an avenging brother? Well, if Lopez came after him, he would be ready.

"Tell you what. I'm headin' north, toward Colorado, come morning. I'll take you with me if you'd like." He patted her belly. "Me, I'd like that just fine."

Renata slapped Royce full in the face. "You think me a squaw that you can pack around until you've satisfied your lust? I am no whore that your silver can buy! What Renata Maria Teresa Sanchez Lopez gives, she gives of her own choice! You, gringo, go and soak your swollen head!"

"Shhh! Renata!" Royce gasped, grabbing her arm. "You'll bring us a visitor."

"Let go of me," she whispered furiously.

"Certainly, *corazón mia,*" and he freed her.

"Do not lie. I am not 'your heart,'" she hissed. "You would not treat the woman of your heart so lightly."

Royce swallowed his amusement. She was trying to trap him into lying about his feelings. He would not be maneuvered by a scheming little flirt no matter how badly his instincts made him want her. "You know what folks say about the gringo trappers who come to New Mexico? We come for pleasure, for pelts, and for silver—not necessarily in that order. If you'd told me you were a virgin, things might have turned out different."

"Then I'm glad I did not," Renata said simply.

"Damnation!" Royce reached out and covered

Renata's mouth with a kiss. There was something about this girl that would make her hard to forget. But just now that did not matter much.

Renata's mouth melted into his as she slowly responded to his desire. Her breasts swelled under his fingers and her thighs spread easily. Suddenly it seemed that she wanted him as badly as he wanted her. That was good. Renata would think about that before dawn. She would come with him; he would bet on it.

"I'm not the marryin' kind, Renata," he whispered into her ear. "But I'll be good to you. I promise."

Chapter 5

Daylight broke over the town of Fernandez de Taos. Kit struggled to his feet in the tiny room he shared with four other trappers and sensed that he was the only man who was awake in American House. A few minutes later the empty drawing room proved him right.

The room was filled with signs of the revelry of the night before: an overturned table, half-empty glasses of whiskey, a few broken plates and some cold tamales that had gone untouched. The smell of liquor pervaded.

Kit's head hurt. He had imbibed along with the rest of the men. To his left, two trappers had propped themselves up against a wall and fallen asleep, their shoulders pushing each other for balance.

He grinned. I guess I'd better get a little more sleep, like them fellas, Kit thought.

He napped.

Later, when he went outside for a breath of air, the town plaza was beginning to fill with people. Packing gaily colored saddle blankets, pottery and baskets

in anticipation of the sales they would make to the
Americanos, the Pueblo Indians were settling down
beneath the few scraggly cottonwoods in the square.
Silver-mounted saddles adorned with ribbon streamers
and tassels hung on pegs outside the blacksmith shop
to encourage the reluctant buyer. Carried on the breeze
was the delicious odor of baking bread, the specialty of
the beehive-shaped ovens that dotted each yard of the
settlement.

"Hy-aii-aay!" The piercing cries were followed a
moment later by the clomp and stomp of dozens of
grey donkeys. Behind them in the plaza came a platoon
of herdsmen twirling lassos above their wide sombreros
and bawling in Spanish at the herd.

Kit chuckled as he watched a balking mule heave
a huge load of firewood from its back, its owner grap-
pling in vain to prevent the wood from tumbling.

The noise and clutter increased as the square
swelled with barterers and farmers. Money had come
to town with the new brigade of Americans, and the
townspeople knew it.

Baskets of pumpkins and red peppers sat beside
piles of Indian leggings and leather shirts. One shirt Kit
saw was made of natural buckskin, its long sleeves
heavily fringed. Along the collar a pattern had been
worked in beads. He paused to look more closely at it.

"Lovely piece of work," came the comment at
Kit's shoulder, and he looked up into the face of yet
another stranger. The man smiled at him, revealing
good teeth behind a brilliant red beard. "Just don't be
lettin' the Arapahos sell you a piece of leather that
hasn't been smoked, laddie. T'will shrivel up and make
a corset around you come the first rain." Before walk-

ing off, the man doffed his hat, displaying his vivid red hair.

"Of all the cockeyed . . . !" Kit began, spinning around to watch the stranger as he went.

"Hold on!" Royce came from around a corner of the square to meet Kit. "What's the matter? Haven't you got no sense at all?" he demanded, when he stood before the younger man. He shook his head. "Don't get mad at him. You know who that is? That's gonna be your new boss! Anyway, why are you bein' so sensitive? That fella didn't do anything but try to help you!"

"I guess you're right," Kit answered, then noticed Royce's disheveled appearance. "What the hell happened to you?"

Royce looked down sheepishly. In his haste to undress the previous night, he had ripped two buttons off the calico shirt he had worn to impress Renata. In addition, he had lost his boots at the pueblo, or, he thought sullenly, he had left them behind when he'd slipped away. Anyway, he was barefoot.

Royce raked his fingers through his hair and then tried to stuff his shirt deeper into his pants. "Nothin' you have to know about, Carson," he muttered.

Kit rested a fist on each hip. "Who you been tryin' to impress? You got some *caballero*'s wife on your string? Whew!" he exclaimed when a gust of wind delivered to him the scent of a woman's perfume. "You'd best bathe before you got half the male population sniffin' after you!" He broke into a grin. "You like your women spicy, that's a fact. Myself, I'd have drowned in that there smell."

Kit burst out with a string of cackles. He would have added fresh insults had he not noted the stony look that greeted him. It was a look that surprised him. Before this, Kit hadn't imagined that anything could shake Royce's amiable disposition. "Who'd you say that hombre with the big mouth was?" he asked to change the subject.

Royce opened his mouth to speak, then clamped his jaws shut and stomped off in the direction of American House.

"Hellfire!" Kit muttered, and moved on. "Some folks ain't got no sense of humor."

By noon American House was crawling with mountain men: Americans, a few Frenchmen, and even two Delaware Indians who stood like sentries on either side of the tall, redheaded man at the end of the bar. Kit pushed his way nervously through the crowd, his eyes alert for the brigade leader of the Rocky Mountain Fur Company. Just as Brant had told him, the man taking down the names and fees of the men in line was the redhead. Kit felt unfamiliar pangs of anxiety in his stomach. He had to have this job. Moving to the back of the line, he watched Royce take his turn in front of the Rocky Mountain Company brigade leader.

"Royce Brant, trapper," Royce announced, and reached for the pen to write his name. "Got my own equipment, Mr. Fitzpatrick," he added when he had signed.

"Everything?" the man known as Fitz inquired with a lift of his brows.

"Well, I could use some galena pigs for making lead balls. They were running low when I came through Santa Fe a week back. Guess you wouldn't know about that," Royce drawled with a slow smile.

Ammunition was the most difficult thing for an American to acquire in Mexico. If Fitzpatrick had found a way to get any at all, it was due to his trading expertise, coupled with his diplomatic skills.

Fitz gave the tall man a hard look before his face crinkled into a smile. "Right you are, then. Galena lead for rifle balls. Amount due: four dollars. Next!"

Kit smoked a hand-rolled cigarette while he waited his turn to face the man whose name was already synonymous with the northern Rockies. Fitzpatrick was tightly muscled, with a direct, blue-eyed stare and a heavy tan permanently baked into his complexion. Kit wondered whether there was a time it had been as freckled as his own.

Fitz was making his own assessments of the youngster who stood before him: short, thin; didn't look like he could hold his own against a Wyoming blizzard. What would Jim Bridger make of the boy? Fitzpatrick wondered. Bridger's business sense made him less sensitive to new recruits. He'd probably say, "There's no sense signin' on a youngster who can't pull his load."

"How do you do, laddie," Fitz greeted. The boy's blue eyes tightened into a squint hearing the leader's unencouraging tone. "You wouldn't be knowin' much of the way of huntin' beaver, I expect." Damn, Fitz thought. There was no good way to turn a man down in front of his friends.

"Mr. Fitzpatrick!" a voice called from the back of the room. Royce stepped forward. "I stuck around just so I could introduce you to my friend here." Royce slapped Kit gently on the back. "This here is Christopher Carson. Folks call him Kit. Well sir, he's the one who took on St. Nair up at the Arapaho camp last evening."

Fitz's eyebrows rose in disbelief. "Took on who?" He turned to the boy. "You mean you're the laddie who felled that big man?" A delighted grin broke his face into dozens of weathered wrinkles as other men who knew Kit now spoke up for the boy.

"Laid 'em flat, our Kit did!"

"On account of a squaw, naturally."

"A regular Davy and Goliath!"

"Faith!" Fitz exclaimed. "I'll be takin' you on just to ride shotgun for us. Put your mark there, my boy, and welcome to the Rocky Mountain Company brigade."

Kit reached out and scrawled his full name in the ledger, grinning at the look of surprise on Fitz's face. "Taming grizzlies ain't the only thing I can do, Mr. Fitzpatrick," he announced. "If you need some figurin' done, you let me know. Trapped in Arizona and California last time out."

"You come with your own equipment?" Fitz asked.

"No, sir, I don't," Kit replied matter-of-factly. "You just set down in your book what I need and what it'll cost me. Be payin' you back before the end of the month."

Fitz ignored the flagrant boast. He knew from years of experience with trappers that most men's wages rarely lasted longer than it took to clear old debts and find the nearest card game. Two weeks of rendezvous, with its temptations of whiskey, gaming, and squaws who needed beads and cloth and other things to make them keep the mountain men company, and a man would most likely sink quickly in debt just buying new clothes for the next season. Too bad, but the boy would have to learn for himself.

"Christopher Carson, company trapper," Fitz stated officially. "Wages: four hundred dollars American. Supplies, to be deducted from wages:

> 4 traps, metal
> 1 mule
> 1 Spanish saddle
> 2 Navaho blankets
> 1 set of buckskins
> Galena lead and powder
> 1 Hawken rifle
> 1 ration of tobacco twists.

Next!"

Kit walked out of American House feeling as light and dizzy as he had after his first tangle with Taos Lightning three years earlier. That particular good feeling had faded when the spirits, combined with tobacco, red peppers, and water, had come back to haunt him for days afterward. But there would be no hangover this time. Four hundred dollars!

"Lord! I'm rich!" he bellowed, embracing the first woman he came to. The rebozo-clad woman shrieked when Kit swooped down to plant a loud, smacking kiss on her toothless mouth. Then he deposited her beside the stacks of pottery she'd set out on the road for sale. Before the day was done he owned the Arapaho shirt he had admired. He'd also bought leggings and a new pair of moccasins. "A man's got to splurge now and then," Kit said to himself gleefully as he returned to American House.

"Bought them big enough?" Royce asked when he met up with Kit before supper.

Kit looked down at his bundle of new belongings. "Which particular thing you talkin' about?"

Royce poked the moccasins. "Those. They shrivel up with wadin'. You'll wake up one night thinkin' you stuck your feet in one of your own traps. A man near got himself shot last season. Jumped up and ran through the camp screamin' like a banshee. Guards thought he was some fool Indian countin' coup on our men. Took him three hours of soaking to get his shrunk moccasins loose enough to come off."

"Yep! They're big enough," Kit answered after hearing Brant's story. He was glad Royce was not holding his earlier teasing against him. "When you figure we ride out?"

Royce shrugged. "Fitzpatrick's talkin' about the end of the week. Way I figure it, tomorrow won't be too soon."

"I'm with you," Kit agreed eagerly. "There's nothin' more I'll ever want out of life than to be a first-class trapper!"

Royce's expression was disbelieving. For him, at least, life had not been that simple, and he suspected that Kit would soon learn that his own life could not remain untouched by trouble much longer. "By the way, you were in such a hurry to outfit yourself that you didn't hear the news."

Kit cocked his head to one side, puzzled.

"Mr. Fitzpatrick decided not to take on St. Nair, after all. Said he didn't much relish the idea of hirin' one good trapper just to lose him in a squabble with another one. Reckon word of your fight with St. Nair set everyone to thinkin'."

"That so?" Kit answered in a cocky tone. "Called me a good trapper, did he? Ain't that a pretty sound? What you figure St. Nair is going to do about bein' left out?"

"I'd say you had a piece of luck there, son. Soon as Fitzpatrick said no to him, another fella—a Frenchman named Céran St. Vrain—offered St. Nair and a few other losers a job hunting buffalo for a new place up north called Bent's Fort. Still, it might be wise if you were to come along with me next light, just so Fitzpatrick doesn't lose his 'good trapper' to some sore loser."

"I'm with you," Kit nodded. "Let Fitzpatrick and the others catch up with us!"

Chapter 6

"Levez! Levez!"

Responding to the now familiar call, Kit rolled over, awakening to a sky greying with the new morning light. The ground beneath him gave a little, a sensation that snapped his lids open.

The softness was from pine needles and other forest foliage. Finally, after more than a month of nearly steady travel, the brigade was off the prairie and into the foothills of the Rockies. It was here that the serious trapping would begin.

Kit flung off his blanket covering, scattering the light mantle of snow that had fallen during the night. "I'll be damned," he exclaimed mildly, reveling in the sight of the quivering snow-covered aspens above him. "Must be this fine mountain air." He rose and stretched, enjoying the sharp tang of frost in the air.

"Just a minute, you darn fool!" Kit roared, hurry-

ing over to the young boy whose job it was to help
with the mule packing. "Been a month, and still you
can't tie a proper cinch knot. One wrong step, my
traps'll be tumblin' down the mountainside." Kit pulled
the boy's knots loose. The "pork eaters," as the trappers always referred to the camp tenders, were usually
men or boys who had no experience on the frontier. To
them fell the labors of rustling grub and tending the
brigade's mules. "Let me teach you how to do this knot
right, sonny."

Amos Tuttle looked at the trapper's callused, capable hands. "Yes, sir. I was tryin' to tie 'em just like
you're doin' now, only the dang mule won't hold still."

Kit shook his head. "If you was expectin' a mule
to set still like a lap dog, you should have took up a
different profession." Kit jerked the last knot tight.
"Now do it right next time, okay?"

Tuttle nodded, and Kit walked away.

It wasn't only knots that Amos couldn't seem to
master, Kit thought to himself. Nothing the boy did
met frontier standards. Kit remembered how, when it
was Amos' turn at the mess, he always had a resentful
word for the quality of the meals. Inevitably, he laid
the firewood wrong or packed Kit's mule so that Kit
couldn't reach the traps without dismantling the entire
pack. The boy was even lazy when it came to scraping
the flesh off the few pelts Kit brought into camp.

Kit stopped in his tracks. Had Amos done anything right? Kit knew he'd had sharp words for the
other tenders who worked for him from time to time,
as well as for Amos. But no one irritated him as much
as Tuttle. Why? He would have to think about that,
but not right now, for they would be making a proper

camping site before dusk. From there, small parties of trappers would set out to camp along the clear mountain streams brimming with thick-pelted beaver. He wanted to be saddled early enough to choose his own spot near the front of the brigade.

The sun set early in the mountains, but Kit was already settled in his site well before the last of the brigade straggled into camp. "Looks like Jackson and a few others is gonna have to slog it a far piece up into them hills to find an empty spot," he said to Royce, who was sharing his campfire.

Royce glanced over to the area where the last of the men were riding in. "Could be Fitzpatrick's gonna need a man ridin' at the back of the caravan to keep those fellas in line. You ought to volunteer for the job, Kit, you bein' so worried for their well-being and all."

"Hell, no!" Kit chuckled. "Ain't never gonna let no job tie me down to where I can't get up and ride out anytime."

"Second in command is a mighty powerful position. Some of the men who rode into Taos with Fitzpatrick tell how his partner, Jed Smith, went under a couple of months back. Fitz could use some help. He's packin' the stock of goods Smith collected for rendezvous last summer."

"That so?" Kit answered with mild interest. "It did occur to me to wonder why we're so loaded down with pack mules when we haven't even caught nothin'. Must be why he hired that useless whippersnapper Tuttle."

Royce smiled behind the tin cup of coffee he raised to his lips. "I'd have thought you'd have a warm place in your heart for that boy."

"Like hell!" Kit barked. "He couldn't find the top side of that mountain yonder without two days' notice and an Indian for a guide."

"Really? And here I was thinkin' how he reminded me of what you must have been like a few years ago," Royce replied, chuckling.

Kit pitched him a sour look. "You spoilin' for a fight?"

Royce shrugged off the suggestion. "Haven't you noticed how the boy hangs on every trapper's words? He's purely hankerin' after a chance to join up."

"Then he should have had more sense than to go and accept a job as a pork eater. Jehoshaphat! The kid ain't got any pride at all!"

Understanding flickered briefly in Royce's eyes. "Carson, if you can't figure out why Tuttle is just like a burr under your saddle, well, I'm not gonna tell you." He reached out to pour himself a second cup of coffee, then continued. "You ready for the evening's stroll?"

Kit's face brightened. "Sure enough. Been waitin' all my life to bait a trap in the Rockies proper."

"You got 'medicine'?"

Kit opened his mouth to lie, then realized the uselessness of it and shook his head. "Last season Cap'n Young supplied all his trappers with the bait scent. Fitzpatrick's been supplyin' me this season."

Royce smiled. He had seen that Kit had been ready to lie. Kit was proud, but he did not often let his pride make him look foolish. "You know what it is?"

"I know it's made from the smelly gland of the beaver," Kit replied, trying to remember more. "Anything else I should know?"

"What to mix with it." Royce set down his cup

and reached into the small sack tied at his waist. "Here, use this." He tossed Kit the sheep horn filled with castoreum. "Let's get at it before it gets too dark."

Kit had scouted out the stream he planned to trap. With his traps slung over his shoulder in the parfleche pouches that were used to check the sound of metal rubbing metal, he left the camp. His tread was muffled by his moccasins. His brand-new Hawken rifle was loaded. He carried it in his right hand with his finger curled tentatively around the trigger. Climbing steadily down the slope for more than half a mile, he soon noticed that his view of the camp had been eclipsed by gold-leafed aspens. Soon, the trickle of water beside his path began to widen as it gurgled along.

Kit breathed in the fresh autumn air. The light snowfall of the dawn had not continued, but he knew that the next morning he might awaken to find himself half-buried in a drift. Still, there was nothing to signal the return of poor weather, and Kit felt he might have rustled up a cheerful whistle had he not known better. There was no sense in scaring away whatever animal life there might be around him. Worse, he might have alerted an Indian eager for a white scalp.

About a mile below the spot where he had found the telltale signs of beaver, Kit stepped off the bank and into the water. The icy splash of mountain water circling his ankles caused him to suck in his breath quickly, but he plunged in anyway until he was knee-high.

There was a sound, and instinct made Kit crouch

and turn as he brought the barrel of his Hawken up for sighting.

"Don't shoot!" The plea was followed by a hasty crunching of leaves as Amos Tuttle scurried out of the shadows of the forest to the edge of the bank. "It's me, Carson."

"That particular news ain't likely to save your skin," Kit grumbled as he lowered his barrel. "You damn fool greenhorn!" he roared. A frightened bevy of quail took off in flight. "Now look what you did, Tuttle. The entire population of the mountain must have heard me yell." Grumbling under his breath in Spanish, he waded back to the bank.

"Gee, Carson, I'm sorry if I startled you," Amos said apologetically. "How was I to know you didn't know I was there all along. I figured you was just ignorin' me." The boy shrugged, wiping back strands of long brown hair from in front of his eyes. "Really, I figured you knew it was me. Lord! You nearly blew my head off."

"Shut up," Kit snapped. "Just what kind of trick were you figurin' to play?"

"Trick? No, sir. No trick," Amos vowed vehemently. "I just wanted to see a real trapper in action." He reddened with embarrassment. "You know, learn how it's done from a professional mountain man."

"Well, you had no damn business following anybody you didn't ask," Kit said, but he felt his wrath disappearing. The boy thought Kit was a full-fledged mountain trapper, not just a first-year man. "Tell you what," Kit offered more generously, "you go on back to camp and we'll forget you came out here today."

For a moment, Amos looked unsure. "How about

this," he said, brightening. "You could just go on pretendin' I wasn't here—like before. That way I won't bother you none and I could watch from the bank."

Kit's smile broadened. "Come here," he ordered, waving Tuttle closer.

"Right out in the water?"

Carson nodded, and Amos stepped forward, yelping when the cold water swirled around his ankles.

Kit waited until the boy had both feet in before he reached out and grabbed his arm. He looked straight into Amos' eyes. "You plannin' to learn about trappin'? You're gonna do it right up close. This here is the first lesson. Never walk on the bank. It disturbs tracks and leaves your own stink on the trail to warn the beaver. The animal ain't near as stupid as you think."

He let Amos go and watched as the boy wandered into deeper water, his knees wobbling.

Satisfied, Kit started off again up the middle of the creek. Only once in the next half hour did he look back over his shoulder. Tuttle had kept pace at a respectful distance, but the boy wore boots that kept slipping on the soft mud bottom. Kit knew he was going to have to be firm, even reproachful, with Amos if he was going to teach the boy properly. After all, that was how he himself had been taught to be a trapper. And he couldn't afford Amos scaring off any beaver.

"One more splash and I'll dunk you," Kit warned the floundering boy.

As the stream widened just beyond a stand of trees, Kit knew he had found the place he'd been searching for. He pushed Tuttle back. There were several beaver lodges along the dam blocking the stream's source. Each one was made of mud and branches from the nearby forest. Kit stared at first one, then another, as he sought the best spots to lay his traps.

The paths the animals made from their homes to their wood source were clearly marked trails on the riverbank, but Kit hesitated a moment. He had seen many trappers simply set their traps in the vicinity of a pond, hoping to draw the beaver with the scent of their bait. But it seemed to him more practical to place the trap in the beaver's way, right where one of those worn paths met the water. He shot one more silencing glance at Tuttle, who had settled himself on a flat boulder in midstream. Then he waded forward cautiously. His plan would require extra care if he expected to get closer to the beaver than most men. One whiff of his scent and they would flee.

Once his mind was made up, Kit went to work quickly. He pulled his first trap from his sack, opened it and laid it on the muddy bottom in shallow water about three yards from the bank. The surface was junked with floating debris from the trees. Kit scooped up a branch, hacked off the limbs in quick movements, drove it into the mud and attached the trap chain. A long while ago, he'd learned that a beaver was not killed by the trap itself, but by the weight of it holding him under water and drowning him. The test of the trapper's skill was in placing the trap so the beaver could be caught in the first place.

For the next half hour Kit worked, testing a new theory. After each staking, he looked around for a supple green twig that a beaver would find difficult to resist. This stick he dipped in the castoreum mixture Royce had given him. Then he sniffed it briefly.

The smell was slightly different than either mixture Young or Fitzpatrick had offered, and a second idea struck him. When he came back to collect his pelts in the morning, he would collect castoreum from the glands of the males. That way he could experiment with his own formula and perhaps improve on his bait. After all, a man's "medicine" was considered a private matter he did not share with even his best friend. More than likely Fitzpatrick and Royce, too, had given him something other than their own personal blend, effective but not first-rate.

Kit staked the twig dipped in scent strategically over the open trap on the river bottom. When the beaver, drawn by the mating scent, stood up on its hind legs to sniff, it would step right into the iron jaws.

"Where the hell have you been?" Fitzpatrick demanded of Amos when he spied him in Kit's company, coming into camp. "You had mess duty tonight. What are you planning to feed the ten men comin' into camp at any minute expectin' a hot meal?"

Kit turned to Tuttle, a scowl deepening on his face. "You been shirking your duties?"

Amos looked from one angry man to the other and lowered his eyes. "Sorry, Mr. Fitzpatrick. I clean forgot. I'll get somethin' together pronto, though!" He turned and fled.

"You don't have exclusive rights to the boy," Fitz said, looking directly at Kit. "Each man is expected to carry his own weight. You find the job too strenuous, you come and settle up with me." Before Kit could protest, Fitz walked away.

"Goddamn. Goddamn!" Kit threw his hat on the ground and stalked off. The fact was that Amos Tuttle—that nuisance—had gotten him in trouble with the brigade chief. "If that kid ever shows his face near me again," Kit vowed, "he's gonna pay for it!"

For the next few weeks, Kit had his wish. Every time he was in camp, Amos was not. Finally, Kit learned that the boy had been assigned guard duty over the pack mules. That meant he'd have to sleep during the evening so he could be alert all night.

Kit's experiments in the field were gaining recognition in camp. By moving his traps closer to the beaver lodges, he had doubled his luck and was doing so well that he had bought three more traps against his wages. Now he had six. Four of the six came up full each morning when he went to check them, and that count more than doubled the other men's percentage.

"You must be doing something right," Royce remarked one night after their traps had been laid for the catch. "You're the talk of the camp."

Kit smiled. "You told me to use my eyes and figure out a few things for myself. Took your advice to heart."

"You made your peace with Fitzpatrick, then?" Royce knew that Kit had been treading thin ice with the brigade leader and that it didn't help matters that he was trapping twice the number of beaver that Fitz's old-timers were.

The men were indeed beginning to talk. They shared no loyalty that could not be bought for the right price. If they had convinced themselves that Kit was a better trapper than Fitz, it would not be long before some of them voiced that opinion aloud. That meant certain trouble.

Kit leveled his stare at Royce. "You and me," he said, "we're the closest thing to friends either of us has out here, but I don't go mixin' in your business. I don't ever ask you what it is that makes you sit and stare at the campfires till they're nothin' but embers. I don't ask you why you mutter about yellow hair in your sleep or why you mention a girl named Renata, either." Kit softened as he saw the bigger man's face redden. "You've got your private business. I'd say that entitles me to mine. Else," he continued, drawing out the word, "I'd advise you to find yourself some pretty little Crow squaw to cool the heat in your britches before it sets you on fire."

Royce sucked in a deep breath. Kit's words had filled him with anger. They faced each other across the breadth of the fire. Neither man lowered his gaze, but neither did either one move to arm himself.

"Where the hell is Tuttle!"

The shout from Fitzpatrick brought Royce and Kit to their feet as the brigade leader came pounding across the camp. His long red hair whipped back as he ran toward them.

"You seen Amos, Carson?" he asked, gasping for breath.

"I have not," Kit answered coolly.

Fitz put his hands on his hips and turned to Royce. "You seen that boy, Brant?"

"Saw him just after sunset. He was pacing out a measure in front of the corral."

"That's what he was supposed to be doin'. Only

when I went to check the mules just now, Tuttle was gone. What's more, two of our mules are missin'."

"You accusin' the boy of stealin'?" Kit asked.

"Think I should?" Fitzpatrick inquired. "Aw, hell! The daft lad hasn't got the sense to think of it." Fitz shook his head. "He probably wandered off to moon somewhere and forgot to tether the animals good and tight. Told him a thousand times that cottonwood corral is just to keep the animals bunched together. It doesn't take much for one of them to knock down a section and scramble away if they aren't pegged to the ground."

"You looked good for Amos?"

Fitz gave Kit a hard look. "You want trouble tonight, Carson, you'll get it. Only you'll have to wait your turn. Tuttle's is the first carcass I mean to chew up and spit out." He swung around and stomped off.

"God help the poor little guy," Royce muttered.

"Ain't got time for prayer," Kit remarked tightly. "Appears Amos is gonna have to make do with a limb o' Satan."

Kit was right on Fitz's heels when Amos appeared suddenly at the edge of the clearing. He was breathing hard, his hair sticking to his damp brow. "I lost 'em, Mr. Fitzpatrick!"

"Lost who? The mules?" Kit asked.

"Indians, Carson," Amos replied. "Chased 'em near half a mile before they got out of my sight."

"Indians!" Fitz scoffed. "You mean to stand there and tell me you let Indians waltz into camp without giving the warning? Saints preserve us! You're a worse liar than worker."

"Honest, Mr. Fitzpatrick! I saw Indians. Well,"

Amos hunched his shoulders, "there was one, anyway. Sneaked up from the back of the corral, near them rocks over yonder. Must have climbed down from above. Never heard a thing till he was headin' for the underbrush. Got two mules with him."

Fitz swore and grabbed the boy by the front of his shirt. "You saw two mules get away—I believe that. But the truth is you're lying about the Indian part." He began moving back toward the campfire, dragging Amos by his shirt. "I've been waiting a long time to settle with you, lad. Somebody get me a length of rawhide. I got some hide-tanning to do!"

The lure of a spectacle brought those few men close in who were not already aware of the goings on. Even as Kit stood there listening, the tone of the crowd grew ugly. He wondered if Fitz would be able to whip the boy and leave it at that, or if the crowd, enthused by the boy's humiliation, would demand another means of punishment that could cost him his life.

He looked up to find Royce at his side. The glances they exchanged told him he would have at least one ally if he broke in to stop the punishment.

"Just a minute!" Kit walked up to Fitzpatrick and put a hand on Amos' shoulder. "You can't whip the boy without first tryin' to learn if he's tellin' the truth."

"He let the mules get away," one trapper muttered.

"It'd serve the pup right, noddin' off on the job," added another.

"Who looked to see if there's any tracks?" Kit asked.

"This isn't any of your business, Carson," Fitzpatrick said under his breath. But he raised his voice to repeat the question. "Any of you boys seen signs of Indians on the trail today?" A murmur of denials rippled through the crowd. He turned back to Kit. "You satisfied?"

"No, I ain't," Kit proclaimed loudly. He turned in the direction of the corral. "One of you men bring a torch. Let's look around for ourselves."

Eager for sport of any kind at this point, the men grabbed up a few burning logs from the campfires and set off after Kit.

"Keep back!" Kit warned as he took a torch and stepped over into the corral. "All them moccasins will spoil the sign." After walking back and forth along the perimeter of the corral, Kit worked his way inward. "There it is!" he shouted after a moment. "Indian sign!"

"What's that?" Fitz jumped the log barricade and came up to Kit.

"Right there." Kit pointed to the ground. "Moccasin prints. Tuttle wears boots."

Fitz shook his head. "Tuttle isn't the only man to work the barricade. Could have been made by any one of us, even you."

Kit ignored the remark. "Ain't nothin' left to do." He threw the burning log over the top of the corral and jumped the top rail.

"Where you going?" Fitz yelled.

"Saddling up!" Kit answered. "Gonna catch me a horse-thievin' Indian."

"Oh no you don't!" Fitz roared, racing after him. "You think I'm going to wait around in this valley while you comb the mountainside for a sham Indian, think again."

Kit picked up his saddle and possibles and slung them over his shoulder. "Don't expect you to wait. I'll find you in a day or two. Don't mean them mules to be docked from my pay."

"What sort of talk is that?"

Kit grinned for the first time. "If Tuttle was lyin', I'll pay for the two lost mules out of my own pocket."

"I ain't lyin', Carson," Amos maintained.

Kit shrugged. "It's *you* I'll be after next if you are."

It took Kit all night and most of the next day before he found the thief. He was camped by a creek. His back was to the water, the mules tethered to a stake in front of him. The small fire had gone out, the last of the Indian's meal in scraps around it.

Kit dismounted and walked his horse back fifty yards. He did not tether it. When he recaptured the mules, he would whistle for his own mount to follow. Checking his Hawken, he moved off. He knew he would have his hands full if he awakened the thief, because this was no Arapaho nor Cheyenne he'd have to deal with. The markings of yellow and red on the Indian's face were clear. He had finally run into his first Blackfoot.

Kit crawled on his belly in the underbrush until he again had the Blackfoot's camp in sight. He smiled when he noted that the warrior's horn bow and quiver of arrows lay before him on the ground. Even if the man had a knife, he was not armed sufficiently to present any real problems if Kit could scare off the mules. Kit watched the slow rise and fall of the Indian's chest. He couldn't swear that it was the breath of real sleep, but he did not care. What he wanted to do was steal—not kill—as quickly and neatly as the warrior had.

Rising to his feet, Kit pulled the Green River from his belt and crept forward until he was within five yards of the clearing where the Indian slept. Then he broke brush at a dead run, his moccasins a mere whisper in the dewy grass. When he reached the mules, he severed their tether with his blade. Then he leaped on the back of the nearest one and kicked it into action.

The mule, startled by the blow to its ribs, bawled and kicked once, but Kit had the lead rope and forced it forward. He ducked low in the seat, leaning his length along his mount's back as he braced for the arrow he expected to whiz past. The explosion of a rifle was a bad surprise.

Kit jerked on the reins, turning the mule around to face his opponent. The Blackfoot lowered his Hawken rifle—probably a prize from a dead trapper—and reached for his bow. That was all the provocation Kit needed. He was tired and hungry, and he'd be damned if he'd let the Indian chase and kill him or call for help from other members of his tribe. Kit swung his rifle to his shoulder, took aim and fired. The Blackfoot dropped.

Kit got down off the mule and walked up to the body. He stood expressionless over his victim. The Blackfoot appeared to be older than Kit, and somehow this made him feel more at ease.

Suddenly he remembered what another trapper, Gibbon, had done to the first Indian Kit had killed. The memory, coupled with the thought that he would have to have proof for Fitz of what he had just done, made him grimace. He shook his head. "I can't do that," he told himself. "I can't."

He pulled out his Green River. His hand began to shake as he bent down over the body. . . .

"The damndest fool thing you've ever done!" Fitz finished, his face reddening in anger. "You killed a Blackfoot and left his scalped body for his tribe to find? Lord love us, you're more trouble than you're worth."

Kit had remained relatively calm during Fitzpatrick's tirade. "Sorry about not buryin' the body. But I didn't have the time. I wanted to prove Tuttle was right about the Indian. That's the only reason I scalped him."

Fitz's Irish temper was not about to be appeased by the admission. "Think it's my fault you had to do it? I know what you're thinkin'. Well, let me tell you, mister, if I'd gone after the mules, I'd have come back with them, but I wouldn't have brought a dead Indian's scalp with me. You're too trigger-happy to suit my taste, Carson. But you'd better keep your rifle loaded. Could be you'll get another chance to turn it on Blackfeet. Once they find that warrior's body, you can bet they'll be lookin' for us to spread our guts from here to kingdom come." Fitz took a deep breath. "Know something about Blackfeet, Carson?"

Kit shrugged. "Can't say I do."

Fitz stared at him. "They're not like Arapaho or Cheyenne, content to count coup and run. The Blackfeet don't mind standing right out in the open and firing at you as long as you can fire back. They fight white man's style—to the death. They catch you alive and they'll make a bit of sport of your lovely self. Probably rip your belly with your own Green River and make you run till you drop. Just be certain you're ridin' right up front when they attack. You like a little excitement? They'll oblige you, for certain." Fitz turned away. He was worried and tired. "Wouldn't have happened had Bridger been with me," he muttered to himself. "Bridger'd have blown the Blackfoot's fool head off first, asked questions second."

"What are you going to do now?"

Kit gritted his teeth as he turned to Royce. "What the hell kind of question is that?"

Royce scratched a patch of whiskers as he said, "You've done what you've been wantin' to do—proved the bourgeois wrong. You can outtrap, outthink, outmaneuver him. You've undermined his authority before his men. I was just wonderin' when you plan to ride on out with his men and his pelts."

"You're joking? I ain't after Fitzpatrick's job. Don't want that kind of responsibility. Only, I ain't gonna back down neither when I know I'm right."

Royce pondered that announcement for a moment. "That bein' the case, I'd say you got a problem. No outfit can have two leaders. From now on the men'll be lookin' for your okay on Fitzpatrick's every word. You won the responsibility. Now you got to live with it."

Kit bristled at the reproach in his friend's voice. "Who hired you to be my conscience?"

Royce shrugged. "It's part of growin' up. Look around you. Most of these men never got that far. You want to amount to somethin' bigger than a mountain goat, you got to think about the consequences occasionally. You've made two enemies this fall. You're gonna have to live with that."

"Thanks for nothin'!" Kit called after the retreating figure. "That son of a bitch Tuttle got me into this. Fitzpatrick didn't give me no choice." And now, Kit thought angrily, Royce thinks I was wrong. Well, I'm right, damnit!

Chapter 7

William Bent watched without comment as his hunters saddled up for the day's activity. As the number of people living in the fort increased steadily, the necessity of providing fresh game had taken on new importance.

There were additional demands. The oxen that pulled the wagons needed care, as did the sheep, milk cows and chickens William had brought into the territory. There were cowpokes to break and herd the fort's cattle, mules and horses. These men never ventured far without their families. William smiled. He had almost grown accustomed to the wail of a baby in the middle of the night. Which was just as well, since Owl Woman, his bride of several months, was pregnant.

"You, there! Cinch that mule a touch!" William's voice carried over the yard. The man tending the mule made an impious gesture at his employer, then turned, grumbling, to comply with the order.

William chuckled. He had learned long ago when to ignore the crude ways of the men in this territory. They were a lawless breed, accustomed to taking what they wanted and going as far with it as their lead and powder would carry them. Violence was an everyday affair on the prairie. There was no sense in provoking trouble. When he did pull his rank, most of the men listened. He tried to be fair, kept drunkenness to a minimum most times, and made certain no large bands of Indians remained inside the fort's walls at sunset.

"Mr. Bent, we're just about ready," one of the hunting scouts called a few minutes later. "Fine day for running meat."

William moved from the doorway of the Traders' Room, where he had been watching his clerks divvying out supplies to the hunting party. With an expert eye he reviewed each man's provisions, including horse and pack mule. When he reached the mule used by Jules St. Nair, he paused, put his hand into the pack sitting askew on the burro's back and pulled out an Indian bow. "What's this for?"

St. Nair looked at the American, and for an instant his dark eyes glazed with fury. Immediately he looked away with a shrug.

Most times William would not have pursued the matter, but he had not slept an easy night since St. Nair had ridden in with the other hunters Céran sent up from Taos. The man was a brute. The evidence was the manner in which he treated those unfortunate enough to cross his path. The fort's butcher, doubling as doctor, had bandaged a dozen different wounds inflicted by the French Canadian. A sly, instinctively nasty fighter, St. Nair took what he wanted and dared anyone to object. To let him get away with a show of insolence would make life more difficult in the long run.

William lifted his head slightly to meet the grinning leer of the huge man. "You think you'll have time to play warrior on the trail when the hunting's finished?"

"Maybe so," St. Nair murmured in thickly-accented English. "This buck, he rides like the Comanches, fights like the Blackfeet. Maybe so he can settle his score like Cheyennes." Then he mimed the losing of an arrow with his hands and swung into the saddle of his sturdy pony. The beast seemed to shrink beneath the man's weight. "You give St. Nair his toy. I bring back many scalp." With a perfect imitation of a Cheyenne war whoop, he kicked his horse forward.

"Damned Canadian!" William roared, backing away in self-defense.

"Not too smart, Will," Charles Bent said as he came striding up to his elder brother's side. "That St. Nair's not quite right in the head. Fellas say he's had the bit in his teeth ever since last summer. Something happened down in Taos. Nobody wants to say what it is, though."

William slapped the dust from his buckskin trousers. "I know what's eating that big boar," he said. "He got bested in a fight over a little Arapaho gal. Brought low by a length of lodgepole, so I'm told." William's distemper seemed to melt away. "Damned if it wasn't a runt by the name of Carson who did it, too. Must have smarted something awful."

"The blow with the lodgepole?" Charles asked. "Wouldn't think that would faze an ox like St. Nair."

"Probably wouldn't have if the man hadn't been soused with rotgut. Must have been one sip this side of perdition when Carson persuaded him to lie down for a bit. St. Nair's pride must still be smarting from the licking."

Charles' brows rose in surprise. "You mean he didn't kill the runt outright?"

William took his brother by the arm and led him back to the storehouse. "That's right, blab it right out in the open for the big galoot to hear. Your mouth, I swear!" He pushed Charles inside before finishing his speech. "I never told you before because I figured you'd spill the beans and get yourself killed. But now that you know, you might as well get the story straight. St. Nair was felled by Carson, that's so. When he came to the next day, Carson had ridden out with Fitzpatrick's Rocky Mountain brigade. Took the best men in Taos. That's why Céran saddled us with this crew. Lord, there isn't much difference between them and the varmints they're after. In a pinch, I'd side with the buffalo."

Charles let loose with a long whistle. "So, you think St. Nair still has it in for this Carson fella?"

William shrugged. "Can't say that I care much one way or the other. I met Carson once. Vicious little savage, swinging a bloody scalp. Figured then he would be dead before the season was out." William's smile was grim. "Bet he thought the same of me. It's men like St. Nair and Carson that keep the territory too wild for civilized folk. Business will suffer if we can't run such freewheeling bandits out of the Rockies before long."

"And just how are you planning to do that?" Charles questioned in a mildly teasing voice. "Think they'll just kill each other off?"

"Don't give me false hopes," William said sourly. "Nope. We're going to have to outtrade and outsmart them. Once we've established the link between Taos and Independence, the free trappers will see the need to come to the fort to trade just like the Indians. Why wouldn't they come? We'll offer better, cheaper merchandise than they can get at rendezvous. Pretty soon they'll be working for us, though I doubt the notion will penetrate their thick skulls."

"Carson and St. Nair, too?"

William shook his head. "No. They're two of a kind, natural-born mean and about as trustworthy as coiled rattlers. It'll be the best thing for the frontier when they've both gone under."

Long after he had returned to the business of running the fort, the nagging thought remained with William that St. Nair was up to no good and that perhaps he should rid himself of the man.

Kit noticed the lead-colored sky and shook his head. "We're in for miserable weather, for certain. Don't even look like snow. Sleet and wind will come howlin' down on us before next light."

Royce's and Fitz's gazes followed Kit's, resting first on the dull grey of the distant mountain peaks, then on the dazzling white tips of the nearby ranges.

"Snow up north," Royce announced.

"Blue norther weather," Fitz concurred, spurring his mount to move on.

"Damned Irishman," Kit muttered. "Can't say two words to him these days. And pushin' too fast for my likin', besides."

Royce shook his head. Things still had not improved between Carson and Fitzpatrick. A tense, unspoken truce had polluted their relationship after the Tuttle incident. Kit never openly opposed Fitzpatrick in matters of brigade policy, but the men were waiting for the moment when he would, as eager as children to see the fireworks renewed. "Can't you just ride for a while and stop trying to steer?"

Kit spat on the ground. "Ain't made any objections, have I? Would've stayed on the last river another two days myself. Fitzpatrick's trying to trap and haul a caravan at the same time. Won't wait till a stream's played out."

Royce nodded. "Know what you mean. But Fitz has got men waitin' for him up on the Salmon River, men who've gone this season without resupplying. They need powder and lead, and he's got it."

Kit turned in his saddle to face Royce. "Fitz, is it? When did you come by that familiar way of addressin' the bourgeois?"

Royce's smile was baiting. "Oh, while you were outtrapping the rest of us, I took it into my head that perhaps I should make friends. Maybe you don't need the good will of the boss, but some of us aren't that certain of the future."

The reminder that Brant might not be doing as well as he had been was unsettling to Kit. "What do you mean? You been bringin' in pelts. I've seen 'em."

"Have you now?" Royce drawled, imitating Fitz's Irish banter. "And when were you liftin' your fine eyes from your own concerns to bother that fair head of yours over my well-being?"

Kit reddened at the comment. "Of course I know you've been doin' well." He looked over his shoulder at both their pack mules. "Your mule is as heavily loaded as mine."

"You've stopped to cache twice," Royce reminded him. "Me, I cached once, in that cave back on the South Platte."

"Oh." The word hung heavily in the air as they moved in file with the rest of the brigade. The narrow trail in front of them had widened to reveal a steep mountain valley. "Don't suppose we'll be headin' down there," Kit remarked after a moment. "That would be too easy. We might actually have a chance to do some real huntin'. Fitz," he continued, hesitating briefly, "he'll be wantin' to stick to the mountain streams. We're likely to freeze our tails off."

But Kit was mistaken. Just about the time the camp was ready to break after the midday stop for food and rest, Fitz gathered his brigade for a talk.

"Been pondering the situation," he began, hands on hips. "Doesn't take a goose to tell you winter is rushing down on us early. We've got to make it into Wyoming before that. Here's what we'll do. We march straight up that valley ahead, keeping just east of the mountains proper till we reach the North Platte. After that we turn west, toward the Wind River Mountains."

"Don't aim to spoil your fine plans, only I seen Indian sign on the trail last three or four days," one trapper volunteered.

"That's so!" another confirmed.

Fitz nodded impatiently. "If you'd had your eyes peeled, you'd know they've been watching us the better part of two weeks." His attention focused briefly on Kit. "Since that trouble we had back south with horse thieves, you can probably expect it's Blackfeet."

The announcement brought a swell of complaints.

"What's the matter, Gibbon?" Fitzpatrick gibed in hopes of lightening the brigade's mood. "You afraid of Indians?"

"Not me!" Gibbon proclaimed, brandishing his rifle. "This here buffalo thrower's been made medicine over. Ain't an Indian that can draw a bead on me, because my gun'll throw 'em first!"

The laughter subsided and Fitz said, "That's it, then. We make the valley our bedding ground come nightfall."

"I wouldn't do that if I was you."

The softly spoken words could not have had a greater effect had they been shrieked instead. Fitz's reaction was instantaneous. He spun on his heels, teeth bared. "Carson!"

Kit moved forward to face the Irishman, his face carefully devoid of emotion. "Blackfeet are on our trail. They're just waitin' for us to show ourselves in the open. That valley would make a fine spot for an ambush."

Fitz's face had already turned beet red. His hand went for his Green River; then, all of a sudden, he froze and let his hand fall to his side. "If you're scared, Carson, you keep to the trees. I'm going up that valley. Any of you fellows brave enough can follow me. The rest of you can stay and play hide-and-seek in the cottonwoods till the spring thaw."

"It was just a suggestion!" Kit shouted at Fitz as he was walking away.

"What do *you* think we ought to do?" Tuttle had appeared at Kit's shoulder, his face puckered with concern.

Kit shouldered him aside. "Got to mount up," he muttered.

"I know, I know," he said to forestall Royce as he swung into the saddle a moment later. "I said I'd prefer the valley to the mountains. But that's asking for trouble. Thought Fitz would claim otherwise."

Royce broke into an understanding grin. "You thought Fitz would suggest the mountains so you could complain that the valley was an easier path. You know, Kit, you can't have it both ways. Either you're goin' to have to revise your opinion of Fitzpatrick and admit he's one smart leader or you're goin' to have to leave the brigade."

"Leave?" Kit blasted sarcastically. "Me? When I'm having all this fun, and when I'm about to get in a fight with some Indians, besides? Royce, you purely amaze me."

Throughout the day, small parties of trappers fell away from the main brigade to try their hands at trapping the gullies that wound through the valley floor. Fitz had made his intentions clear. Any man disobeying his directions was taking his life in his own hands. They all knew it, including Kit, who rode right behind the Irishman. This was as close to an admission of

Fitzpatrick's command as his pride would allow. Their number had dwindled to less than twenty by the time camp was set on the narrow valley floor. No wider than a canyon, the location made protecting the camp difficult. To counter that disadvantage, extra guards were ordered up after supper.

"Keep those rifles ready," Fitz warned, ordering every man's Hawken checked to make certain that the powder was dry and the ball was properly set. "If we make it through the next day without trouble, we'll be safely into the hills again."

Kit took his rifle and settled into a place nearest the ravine at the back of the camp. If the attack came, it would be from that direction. He rested his rifle in the crook of his left arm and curled the forefinger of his right hand around the trigger.

At midnight, after hours of huddling in his wool blanket against the brutal bursts of frigid air that came down the canyon walls, Kit felt a hand on his shoulder.

"My turn," Royce said.

"Lucky I recognized your step, Brant," Kit commented wryly. "In this light you look just like an Indian."

"Grab yourself forty winks, Kit. The best sleepin' is after the first part of the night." Royce wrapped his buffalo robe around his long frame—fur side inward—and began pacing.

"What's that all about?" Kit called sleepily after him.

The signal went up only minutes after Kit had dropped into sleep.

"Levez! Levez! Indians! Indians!"

He heard the first shots just as he leaped to his feet. He automatically pulled his rifle to his shoulder even before he sighted the enemy. In a moment they were in front of him, racing against the thin light of dawn hoping to scatter the first line of trappers who ran forward to defend the camp. Even as his rifle recoiled against his shoulder, Kit noted with mild surprise that the Blackfeet had not waited for full daybreak.

Their faces were streaked with the telltale yellow and red warpaint. There were perhaps twenty, all on horseback and moving through the camp like rolling thunder.

The trappers' cries and those of the savages clashed as Kit ran, rifle in hand, to pull a Blackfoot from his saddle. He was successful. Before the Indian had time to react, Kit smashed the butt of the Hawken into the back of his head, knocking him unconscious.

"Carson! Help me!"

He whirled sharply to find the source of the cry for help. Just in time, he saw by the moonlight that Amos had fallen in front of a mounted Blackfoot's horse. The Indian had slipped to the ground and seized the unconscious Amos by his hair. The intent was clear. In a moment he would have scalped the boy with his skinning knife.

Kit reacted quickly. He jerked his rifle up, raced the short distance to where Amos was being held, and swung it against the Indian's back. The Blackfoot gasped, arching up suddenly and then stumbling away into the darkness.

"Get up, you darn pork eater!" Kit yelled, prodding Amos with one foot as he searched the camp for other attackers.

But the camp was settling. The Indians, some injured and some not, had fled. The assault had ended as quickly as it had begun. An uneasy silence pervaded the clearing as Kit dropped to one knee beside the still boy.

"Amos, come on, don't play possum on ol' Kit." He reached down to draw the boy's head up against his knee. There was a steady but weak pulse at the youngster's temple, and Kit shook Amos' thin shoulder gently. "Come along, sonny. You can't get off from a day's work because some worthless Blackfoot tried to tickle your scalp."

Amos snapped out of his daze, instinctively throwing his arms over his head in protection from what he thought was another attack. "Easy," Kit urged, surprised at the relief he felt when the boy moved. "It's over. Them Blackfeet cleared out. You ain't even got a scratch to show for it neither."

Amos blinked several times before steadying his gaze. "Mr. Carson?" he asked innocently, "did they get my hair?"

Kit laughed. "If you were in need of a haircut, you might have asked one of the tenders instead of waiting for the Indians to do the job for you. No, boy. You still got enough hair to shame a beaver. Though, mind you, you'd have lost it, for sure, if it hadn't been for me. Sent that Indian away shakin', just to please you."

Amos was wide-eyed as he stared up at Kit.

"Ain't never seen nobody like that Indian," he murmured.

"Well, let that be a lesson to you. You got to learn to fight if you're gonna make a proper mountain man."

Amos wagged his head slowly. "Don't think I'm mountain man material. I can't . . . couldn't have done what you did. I just couldn't."

"Well, I wish you'd told me that before we came out here. You said you wanted to be a trapper. I imagined you'd learned your lesson and were gonna make a first-rate frontiersman. Looks like I was wrong."

"I done what I could," Amos replied, trembling. "Brought Mr. Fitzpatrick his extra rifle without being told to. I could have run and hid, but I didn't."

"No," Kit nodded. "You didn't. That's why I figured you ought to live long enough to get a chance to get even with the body who forgot to teach you how to shoot. First thing when we set up a new camp, you come to me. I aim to teach you just how to plant a lead ball right between the eyes of the next red man who takes a hankerin' to your scalp." Kit turned and walked away.

Now why did I promise to teach the boy to shoot? Kit wondered. Maybe it had something to do with seeing a defenseless soul in danger. No man should have to forfeit his life because he doesn't have a skill as necessary to the mountains as breathing. At least he could cure that deficiency in the boy. "Besides," he said out loud, "it'll keep me from havin' to play nursemaid."

"Guess you're feelin' right proud of yourself."

Kit did not even lift his head in answer to the familiar voice. "No sir, I ain't, come to think of it."

Fitz stood in front of Kit, arms akimbo and legs squarely planted. "Hope you're satisfied. Those Indians that got away on the trail cost me a man."

Kit followed the Irishman's jerk of the head to the spot where two men were rolling a body up in blankets. "They killed Dawson. A life for a life, since we got one Blackfoot. Must have been satisfied since they didn't do much more than ride through."

Kit looked hard at Fitzpatrick. "I did the right thing, just like you did by comin' into this valley as a shortcut."

Fitz looked visibly shaken. "Am I hearing you right, Carson? You're admitting I could make a decision you might approve of?"

Kit ignored the remark and pitched a final glance at the dead man. "Dawson knew his chances. Sooner or later we all go under. Reckon he knows we evened up the score for him."

Wearing a grim expression, Fitz looked off to the right where the lone Indian's body lay. "So, one Indian was killed. If you hadn't killed one a while back, we wouldn't have been attacked. Sorry, Carson, you get no thanks from me. Now let's get the hell out of this valley before trouble decides to pay us another visit."

Kit walked the length of the camp to get to his equipment. Three men had been wounded; one had died. Something bothered Kit about the attack, something he could not pin down.

"What you got there?" he asked, seeing Royce head toward him with a red silk bandanna in his hand.

"One of our Blackfeet friends is partial to the finer things in life, I'd say. Picked this up by Dawson's body." He handed the scarf to Kit. "I'm curious. Did you notice the number in that raiding party?"

"Yep. There were no more of them Blackfeet than there were of us." Kit ran the scarf through his fingers, a memory playing at the edge of his thoughts. "That don't set right. Indians usually like their odds heavy in their favor, like three to one. Maybe Blackfeet are different, but . . ."

"Yeah?" Royce prompted.

Kit's eyes darted up to meet the taller man's gaze. "Did it bother you that they attacked before sunrise? It ain't like Indians to do that. And all of them had rifles and didn't take anything, did they?"

Royce shook his head. "Nope. Fitz couldn't decide whether to be mad over the whole matter or jist plain grateful."

Kit fingered the red silk. "This here is a voyageur's scarf. Don't see that many this far south. In fact, the only man I've seen wearing one this year was that—hey!" Kit's eyes narrowed. "You don't think that . . ."

"It's possible," Royce interjected, knowing exactly what was on Kit's mind. "But it doesn't make good sense for a man to shoot up a whole camp just on the off chance of killing one man. Besides, the one that was killed was one hundred percent Indian."

"St. Nair's a mean son of a bitch. Could be he's just waitin' for a chance to make your acquaintance again. You got to figure that's so. Carson," Brant added, solemnly shaking his head, "you been making enemies right and left since the day I met you. I guess you got to figure that one of them will cash in on the acquaintance sooner or later. It'd be a shame if your friends—however many you got—have to suffer for the poison someone's feelin' particularly for you." Royce paused. "Wouldn't have thought that even St. Nair had that kind of meanness. You never can tell about some vermin, though. Funny thing about that scarf."

"Funny," Kit echoed as he walked away. The notion that he'd made an enemy who wouldn't meet him in the open settled in his stomach like bad meat, churning his insides long after the brigade had saddled up to move out of the valley.

He expected to meet trouble head-on. The only things that might legitimately sneak up were wolves, grizzlies and Indians. A man who was sorely grieved didn't think twice about walking right up to someone and shooting him in the head. That was natural, Kit thought. But dressing up Indian-style and raiding a campsite just for the sake of mischief was something else entirely.

"Can't prove it," Kit muttered to himself uneasily. Then another possibility came to him. Dawson had a small frame, like his. Same sandy hair and beard, too. In the grey dusk, there might have been a mix-up.

Kit scratched his beard thoughtfully, remembering the reason for the whole mess—the beautiful Arapaho girl with the wide dark eyes and supple body.

She had been too young for him then, just a child, but something in the way she had looked at him made Kit remember her now, months later. He had been greatly excited by her.

"No use studying on it," he muttered as he rolled up in his blanket that night. "Still, I wish I'd gotten to

know that sweet thing. It would have made the thought
of St. Nair a bit easier to swallow." For that girl's sake,
Kit thought, wincing, I may have loosed a madman on
myself.

Chapter 8

". . . was froze so hard, if this hombre didn't get a handful of quills everytime he scratched his head, I'm a gopher!"

When the laughter diminished, a new tale was taken up.

"Ever tell you boys about the time I went out scoutin' for Cap'n Bridger and ran right into an Indian war party? Hell! I'd made my way down the draw of a pretty little canyon, upstream on the Snake. Before I reached the bottom, I heard this caterwauling behind me. Turned my head and saw this plume of dust risin' from the lip of the canyon. Made a run for it, I did. But my old horse, Bess, was kind of tuckered out, seein' as how we was two days without water and three without meat. Took my best shot, emptied my Hawken into the nearest Indian that came upon me. Then I looked up and found myself racing right into the sheer rise of a wall. 'Box canyon, by damn!' I roared. 'Ain't no way out, Bess!' "

A long silence was punctuated by restless coughing and stretching while the narrator refilled his pipe.

"Come on, Meek. What happened!" a man cried at last.

Joe Meek looked up, a trace of a smile on his sunburned features. "Why, them Indians killed me, of course!"

Whoops rang through the confines of the tepee.

About twenty trappers had crammed themselves into the small area to share the warmth of the meager fire. The favorite pastime of swapping stories always seemed upgraded when Meek added a tale or two.

It didn't seem to matter, Kit noted, that though they were shoulder to shoulder, hardly able to find sufficient ground to squat, the trappers were as cheery as they would have been in more luxurious accommodations. Overruled were any scruples a man might have about the peculiar odor of the acquaintances rubbing against them.

The steady snow that had begun before the brigade reached Wyoming had turned into a blizzard by the time it reached the wintering grounds of the Salmon River.

Kit rolled a cigarette. It felt good to relax. The construction of a network of sapling frames had taken more than a week. It was over the frames that the scraped pelts had to be stretched to dry. Trapping in the warmer climates of Arizona and California with Young had taught Kit that skins should be regularly unpacked, beaten and aired to prevent moth damage and rot. But this was not so in the high, dry altitude of the Rockies. They could be packed on the mules and, barring rain or river crossings where they might get soaked, be left bundled together until the end of the season.

The camp work had not kept Kit from scouting out the area in southern Idaho where Fitzpatrick had led them. It was a mountain basin, sheltered by a ridge to the north and heavily wooded. Kit registered these two important points carefully in his mind. The valley sloped southward so that the prevailing north winds drove the snow away from them. The woods provided fodder for their animals. Cottonwood bark was a particular favorite when the ground was covered with snow, and it also made for good hunting. Kit patted his full belly. He had bagged an elk just that morning.

"Hey, Meek! You got any more of them tall tales?" a trapper inquired, jarring Kit from his thoughts.

"Yeah, Meek, but seein' as how you done 'gone under' in the last one, any story you tell had better be about somebody else." The voice that made the complaint was a deep dry bass, and Kit craned his neck to find its owner.

Jim Bridger had joined them. He was seated cross-legged near the campfire, within reach of the stew boiling on its tripod. Heavy, sun-streaked hair fell below his shoulders, and even though Bridger was seated, Kit measured him at more than six feet. His skin was darkened by the prairie sun. Above wide cheekbones and a long, straight nose were his vivid blue-grey eyes.

So this was the famous Jim Bridger. Kit sensed that Bridger was only partially enjoying the company of the men around him. Something else was working actively behind his stare. Perhaps he's planning the spring hunt, Kit speculated. Or perhaps he's deciding who to keep with his brigade and who to fire.

"Since none of you boys are willin' to hear top-rate adventure, I'll have to teach you about this new method of tree climbing I got from Milt last year." Joe Meek grinned as the man next to him groaned in mock pain. "That's right. This here fella, for those of you who don't know him, is Milton Sublette." He slapped the back of the man next to him.

Milt Sublette looked up, revealing a roguishly handsome face. It was an attribute that was known to keep his bedroll filled with local Crow and Nez Perce squaws. "You ain't got to tell it," he moaned.

"No, that's a fact," Joe conceded. "But I sure as hell am goin' to!" He cleared his throat. "You see, it all started with a buffalo hunt. Leastways, that's what the rest of us was doin'." His gaze shot sideways to Sublette. "With Milt you never can tell. Might have caught the scent of some half-naked Indian girl in the woods and took off after her. Anyhow, we're blastin' away, making buffalo come faster than flies to honey when I hear this screech."

Milt groaned, much to the delight of his audience.

"Now, now, Milt, we're just gettin' to the best part," Joe assured him in a voice that made the other man squirm. "Well, I look up in time to see Milt make a bead on somethin' at the edge of the cottonwood thicket. His rifle kicks back, and whatever he hit couldn't have been madder than the grizzly sow that came scramblin' out of that thicket after him. Milt, bein' sort of smart, lit out of there like his breeches was on fire. Course, mama bear wasn't pleased about

that and took off after him. Meanwhile it comes to me
that Milt might need a touch of help. Not that I like
spoilin' a man's sport, you understand. It's just that
this time I wasn't quite certain how Milt figured he was
goin' to reload at a dead run. So I came runnin' up to
within three hundred feet or so, took aim and blasted
that mama bear. A second later that bear ran into the
cottonwoods just behind our friend Milt."

Joe took a deep breath. It was a trick he had
learned to make a story all the better. "I stood there a
second, scratchin' my head and wonderin' what to do.
If I'd thrown that grizzly, it was layin' up in the thicket
dyin'. But if I hadn't planted my ball square, I figured
Milt was in for a bad time. Grizzlies don't take to two
balls in their meat sack quite as meekly as you and me.
Still, Milt was a friend. So I took off into the woods.
And what do you think I saw when I got there?"

"Milt waltzin' with mama bear!" one man offered,
and the tepee shuddered with lusty laughter.

"Now I wish I'd thought of that," Joe remarked
gently when he'd gotten his audience back again. "Still,
truth is near about as good. I found the grizzly
sprawled at the edge of the thicket, still quiverin', but
dead meat for certain. So naturally I start lookin' for
Milt. He can't have gotten far, the way I saw it. Then I
spotted him." Joe shot his victim another glance.
"There's brother Milt, sitting fine as you like, at the
base of a big cottonwood. Only there's something
mighty peculiar about the way he's sittin'. He's got his
arms and legs wrapped around that tree trunk tighter
than he ever wrapped himself about that Crow gal he's
keepin' this winter. Says I, 'What you huggin' that tree
for, Milt?' Well, Milt looks back over his shoulder in

surprise and answers, 'Hell, Joe! Thought I was thirty feet up the son of a bitch!"

And so it went. Story piled upon story until the tepee yellowed with smoke.

Weary, Kit was one of the first to break off from the pleasant company. He quietly rose and let himself out of the lodge, only to be greeted by a gust of bitter-cold air that made him gasp for breath. Kit pulled the hood of his capote up over his head. Then he made his way from the main lodge belonging to the Rocky Mountain Fur Company partisans to one of the smaller tepees he shared with Royce, Tuttle and the Nez Perce girl they had agreed to hire to keep house for them.

The ground crackled under his moccasins, the hard-packed snow gleaming in the dim winter light. From the corrals came the snorts and brays of cold mules. Kit paid little attention to the sound. The trappers were nearly two hundred strong in the winter camp. That count did not include the villages of Nez Perce and Flathead Indians who had chosen to share their wintering grounds. Nothing dared bother a herd that heavily flanked with men able to fight.

"The Indians give us as much protection as we give them," Fitz had remarked in one of the rare moments he and Kit found themselves in conversation. "Besides, think of the joys to be had in the company of their lovely womenfolk on these long, cold nights."

Kit had been thinking about that more and more these last few days. Men like Milt Sublette, and even Jim Bridger, he suspected, made no show of their prowess with women, but were famous for it anyway.

For Kit, things were not quite that simple. He had no fancy words to woo the girls. And when it came to money to buy the beads and rings and bracelets the Indian girls expected in return for their favors, well, he had vowed in Taos that he had spent his last coin on that sort of thing. Life was just beginning to show profit. He would not trade it for a few hours—no matter how pleasant—of pleasure from some sweet Indian girl. "Keeps a man off his stride, howsomever," he muttered, feeling a growing excitement at the thought of the smooth touch of a woman.

The Nez Perce girl who usually went back to her family's village after supper was sitting by the door flap when he returned to his tepee. Kit frowned. He had wanted privacy. The girl jumped to her feet when he entered. Some of the night chill seeped in with him.

"You are cold. Need hot food," she voiced in the stilted English she had learned from the trappers. "Good for belly." The girl picked up a wooden bowl and filled it to the top with the last of the elk stew she had prepared.

Kit accepted the stew without looking at the girl. Then he hunkered down and polished off the contents without a word. When he finished eating, he put away the bowl and reached for his buffalo robe—one of the few luxuries he had allowed himself. The feel of the thick, deep hair against his skin when the temperature dropped below zero made the expensive purchase worthwhile.

"Better go home," he suggested as he rolled up in the robe and turned his back to her.

"No home. Too cold. Die outside," the girl replied softly.

Kit raised his head in annoyance. He was tired. The stew had satisfied him and he was in no mood for a temperamental female. "Then take that blanket and go to sleep." He pointed at his wool blanket and lay back down.

He did not have to be watching the girl to know she had rejected his offer. "No good," she said. "Sweet Blossoms turn to ice like water on river. Too cold to move when the sun returns."

Kit cursed under his breath, flung back his blanket and leaped to his feet. "Then what the hell do you expect . . . !" he stormed, but got no further.

Sweet Blossoms stood before him, her head slightly bowed, naked as the day she was born.

She was not beautiful. Kit did remember thinking that. But her golden-brown skin shone in the dying firelight as warm and inviting as any he had ever seen. Slim-legged and narrow-waisted, the girl stood quietly, her breasts gently rising and falling.

The feel of a woman had long been missed, and it aroused him immediately. The taste of Sweet Blossoms in his mouth was like nectar. Hungrily, Kit caressed her breasts, and she offered her body as eagerly as he accepted it.

He had been too long without a woman to expect anything from himself but quick release, but Sweet Blossoms seemed content with his hasty lovemaking, and soon it was over. She curled tightly against him when he rolled off from her, clamping her arms about his neck and laying her head on his chest. Within minutes they had both fallen asleep.

It was late February when Fitzpatrick finally made up his mind to seek Kit out. He had been watching the young man closely. In his opinion, Carson was in for a bad spell if he didn't learn to bend a little; but he conceded to his partner, Jim Bridger, that Carson was making a fine, first-class trapper.

"Appears to me you've come to some decision," Jim had said to his best friend earlier that morning while they shared a pot of coffee.

"Made it, all right," Fitz admitted. "Trouble is, am I going to regret it?"

"Could be," Jim said, nodding. He and Fitz had been together so long they thought the same thoughts on occasion. "Can tell you now he won't accept."

Fitz looked up. "Won't accept? Do you know how many of this crew would dearly love the chance of being asked?"

"All the same, he won't accept."

Fitz swore and dumped the last of his coffee back into the pot. "Did you ask him?"

"Didn't need to." Jim looked across at the Irishman, his face beginning to beam. "That cub's got the hair of the black bear in him. Nothin's gonna tame him completely. If riding with you hasn't done it, nothin' much can. Some folks are natural-born randy-footed. My pa was. Dragged my ma and kid sister and me halfway across the continent before the putrid fever put a period to his life. Might have took up trappin' himself had he lived. Me and you, we're the lucky ones. We found our place. We're in for it up to our ears, gonna fight for it, territory and trade. But men like Carson—I figure he'll make a name for himself, but you watch. He'll never call anyplace home. It's just not in him."

Later, as he stood in the clearing waiting for Carson to pass by, Fitz remembered that conversation. He smiled. Carson was no fool. He had underestimated the lad, equating size with strength and determination. They had had their disagreements, and except for the Tuttle incident, Fitz still felt he had been right at every point. But a man learned to take into account other things, things like the loyalty Kit had shown in the end when the Blackfeet attacked them, the conviction he had shown in his willingness to defend Tuttle, and the intelligence to see that a little money might be made on the side by setting up shop in the winter camp.

Kit had taken to repairing saddles once the major portion of winter labor was complete. He had even tanned some hides to help in the repairs, charging an otter skin here, a few fox tails there, according to the extent of the work. That kind of determination Fitz could put to use, even if their personalities didn't blend well. And, just as important, Carson had won the respect of the men around him.

Kit threw back the flap of his lodge and saw Fitzpatrick standing under a nearby tree. At first he was confused. He knew that the Rocky Mountain partner did not need his services. While the Irishman might not know trapping as well as he, Fitz knew the country and could handle himself and all that he owned with an expertise that Kit admired. While absorbed in friendly conversation around the campfire, Fitzpatrick could dismantle his Hawken, oil it, then put it back together without directing any more attention to the weapon than an occasional glance down at his busy hands. If Fitz wanted him to stay, it was for something mighty different.

Kit took his time collecting his things, stopped once to plant a soft kiss on the lips of a smiling Sweet

Blossoms. Then he counted to ten before leaving the tepee. Fitz was still outside, smoking a black clay pipe.

"Good day to you," Fitz hailed merrily. "It's a talk I'll be having with you if you don't mind," and he fell into step beside the smaller man.

"I guess it's okay," Kit mumbled. Fitz's blarney, he had learned, either meant the Irishman's temper was aroused or he had something for the day ahead. "You want to talk, we'll talk walkin'."

Fitz exhaled, his breath hanging as thick as cotton in the cold air. "Have you turned in your catch for the season?"

Kit gave Fitzpatrick a sharp look from under the brim of his flat-crowned hat. "You know I haven't. Why?"

"Then you haven't signed up again."

The young trapper shifted the weight of the two saddles he bore on his back. "Don't aim to, anyhow."

That announcement made the Irishman pause. "Why not?"

Kit stopped short. He turned to face the bigger man. "I've learned a thing or two. Seen how you pad your pockets on the extra profits to be made by hirin' a man by wages instead of paying him by the pelt. I got seven hundred dollars worth of pelts I've already agreed to sell to you for four hundred dollars minus expenses. That makes me about two hundred dollars richer than when I started. And I ain't even resupplied. Got to do that, too. And you're sellin' what I need. Way I figure it, you get it all back and I get nothin'. No thank you, I can cheat myself without your help."

Coming from any other man, Kit's accusation might have earned a ball of lead in the head, if not a quick trip up Green River. But Fitz merely chuckled. "Gabe said you were full of the black bear."

Kit had heard Bridger referred to by the name "Gabe" since arriving at the wintering grounds, and news that the consummate mountain man would have such high praise for him, a first-year man, made Kit smile in spite of himself. "Do tell."

Fitz, sensing the advantage his remark had given him, pressed on. "Staying would give you a chance to keep your woman. Hear me out," Fitz sputtered quickly, sensing that Kit was about to wave him off. "The usual procedure for the Rocky Mountain Company brigades is to carry with them women and children of the trappers the company employs. Your little lass would be more than welcome."

"I don't pack a squaw," Kit bit out tersely. The phrase had become synonymous with buying a cook and mistress who was to be traded back to her family whenever the white man who kept her grew tired of her company or found a better bedmate.

"Didn't mean to suggest the lass held anything but a sweet place in your heart, lad. Don't give me that storm-and-thunder look. Ah, Carson, a man can't put five words together before you're calling him a liar and a cheat." Fitz gazed upward. "May the Saints witness the truth of my words. I'm asking you to join us, me and Bridger and the rest, as a partner."

This was not what Kit expected to hear. Yet he shrugged off the notion calmly. "Don't want to, thanks."

"Don't want to!" Fitz nearly choked on the words.

Kit's sense of humor returned as he watched the

man struggling with his temper. "Don't take it personal, Fitzpatrick. It ain't you, the man, I'm turnin' down. I wouldn't work for no other man after this winter. It's just that I gotta try this business for myself."

Fitz swallowed. "You're not serious? Trapping this territory alone? You'll not last a year. There's Blackfeet on the warpath, not to mention our own trouble with St. Nair and that big company back East trying to run us out. By damn! If you're thinking of coming up against us, I'll settle that for you right now." Quicker than Kit could have expected, he was staring at the naked blade of the Irishman's skinning knife.

Kit set down his load slowly, glad that their conversation had not drawn the attention it might have later in the day. "If you're plannin' to use that thing, go right ahead. Else you better put it away before I take exception to your poor show of hospitality." Kit's eyes never left Fitzpatrick's face as he continued to speak in a flat-toned voice. "If I was fool enough to want to come up against you and Bridger, I'd keep it to myself. As is, I'm going back south first thaw. Colorado is more to my liking. You left a powerful lot of streams untrapped last season. I'm willin' to correct that mistake on my own time and for my own profit."

Fitz hesitated, remembering Bridger's pronouncement—natural-born randy-footed. He'll never call any-place home. Fitz shoved the knife back in its sheath. "Give it some thought, lad. We've another month before the thaw. The money's good. The companionship, better."

Kit reached down for his bundles and slung them over his back. "It ain't the money," he protested, turning away. "I got to do it for myself. Got to make it alone."

"Nobody's ever done that, Carson," Fitz called after him. "Every man needs something besides himself."

Fitzpatrick's words hung in Kit's thoughts and stayed with him for the next few weeks, long after he had turned in his fall catch and received his wages without renewing his name to the Rocky Mountain Company roster. But the words didn't change his mind. He had to make it alone, to be free, to win the test for survival.

If he clung to someone else's ways, carrying the extra burden and protection of the company with him, he could never judge whether it was his skill and determination or theirs that was bringing him success.

Of course, when he broke away, he would have a few men of his own with him. No matter how much he'd like to be completely by himself, common sense forced him from the notion. No single man could trap and hunt sufficiently and make the profits he hoped to realize in the next seasons. He would need a few independent men, self-contained and just as eager as he was to meet success or failure on their own terms.

Failure. Kit flinched every time the thought flashed through his mind. Whenever he saw Bridger striding through camp with a parcel of men at his heels, he wondered what it would be like to exchange places.

"That Mr. Bridger, son, when you're riding with him you know your life counts for something," one of the old-timers had confided one night around the campfire. "Seen Gabe snatch a half-dead man from the claws of a grizzly and then wrestle that bear to the ground. He staked him out to dry, meat and all."

The tale was a whopper, but it was indicative of how Bridger's men felt about him. To them, he was capable of defending their lives against all odds. If Kit had accepted the offer of partnership, he knew that he too would have been expected to fulfill the same kind of loyalty.

"Don't want anybody lookin' to me for their life," Kit asserted to Royce later as the two men lay in the darkness of the tepee, wrapped in their robes. "Can't abide a body that won't take care of his own." Kit stroked Sweet Blossoms' hair as she lay nestled in the crook of his arm.

Royce smoothed the fur of his bed of fox and muskrat pelts. "Then why have you been teachin' Amos to shoot?" he asked, snuggling under the heavy bearskin that topped the pelts. "Why did you go after that Blackfoot that stole our mules last fall? Why you tryin' to convince me? I believe you."

"Sounds like I hear a lecture comin' on."

Royce shook his head impatiently. "Not from me, by God. You're just crazy, that's all. First you go out of your way for people, plenty. Then you say you don't want to do that and tell me that's why you turned down a permanent position of guaranteed prosperity. Seems to me you want to go out and be a failure, and a dead one at that. Logic like you've got doesn't need any explanation; it's askin' for a lodgepole across your thick skull." Royce slung the bearskin over himself and turned his back.

"Sounds to me like you're jealous." Kit grinned, amused by his friend's reaction.

Royce flung back the cover and turned to meet Kit's eyes. "You think you're so damned smart, don't you? You're so smug it makes me sick. Sure I'm jealous, but not in the way you think. I'm mad as hell because you're throwin' away a chance a man like me hungers after. A permanent life to look forward to, a place to come home to. I'd take it in a minute."

"You're serious," Kit replied in amazement. "If you want to settle down, why didn't you marry that little señorita back down Taos way last summer?"

"Didn't want me," he whispered after hesitating a moment. "And don't press your luck, Carson. We came close to trouble last time you brought up Renata. Don't aim to have her mentioned again."

"Get yourself another woman," Kit returned, running his hand along Sweet Blossoms' thigh under the cover. "It makes life a lot simpler."

"That's all you know about it," Royce grumbled. "You wait. Some little gal is going to get into more than your britches. Some little gal is going to get into your blood. You come tellin' me about women then."

Kit was silent in the darkness a long time before he spoke again. "That mean you ain't for comin' with me?"

Royce raised his head immediately. "Who'll keep you out of trouble if I don't?"

Chapter 9

"I said no, and I mean no!" Kit shouldered his way past the band of men who had collected outside the Rocky Mountain Company tent to enlist for the spring hunt.

The air was softer, though snowflakes still danced through it. The ground, covered with a winter's fill of ice and hard-packed snow, had a give to it that announced spring even to the light pressure of a moccasin. Within another week, the hibernation period of the beaver would end.

"It ain't fair!" Kit heard behind him. Amos came around Kit to block his path. "You said yourself I'm a good shot. I know the mules. I'm learnin' to use the traps. Why can't I come?"

Kit looked at the boy with a critical eye. Between Kit's saddle repair enterprise that drew a brisk business and the many smaller jobs that he had hustled, he had managed to keep his promise and taught Amos to shoot. But he had not paid particular attention to Amos himself.

It was obvious that the wintering season had been a time of growth for the youngster. He had been as tall as Kit at the beginning of the fall hunt, but now Amos had to angle his head slightly lower to meet Kit's gaze. And there were other changes.

The stubbly hair on the lad's chin indicated that in twelve months time, Amos would be sporting a beard. His wool trousers had risen up over his ankles, and his features were sharpening.

"How old are you now?" Kit asked suddenly.

"Fifteen, next birthday," Amos replied promptly.

"Wasn't your birthday last month?" Kit recalled with a grin.

"Yes, sir," the younger man returned grudgingly.

"Fifteen's a fair age. Was learnin' to drive mule teams for the Gila River copper mines not much older than that," Kit reminisced.

"Don't want to be a teamster," Amos grumbled under his breath. "How did you feel about doin' it?"

"Hated it," Kit replied too quickly to catch himself. "All right," he snorted, annoyed by the trap he'd stepped into. "So I hated it. Done plenty of things I hated in my lifetime. Wasn't anybody to hand me nothin'. Had to wait my chance. You want a chance, you got to wait for it."

A confused look clouded Amos' eyes. "Nobody ever done nothin' for you? How come?" Unwittingly, Kit's thoughts rested on Ewing Young. Young *had* taken a chance on him, and more than one if a body counted the job as cook.

"Wasn't the same thing," Kit muttered. "Anyhow, you don't know the first thing about stayin' alive. You go out with your arms wide open expectin' somethin' to point the way. You can't live like that out here. You gotta be watchful, gotta use your wits and instincts, figure everything possible that could happen and provide against it. It's a wild, unforgivin' kind of life that takes everything a man can hold onto with his bare hands and courage. This country'll swallow you up whole so there'll be nothin' left to tell folks what happened. You're a swell kid," Kit conceded, then added quickly, "but you're not ready for the wilderness. The frontier'll kill you. Mark my words."

Amos swallowed hard to keep the tears from slipping onto his cheeks. "Well, if you don't take me, I'll strike out on my own. Plenty men do it. Old Bill Williams has been tellin' me how he ain't scared of livin' alone. If that old-timer can do it, so can I." Amos bolted away.

Kit kicked the ground. Damned if these good-byes weren't heart-wrenchers! Kit had just come from the Nez Perce camp where he had said good-bye to Sweet Blossoms. She had broken into tears and clung to him.

Kit had enjoyed the times Sweet Blossoms and he had shared. He was pleased that her presence in his lodge had given him status in the eyes of the other men. And the personal comfort and joy she had afforded him were irreplaceable. Sweet Blossoms had known how to make him happy.

Now Amos had gone. Guess it's just as well, Kit thought. He knew that what he needed was another expert trapper—a man like Royce—who could take care of himself. Only where would he find that second man?

"Five shots. Three rifles! In the three passes or I'm a walleyed racoon!"

Kit swerved just in time to see the trapper with the booming voice heading his way. He was six feet two inches of almost meatless bone, with an incredible wealth of long black hair. The man wielded a rifle in one hand and a bottle of *aguardiente* in the other. He strode past Kit and headed toward the corral. A dozen men trailed him. Intrigued by the presence of someone new in camp, Kit followed.

"That's how it'll be, by damn," the newcomer declared, "or my Green River'll do the talkin' for me." He reached out an arm, the bottle tucked under his other elbow, and clamped one huge hand around the neck of the man nearest him. "You hear me clear, Wooten?" The lanky trapper reeled a bit, rocking back on his heels. "Where's my horse? Here's for lead!" He released the man to wave his bottle in the air. "Saddle up, Wooten. Show us what makes you shine with the crowd."

The second man, at least as large as the boisterous one, had remained silent even when manhandled. He swung onto the bare back of the horse that had been brought out for him to ride. Next, he put his rifle in his right hand, wrapped two turns of the rope looped onto the horse's muzzle around his palm, and kicked his mount out toward the edge of the settlement.

"Can't ride no horse like that," one man put in.

The braggart only laughed. "That there is Dick Wooten, damned orneriest devil spawned out of these here Rocky Mountains. He's gonna take all your possibles, horse and beaver. Bet on it?"

"This is sure gonna be somethin'!" a familiar voice exclaimed from behind Kit.

"Where the hell did *you* come from?" Kit queried, wheeling to find Amos Tuttle standing at his side. "Never mind. Who's that long-armed gorilla with the ten-foot mouth?"

Amos grinned. He knew the answer and was proud to give it. "He and Wooten came in just before first light. Didn't take 'em long to see themselves to easy pickin's."

"How you figure that?"

The boy shrugged, secretly enjoying the full attention of his idol. "Folks don't seem to pay much mind to my kind," he began. "Was settin' the breakfast fires when they rode in. Took a cup of coffee at my mess. Rube said to Wooten, 'Here's for pelts, Dick. I'm doin the talkin'. You'll do the shootin'. Nice and pretty, now. Ride on a hundred dollars richer.' That's what they said, a fact."

Kit didn't reply. Instead, he followed the other men who were moving to the flat stretch of valley floor just beyond the camp. There, poles had been sunk to make the framework for hanging dried meat.

"This one, that one, and that one," Rube Herring called out, pointing to three of the poles which seemed evenly spaced. "Five passes, five rifles, any three shots that hold in the wood."

The assembly was growing fast. Not many wanted to miss a rare demonstration of skill, especially when the ground still held ice and the man was riding bareback. Rube took up bet after bet. "How they plan to pay if they lose?" Amos asked innocently.

Kit smirked. "They'll be hell-bent for leather if

this don't work. There's nobody expectin' they can win. Just be certain you duck when that big fellow Wooten misses his shot. He's gonna wish he's about the size of that skimpy lodgepole once they begin firin' at him."

At last everything was ready. Wooten had fallen back a full hundred yards. The first pass was an easy one—one shot, one hit. But the crowd was not pleased.

"Ain't ridin' sidesaddle! Can't he get an honest gallop out of that old horse?"

"Too slow! My Hortense can trot faster than them bullets he's lettin' loose!"

"I could throw them bullets faster than he's firin' 'em!"

Round two proceeded at a faster clip. No words were exchanged between the two men when Wooten missed his next two shots. The fourth shot held in the wood.

"Get ready to duck, son," Kit reminded Amos. Wooten picked up his fifth rifle and, as if seized by a demon, suddenly let loose with a war cry. Yanking his mount into a wheeling rear that kicked up ice and snow, Wooten then let it out at a flat gallop as clods of frozen earth were sent flying out by the horse's hooves.

The crowd cheered as his shot rang out, pleased with the show of spirit and not caring just then whether he had hit or missed. He had hit. That was obvious as one of the poles cracked and broke off five feet above the ground.

"Two shots at the same pole!" Rube declared in glee. "By damn, Wooten, you didn't have to show off!"

A smile spread across Kit's lips. When the men retired to the warmth of the camp, he invited Rube and Dick to join him. There they were—two good men.

And, he thought after reconsidering, perhaps he could afford to take Tuttle after all.

By late spring Kit's party of four trappers and a campkeeper had roamed over a good deal of northern Utah. They followed the Bear River south, then north again, heading into Wyoming on the Green River, and then finally approaching the Laramie Plains between the North and South Platte Rivers.

As the ground beneath them transformed into open plains once more, Kit felt the relief that comes from leaving one kind of danger behind. For weeks after they left the Salmon River wintering grounds, he knew their group was being followed, their progress measured by the silent tread of unseen, unfriendly faces. Blackfeet, perhaps, but never enough to warrant fear of an attack. The threat, though, had kept Kit moving, leaving little time for the sort of trapping techniques he had wanted to test. But once they were on the open plains of northeast Colorado they felt more secure. They were able to slow their pace, to stretch out their trap lines and leave them until beaver no longer left sign of their presence on the muddy banks.

One morning, Kit moved out ahead of the rest of the party. His men were fine companions, but he had need of the kind of peace that came to him only when he was alone. He was riding in a broad valley rimmed by distant mountains, the floor a lush green of spring grasses interspersed with columbine blue and poppy white and daisy yellow. Above his head the sky was cloudless. Sunshine poured down, making him squint.

A morning so pretty it'd make a man think of God, he thought to himself. It wasn't that he was particularly religious, but something had to have a hand in such perfection. It just made sense. Alone in the wilderness, such surroundings made a man think thoughts he couldn't put proper words or feelings to. He knew then that this was why he had come, why he would always stay on the frontier. Whatever happened, he could never find in another place the contentment he was feeling now. His life—no matter what happened to it in this glorious, wild stretch of earth—was his own.

Kit's band followed the South Platte to where it meandered into a grassy basin. There the men stopped to perform the arduous task of bundling their catch. It took several days to lay out the framework and cover it with rough-cured pelts. Then, for a day or two, the pelts were stretched on willow loops and left to dry. Then each was folded, fur inside, marked by its owner, and stacked for pressing into separate hundred-pound bales.

"If I pack another rock across this camp, my back'll be sprung permanently!" Rube growled as he dropped a fifty-pound boulder on top of his pack of furs.

"Looks heavy enough to me." Kit surveyed the log-and-stone press they had made to squeeze their packs. "This here is the last. The mules ain't gonna be too happy about the weight, but at least they won't be stumblin' along for lack of a view."

Kit looked about their small camp where at least a dozen packs lay on the ground. Each hundred-pound pack carried about eighty pelts, and each pelt was worth two to three dollars.

Four of the packs belonged to Kit. He beamed as he thought again that he had made close to nine hundred dollars since the spring thaw. "Fine doin's," he pronounced. "Mighty fine."

"Somethin' wrong with you, Royce?" Kit asked his fellow trapper when the other men had retired for the night. He had been watching Royce for several days.

Hearing Kit's question, Royce made a sour face. "Nothing stranglin' Wooten wouldn't cure." He directed a sigh and a glare of exasperation toward Rube and Dick. The two men were bedding down under a scraggly cottonwood nearby. "For a quiet man, he makes a powerful lot of noise."

Kit knew instantly what Royce meant. Wooten had the annoying habit of singing to himself in the middle of the night when it was his turn as lookout. If you could call it singing, Kit thought. Wooten liked to sing "Indian," as he called it, whooping and wailing while banging out accompaniment on a tin plate. But was this what was really disturbing Royce?

"He eats us out of house and home, too," Royce commented, continuing with the complaint he'd already begun. "Never seen a man that could put away a whole side of buffalo, polish off two gallons of cured fat, and then begin nibblin' on a length of raw buffalo guts." Royce shuddered at the thought.

Kit laughed. "Beats the thing I saw up at wintering. Some Crow Indians had come upon a buffalo carcass. Dumb beast had fallen through the ice of the river. You could smell the damned thing clear over the next mountain. Thought they was gonna bury it, but you know what they did? They carved up that green, spoiled flesh and took it home. Said it was good that way, so ripe and tender it didn't take no time boilin' before it was done!"

"Well, I'll be damned!" Royce exclaimed. He threw his buffalo rib supper into the fire. "What do we talk about now? Weather's turnin'," he said, answering his own question. "In another month it'll be so warm that hair'll be fallin' from the beaver. Where are we taking our catch?"

"Haven't decided yet," Kit answered.

Watching his friend carefully, Royce said, "I heard about a trading fort been opened down on the Arkansas, near the Purgatory River. Bent's Fort, somebody called it. Heard they're payin' a pretty price for beaver, buffalo hides and anything else with a valuable skin."

"Ain't tradin' with Bent," Kit snapped.

"I know it's gonna cost me askin' why, but it's a quiet night. I'll take my chances."

Kit took his time rolling and lighting his cigarette, but Royce knew him too well to be put off by the Indian dodge of silence.

"Met the man once," Kit answered finally. "Me and some Taos boys went out to the Cimarron a couple of summers back to save Bent's neck. Comanches had his wagon train pinned down in the sand. When it was over, Bent took exception to my trophy."

Wisely, Royce kept his mouth shut.

"I didn't take the scalp myself. It was my first killing—an Indian boy about my own age. This Gibbon fella came along. He told me I done fine work, and scalped him. Well, I ask you, what was I to do? I took the damn thing! Only Mr. Bent," Kit said sarcastically, "he saw me comin' into his camp with the bloody thing and put up more of a fuss than a St. Louis housewife. The man's a merchant! Thinks he can set up shop on the Arkansas like it was Main Street in Boston. Can't abide city doin's. Never could."

After a moment Royce asked quietly, "So? What's to do?"

Kit's quick grin flashed clear to his eyes. "Me, I'd purely love to waltz into Taos. Like to see them lovely señoritas droolin' over this hombre!"

At the thought of going to Taos, Royce shuddered. "You can't trade in Mexican territory," he pointed out.

"Maybe I can't," Kit agreed, "but Ewing Young can. Got himself a Mexican citizenship, so I hear. We trade to him, he trades with the Mexicans. Nothin' simpler. Besides, this Bent fella's in competition with Young, and Young's the better man. I owe him.

"Ain't you even a little curious about your lady friend?" Kit teased, a wicked gleam in his eye. "I know," he held up a hand before Royce could answer. "I ain't supposed to talk about her anymore. Only, you got to wonder what happened to her."

Royce didn't answer, but when the camp had settled down for the night, he thought about Renata. Actually, he thought about her every night. He could have forgiven her for anything, even her refusal to come with him. What stuck in his craw and would not go away was how quickly that evening had passed. He'd felt used, like a prime bull who had been let in to service a young heifer and then turned out as soon as he had performed.

"Damn your eyes!" he whispered viciously, for they were what haunted him. Somehow, they had promised safety, a life with a purpose, a home.

Yanking his buffalo robe over his head, Royce turned to his side. What happened with Renata had made him dissatisfied with the new life he had chosen. He detested her for that. He had wanted it all!

A week later, Kit rode out at dawn to scout for a new campsite. The gentle, treeless roll of the terrain gave way to steeper, tree-lined hills along a little stream called Cripple Creek. The rocky ground descended into a tree-rimmed basin, then farther south into a magnificent gorge filled with blue spruce and aspen.

But the splendor of the view held only secondary appeal for Kit. At that moment, he was evaluating its potential as a prime trapping ground. Following the aspens with a practiced eye, he searched for telltale signs of gnawing—a split log half-stripped of its bark, or even meager piles of shavings.

Beaver loved the tender treetop shoots, almost as much as they relished the inner bark of a limb when the dried outer portion had been stripped away. So these signs, plus the other more obvious signs of slides and tracks, kept Kit's eyes on the trail until the sun was at its peak. What greeted him when he rounded a sharp turn in the winding natural path and skirted a small outcropping of stone made him dizzy with joy.

There were beaver in the wooded canyon all right. Hundreds of them! The dams they had built divided the creek into multiterraced pools. Each was supported by a dam and filled with plaster mud-and-stick lodges;

all in all they covered perhaps a half mile of the canyon floor.

Imagining for a moment that the sight might be nothing more than a poor man's vision of paradise, Kit jumped from his horse, tethered it quickly to a nearby limb and struck off toward the beaver community. If he was alone in his discovery, he and his men could settle in until the season was finished, trapping to their hearts' content. And they could plan to return to Taos with more beaver than any four men had ever brought to any trading post.

Kit's tread was quick and light. Leaving as little sign as probably anyone ever had, he looked around for a position from which he could survey the entire area. "We just gotta be alone," he murmured to himself, Hawken in hand. "We just gotta."

A nearby hillside provided Kit with the view he needed. The stream entering the canyon at its far end wound unevenly back and forth along the floor of the gorge, widening into the beaver community, and then almost ending, only to widen again and pick up a thread below the ponds.

Kit sighed deeply, relieved to sense no human life around him. Nothing Indian had set its mark on the land either. The only thing alive was that beaver village.

The crashing in the underbrush behind Kit gave him only a second to respond. He swung around and brought his Hawken to his shoulder and, in the same instant, saw sixty pounds of wolverine break cover. The thick brown fur stood raised on its back. The wolverine's foot-long tail was held high as it ran.

Clamped in its powerful jaws was a freshly killed beaver.

Kit hesitated, concerned about the effect the noise of his rifle would cause in the stillness. By then the animal was almost upon him, its musky scent tickling his nostrils.

Kit jumped to one side and fired. The shot caught the animal squarely, throwing it several yards at an angle to the path it had been pursuing. Wolverine fur was worthless on the market, and the beaver the animal had been carrying was a bloody mess, useless for trading purposes. Kit had made the kill to protect himself, but was sorry he had.

The rush from the underbrush could not be covered by Kit's rifle. The single shot had been spent. Kit spun toward the sound he heard and saw two grizzlies break into the open a few yards from him. It didn't take him long to realize that the wolverine had stolen its prey from the bears. They appeared not only angered, but hungry—a deadly combination.

Kit dropped his rifle and ran.

Two monstrous growls increased in volume, indicating that he had been seen. Kit knew the grizzlies would veer off in his direction, picking up speed as their claws—sharp as razors—dug into the earth. They'd be on him in a minute if he didn't find shelter. Desperate, sweat making a sodden mat of his leather shirt, he leaped up to catch the lowest bough of the first large tree he came to.

The limb gave easily under his weight—too easily, in Kit's opinion. No sooner did he vault onto the branch than it dipped, dangling him over the heads of his would-be attackers like a carrot on a stick.

In an effort to move over the limb and reach a higher perch, Kit twisted his body upward. Just then one of the bears reared on its hind legs and took a swipe at him. Kit felt the sharp claws brush across the back of his head as he swung up and away. If he had lost his scalp, he thought as he grasped a higher branch, at least he had saved his life.

Blood trickled into his eyes as he braced his legs between the tree trunk and the limb that he'd just escaped to. Gingerly he put a hand to his scalp, gratefully convinced, a few anxious moments later, that the bear had gotten nothing more than his hat while plowing through his hair. Even though they were fairly deep, the cuts would heal.

But Kit's assailants were not ready to concede defeat. Enraged that their prey was so close and yet out of reach, they began climbing up after him.

"Now wait one damn minute!" Kit roared, reaching around to whack off a switch with his Green River. Each bear outweighed him fourfold. They would bring the tree down for certain. "This here tree ain't big enough for you and me," Kit thundered. "Now get!" With quick jabs, Kit poked the tenderest spot available on the climbing bear—his snout.

The offended grizzly drew back, roaring, then dropped to the ground. For the next few minutes it was poke and growl between the adversaries until finally the bears gave up the idea of climbing the tree. Kit's relief was short-lived. No sooner had both grizzlies given up climbing than they decided to bring Kit down by other means. Tearing at the ground around the base of the tree, they began digging frantically to pull up the roots.

"I'll be a jack rabbit fried!" Kit exclaimed. He had heard of such things, but never before had he believed those campfire tales about bears digging up trees.

If they do bring the tree down, Kit thought, it might be possible to scramble to a stouter perch. A large aspen would make for better climbing than the puny specimen he was sitting on now. And if the bear climbed that tree too, he could always cut another switch and poke noses till his arms fell off. The idea, strange as it was, made him laugh. Then he began to shake his head. No, he thought, this really isn't funny.

Suddenly a rifle cracked in the distance. Screaming in pain, one of the bears swung and dashed back into the forest where it had come from. The other bear seemed surprised by the desertion. As if to make Kit pay, it reared up on its hind legs and shook the tree.

Instinctively, Kit embraced the trunk, pleased to hear a second shot ring out. In no time, the second grizzly had lunged into the stream close by, collapsing in the shallows and frightening a family of beaver.

"Well, sir. Now I've seen it all." Royce Brant's face smirked up at Kit.

"Took your goddamn time setting that second ball," Kit jested.

"Well, didn't want it to go queer on me. Figured I wasn't gonna get a third chance." Royce shaded his eyes with a hand. "You in love with that tree or are you comin' down?"

Kit released the trunk and jumped down right on top of Royce, the impact sending them both sprawling.

"If it was anybody else stuck up there, I might have left them," Royce gasped out between peals of laughter. "Phew! Hope I live long enough to tell about this one."

"You open that mouth of yours about this, you won't live long enough to regret it," Kit muttered. Then the absurdity of what had happened struck him, and they both began rolling in the grass, holding their sides in laughter till tears plastered dust to their faces.

"You see that?" Kit asked finally, pointing to his find.

Royce nodded. "Hog heaven trapper-style."

"Know what we're gonna do?" Kit said after a moment. "We ain't goin' anywhere this summer. Instead, we're gonna cache down a bit farther south, maybe near the Arkansas. Then we'll head north into Wyoming, see what's going at rendezvous. First sign of fall, we'll hightail it back down here to our own private preserve. Then, this time next year, we'll dig up our old cache and add it to the new catch we got. Can you see us? We'll just about be able to buy all of Taos!"

Royce stifled his objections. He had known Kit too long to not realize that any opposition would be met with bullheaded resistance. "That's a lovely thought. Only, how are we goin' to resupply ourselves?"

Kit had an answer ready. "You got somethin' left of your fall pay? Me, too. We go to rendezvous with a few pelts, tell 'em we had a poor year, then buy what we need and set out early. Poor trappers is in a bigger hurry than wealthy folk."

"Okay." Royce nodded. "What about Wooten and Rube?"

Kit broke into a sly grin. "Would purely like to

see them sucker in a few more boys with that shootin'
trick of theirs."

Although Royce understood that Kit wanted the
two to make their own money to tide them over, he
wasn't convinced it would happen so easily. "They get
one look at this place," he appealed, "and they're liable to blab all over rendezvous that we've hit big."

"Rube and Dick won't tell," Kit replied. "They're
sons o' bitches, sure thing, but even a son of a bitch
will watch out for himself."

Two weeks later, Tuttle stood guard as the four
partners began building their cache. They had found
an area of level ground close to the Arkansas River,
but far back enough that periodic flooding would not
ruin their pelts.

First they cut the sod out in pieces. Careful not to
damage it, they laid it nearby. Then the real digging
began. The entry was small by design, and the hole
widened the farther in they dug.

"This is too much like real work, I'm thinkin',"
Rube complained as he carried a load of the dirt to the
riverbank in a buffalo blanket, then flung the telltale
sods into the water.

"Just make sure you ain't droppin' none of that
dirt," Kit commanded. "I ain't bustin' a gut so we can
leave a trail for varmints."

Wooten, in a subdued mood as usual, was out collecting branches for lining the hole. He picked up only
the fallen ones so that there would be no sign of cutting and stripping left behind. Once the hole was finished, it was unsparingly lined with twigs and leaves,
and the pelts were packed tightly in. Then more

branches and dirt were added, and finally the carefully preserved sod was replaced.

"Mighty fine work," Kit commented when they were done. "A body would never know we'd been here. When we're finished, I'd be willin' to bet that even Rube couldn't say exactly where we dug. So, let's set camp right here."

"On top of the cache?" Wooten asked, astonished at the suggestion.

Kit wagged his head at the big Missouri trapper. "Nobody in his right mind would mark his cache so plainlike, right? Well, then, that's exactly what we'll do. A heap of trappers will likely be drawn to this spot to camp. But not one of them will think to dig under his feet. Unless there's a jay with a big mouth in them trees yonder, our cache is as safe as if it were tucked under my arm."

Kit picked up his hat and wiped the sweat from his brow. It was hard, dirty work they had done. He was not suited to it. Now trapping, that was different.

"Why you starin' at me?" Kit asked Royce when he realized his friend was watching him.

Royce shrugged. "I'm just tryin' to decide when you took that step over the line from stupid to stupefying."

"Don't go usin' them ten dollar words on me!" Kit clamped his hat down on his head and reached for the tobacco in his possible bag. Despite it all, he was pleased—as pleased with himself as Royce was. He had made a smart decision. They all were going to be rich and they would get that way because of him. Life was looking very fine, indeed. He would buy another of those Spanish saddles. This one would have all the fine silverwork on it he had coveted since his first day in Taos. He would buy a new mule too—no, two new mules, and a fine Indian pony to carry him as well as the extra dollars in his possibles. Sure thing. He would be more of an attraction than a Santa Fe whorehouse on a Saturday night.

"Next year," Kit promised himself out loud. One more year and he'd reach his goal.

Chapter 10

The musky smell of the fire mingled with the turpentine odor of sagebrush, damp at daybreak. To the west, a narrow ridge of purple mountain peaks rode the horizon. Grass Singing stood with her back to the dawn, stirring the pot of stew that was hanging on a tripod over her family's fire.

It was nearly summer. The quick chill of night was lifting from the river valley in wispy strands of mist. To the north, less than half a mile away, stood a white-walled fort. It was to the fort that Grass Singing's attention kept straying. Her people had come to trade there.

For three days now, emissaries from her tribe had gone to the fort and been received with the ceremonial hospitality so appreciated by the Arapahos.

No women had been allowed to accompany the council chiefs, but today that would change as the purpose of their journey—the trading—would begin. Grass Singing stared a moment longer at the walls of the huge fort. Never before had she seen a structure so large. It seemed as if her entire tribe could be housed within it.

She lay her spoon aside and pulled from beneath her buffalo robe the "magic" that she had received from Turtle Eye the night before. The small deer's tail did not appear capable of the power which the medicine man assured her it contained. When worn where her love could catch a whiff, she would be irresistible, the man had promised.

Grass Singing turned the little piece of fur over and over in her delicate palm. Two years was a long time to ache for a man she had seen only once. But ever since that night two years ago, she had wanted to be with no one else. Turquoise Eyes, that is what she called him. She knew no other name.

Last summer she had traded three of her best robes for the turquoise-studded bracelet that circled her left arm. It reminded her of her trapper's eyes. Would she ever see him again? If he didn't come to the fort of stone, she might not. There was no name she could ask for that the white man would recognize. Yet Turtle Eye had promised they would meet.

Twenty miles down the Arkansas River where the Purgatory forked from the main stream, Kit, too, was thinking of the past. He had awakened an hour before dawn, a strange dream disturbing his slumber. The dream had taken place in a deep forest, where the rays of the setting sun laid golden stripes between the trunks of the slim aspens. Spotting a doe, he'd lifted his

Hawken to his shoulder to squeeze off a shot. The animal had started and pricked up its ears; then it froze. An almost-forgotten memory was rekindled by the deer's action, stilling Kit's finger on the trigger. The animal had lifted its head. Its dark, gentle eyes had made him remember back to a simple evening's pleasure when he had danced with a fawnlike Arapaho girl whose eyes looked the same.

Now, in the clear air of early morning, Kit pondered the dream. He had not thought of the girl in a long time. How strange that the memory of this particular girl would visit him now.

"Must be your doin'," he muttered to the yellow moon slipping down the western edge of the sky.

Dismissing his wonderings, Kit drained his coffee cup and stood up, stretching. Damn, he was pleased with himself! Exactly a year ago, in this spot, he and his men had buried a sizable cache. Yesterday they unearthed it, whole and undisturbed. Those bales, added to the new year's catch, amounted to well over two thousand dollars worth of furs for himself alone.

"Feeling kittenish, are you?" Royce commented as he sat up from his bedroll and reached for the coffee pot.

Kit grinned. "Been doing some figurin'. We've got a king's ransom worth of pelts here. Maybe we ought to take them all the way back to St. Louis ourselves. Hear tell the American Fur Company is outbidding every other trader in the territory."

Royce choked on his coffee. "You crazy? Them company folks have been tryin' to run Fitzpatrick and Bridger's boys out of the mountains for the past three years."

"I know it. But I don't mix sentiment with business, and this is business." Kit had risen to his feet and stood there scowling, as if waiting for Brant to protest.

Royce looked down into the black liquid in his cup. "It'd be like knifing those Rocky Mountain boys in the back."

"If that's the way you feel, we'll take the pelts to Taos."

Kit picked up his belongings and walked over to saddle up. He did not permit himself to look victorious until he could hide the smile by turning his back.

Royce had been after him all spring to take their pelts to Bent's Fort. It was closer. It was safer. It made good sense. All those things Royce had said were true. What Kit could not make his friend understand was that trading with Bent would be like trading at a feed store back in Franklin, Missouri. That wasn't frontier-style trading. That was shopkeeping!

If this idea sounded like nit-picking on Kit's part, he didn't care. He didn't want to explain it to anyone. He was the leader. Everyone had agreed on that when they cached their pelts last year. Well, although he didn't want that title before, he had it now and meant to make them remember it. Rube and Wooten, Royce and even Tuttle. . . .

Kit looked about. Where was the Tuttle boy? he wondered. He had sent him south to scout for Indian signs on the trail they would be taking at first light.

Amos rode into camp a minute later and, watching him, Kit reassessed his use of the term "boy." Amos was almost as tall as Royce and Rube. He did not have the wide shoulders or body weight of either man, however, and that was what kept Kit thinking of him as a growing boy. Amos would have to fill out, add solid muscle to his frame, before anybody would think of him differently.

Tearing the hat from his head, Amos swung a long leg over his mule's back. "A clear trail, Cap'n Carson!" he sung out as his feet hit the ground.

"Here's for poor bull news," Rube answered. He looked up from where he sat, his long, leathery face hanging in disapproval.

"What's that supposed to mean?" Amos hitched up his trousers and stepped toward the big man.

Rube worked the piece of tobacco in his jaw for a moment. "Sign's there. This horse been drawed a sight too often not to know when Indian sign's been put down."

Hearing the derision in Rube's voice, Kit spoke up. "If you know somethin', Rube, you spit it out."

Rube pushed back the felt hat that sat atop his long black hair. "Arapahos are camped up the river a ways—whole nation of 'em. Cheyennes ain't much farther away. Faces painted black. Been warrin', for certain. It's runnin' season for buffalo. The Comanches'll come for 'em." He turned his head to look up at Amos. "You know nothin' about it, do you, sonny?"

As he finished saddling his mule, Kit pondered the old-timer's news. He knew the Cheyennes and Arapahos were camped nearby. Bent had bought their confidence for a while, trading regularly with them. He'd even married a Cheyenne girl, according to mountain talk. Still, it sounded like Rube had more in mind than just a recital of Indian sign. "You ain't takin' up a sudden partiality to your hair, are you?" Kit asked at last.

The big man jerked back, surprised at this attack

on his courage. He rose slowly, as if he had no pressing need to reach his feet. When Rube finally stood up straight, Kit saw a silver blade in his right hand. "I been too long on the prairie to be scared by any kind of vermin what shows its face in the light of my campfire. Indian or white, never mind, this child'll raise his hair, sure as shootin'."

Kit had been ready to mount the mule, his hand laying casually across the saddle. Now he moved his hand down slowly toward his rifle, which was hidden from Rube's view by the mule.

"Appears to me you ain't happy with us anymore, Rube. That so?" Kit's hand closed over the barrel. As usual, the Hawken was loaded.

The bigger man shook his head. "Like as not, that's so. Me and Wooten, we figure to settle up now. Take our cache on up to Bent's Fort. No sense traipsing all the way to Santa Fe for new gear."

Out of the corner of his eye, Kit caught Wooten rising to his feet and Brant reaching for his rifle. There was going to be trouble if he didn't act quickly.

"You want your share, take it," Kit said. He had his finger around the trigger now. One small sound and he would bring his rifle up and fire.

Rube directed a worried look toward Wooten. "You're sayin' we can just pack up and ride out, no hard feelin's?"

Though a sense of urgency told Kit to break his rifle free and fire, he shrugged instead, getting ready to mount. "No hard feelings," he echoed. "That is, unless you take one pelt more than you're entitled to. You do, and I'll blow your ugly head off." Kit swung into the saddle. "Got some scoutin' of my own to do." His attention focused on Amos.

"Hitch up them mule packs, Tuttle. We're turnin' south when I come back." Then, giving his mount a gentle nudge with his boots, Kit cantered out of camp.

"You're damn lucky, that's all," Royce told Kit as they rode together. Amos was bringing up the rear. "Rube and Wooten could've decided to fight for the whole cache."

Kit squashed his hat tighter on his head to keep the steady prairie winds from lifting it away. "They didn't. That's all that matters." He turned his head to look at the man riding by his side. "Besides, you and Tuttle could've settled with 'em, need be."

Once the Arkansas was left behind, so was the sheltering safety of the cottonwood groves that sprung up naturally along the banks of rivers there. The noonday sun raised sticky perspiration on the necks of men and animals alike. For every mile they traveled, the heat rose a degree or two.

Kit began to worry. The few scraggly cottonwoods had given way to sagebrush and pinyon. Finally, at the edge of the Cimarron Desert, the land was hilly but bare. It was the season for Indian hunting expeditions; and hunting expeditions could too easily turn into war.

One morning, camp was made in the shade of a single windswept tree. Its branches drooped over one of the rivulets that carved out a narrow path in the sandhills of the parched prairie.

"Riders! Three of 'em. On the horizon," Brant warned.

"Damn!" Kit swung his Hawken to his shoulder,

not eager for any trouble. He had believed that Rube and Wooten would barrel straight for Bent's Fort. Kit shook his head. No, he thought, it isn't *them* coming. That would account for two riders, not three.

As the three black dots on the horizon approached, they soon transformed into men. They were bare-chested, the one in front entirely naked except for a breechcloth. Their long, unbraided hair was flying out behind them. Indians. As they came within rifle range, Kit ordered, "Hold fire!"

Tuttle spun around, his face pale with anxiety. "Don't shoot?" he asked.

Kit held his rifle under his folded arms. "They're riding easy, not on the attack. There's no way of knowin' if they're bein' followed. We wait—talk to 'em."

When the riders reached the camp, they reined in, their rifles in view but not held in readiness. Kit stepped forward and made the Indian sign for friend. The riders did not identify themselves, and though the marks on their mounts were Comanche, they were not dressed in enough clothing to make a guess worthwhile.

The Indians seemed amused. Almost simultaneously they burst into raucous laughter.

Kit swore under his breath. Suddenly he reached for the reins of the Indian nearest him. But the big man jerked the reins from out of Kit's hand and, in the same motion, leaped to the ground. Kit had just enough time to draw his blade before the Indian jumped up and knocked him off his horse.

A plume of dust rose above them as the weight of the man carried them into the ground. Kit was prepared for impact and rolled away when the jolt momentarily loosened the Indian's hold.

Jumping to his feet, Kit riveted his gaze on his opponent. Swarthier than the two warriors with him, this Indian was taller than the average Plains brave. Kit wondered if he had been mountain-bred, yet when he looked at the brave's face, a tiny shock of recognition startled him. The man's eyes were blue. He looked like a white man.

"You're white!" Kit exclaimed.

"Bill Mitchell?" Royce's voice was tentative as he edged closer.

"You know this hombre?" Kit asked, his brow furrowing.

"You've heard of him yourself," Royce replied, lowering his rifle. "Been livin' with the Comanches, rumor has it."

"No!" The warrior's grimace relaxed into the lines of a smile. "Me Comanche warrior. Take little white man's yellow scalp. Make plenty good trophy for counting coup." Lunging forward, the Indian took a wide swipe at Kit with his skinning knife.

Kit fell back and did not attack. He had learned at the age of thirteen that a man did not launch himself at a larger opponent. He let the mountain move and then used that momentum to his advantage.

"You scared, little man?" the blue-eyed Indian jeered.

Kit did not reply. If the man wanted to test his mettle, he would be ready with a trick or two of his own.

The two began circling one another. When the Indian slashed out a second time, just missing Kit's midsection, Kit backed up again. He felt himself suddenly cooled by the shade of the cottonwood's branches, and smiled. The brave kept coming toward him, just out of slashing range but close enough to keep Kit from turning or suddenly attacking. Kit felt the rub of the bark against his back. He stopped.

"Little man plenty stupid. I pin to tree, then scalp. Just like skinning skunk." The warrior crouched low, a growl rumbling in his throat. Then he launched himself.

At the same moment, Kit dropped to his knees and pitched himself to one side. The Indian, thrown off guard, fell heavily against the tree trunk. By that time Kit had recovered, rebounding with such force that he landed squarely on the Indian's back.

Kit's blade settled threateningly against the man's throat. "You want to die?" he whispered breathlessly. "You just take a deep breath, you got it?"

"You sure your mama knows you're playin' with that there Green River, son?" the man replied unexpectedly. "Like as not you're gonna get in trouble if she finds out."

"You *are* white!" Kit exclaimed.

The big man started to move. Feeling cold steel biting at his neck, he said, "You get this son of a bitch off me, Royce, and we can talk."

Royce hooted in laughter. "You're gonna have to kill him, Kit, or quit huggin' him before you lose your reputation."

Kit withdrew his weapon. "Hell!" he exploded.

A little later, between gulps of black coffee, Bill Mitchell had stories to tell. "Stole away from them dog-eaters last fall. Still, there's plenty of reasons to go back. There's heaps of . . . pelts to be had in Comanche territory." Bill swallowed a gulp of coffee, galled that he had almost slipped and made mention of the gold he knew was there. That was the real reason he had left his adopted tribe. When the time was right, he was going prospecting.

Neither Royce nor Kit was fooled by Mitchell's stumble; they had heard the hesitation in his voice. But his secrets didn't matter to them—as long as they weren't about trapping. Trapping news was the only sort that had appeal.

"Where to now, Bill?" Royce asked. "Season's over."

The expression on Bill's face never changed as he stared at the stacks of bundled pelts. "So I noticed. Me and Manhead and Tom Hill are goin' to Taos."

Kit's gaze shifted quickly to Mitchell's two Indian companions, who had seated themselves a short distance away. "Who're those two? Don't tell me they're your brothers."

Bill's bear-greased, long black hair flapped around his mahogany features as he shook his head. "They're Delawares. Talk better English than you and me. They came out with the American Fur Company folks, decidin' to strike out on their own. Two better trappers you ain't likely to find. Good shots, besides."

Kit digested this along with his last bite of jerky. "Goin' to Taos, you say?"

Bill nodded.

"You in need of a few extra dollars?"

Again a nod.

"You got a job. We're takin' these pelts to Ewing Young in Taos. Lost two of our men last week. Too scared to cross the Cimarron. You want to ride scout, be mighty obliged."

Royce's look reflected his astonishment.

"Well? He's your friend," Kit answered.

Bill Mitchell looked from one to the other. "Tom and Manhead included in that offer?"

Kit shrugged. "If you trust 'em, I do."

For the next two days they rode steadily south. Bill's familiarity with the terrain overruled Kit's trail-blazing expertise in territory where one sandy rise gave way to another, mile after thirsty mile. Alkali dust burned in the men's throats until they turned raw. Their eyes teared uncontrollably.

More than once, Bill appraised the shorter man at his side. In stature, the Missouri man was shorter than most, and very slender. But what muscle the trapper did have was as taut as a well-strung bow. Carson might look like a boy with his fair hair and freckles, Bill thought. But there was a survivor's instinct, as well as an intelligent bearing, in the young man. That was the reason he had decided to ride a few miles with the Carson brigade. Kit had fought him gamely enough. Now he wanted to see how Kit would stack up against real Indians.

On the third day, about midmorning, Bill was out scouting when Kit saw him rein in and shoot his hand straight up in warning. Squinting into the heat shimmering over the sand, Kit thought that he, too, saw movement on the rise. Then he heard Bill shout a confirmation. "Indians!"

Amos and Royce had been in charge of the mule train and were a quarter of a mile to the rear. Kit swung his mount around and headed back toward them at a gallop. If it was indeed an Indian Bill had spotted, they would not have long to make preparations for a fight. The land offered no protection, so he could only hope the war party would be small—ten or less to their six.

"Rein in!" he cried as he approached the mule train. Immediately he was obeyed, the two Delawares responding to Kit's command just as quickly as Royce and Tuttle. "Circle them mules! We'll use them as a blind."

This time, no one moved. "Look!" The single word spoken by Amos was filled with horror and disbelief.

Kit turned, the hair on his neck bristling like porcupine quills. "Lord Almighty!"

In an arch that filled nearly half the horizon, dozens of lances burgeoned forth, swaying in the prairie wind like buffalo grass. Behind them rose an impenetrable line of a hundred mounted warriors.

Fear ravaged Kit, squeezing sweat from every pore. There was no place to hide. They could not outrun their attackers; their horses were too thirsty and exhausted. Besides, the thought of turning tail in front of an enemy that knew you could not possibly escape left Kit trembling with anger. If those Comanches wanted Kit Carson, they were going to have to come after him and face the barrel of his Hawken.

And then the idea came to him. Pulling his Green River from his waist, he jumped down and grabbed the lead line of the mule nearest him. Then he sliced the beast's throat with the edge of the blade. The animal buckled, kicking Kit's horse, but Kit jumped tree and turned to the second mule. Without a word, the other men pulled their knives. They repeated Kit's actions until they were standing in the midst of dead and dying mules. Kit grabbed the leg of the first bloodied mule he had killed and dragged it in front of him. "Fort!" he cried and reached for a second, still quivering, carcass.

Bill joined them then, his horse bucking and rearing at the smell of fresh blood so nearly like its own. "What the hell you do that for?"

Kit waved him off. There was no time for explanations. The Indians on the distant rise had begun to move toward them, a chorus of war whoops surging in advance over the heated plains.

The trappers threw themselves behind the barrier of dying flesh and put their rifles to their shoulders. Sweat turned cold on Kit's skin as he saw the number of naked, painted bodies thundering toward them down the sandy slope. The pounding of hooves made the ground beneath him quake.

The Indians were magnificently mounted. Painted and plumed in eagle feathers, with colorful blankets beneath their bare bodies, Kit couldn't help but admire them.

Strangely, the admiration buoyed his flagging courage. These Indians were Comanches. Better riders—better opponents—never lived on these plains. But one thing was certain. If they took Kit Carson, there would be a few of them coming along to entertain him in hell. That promise made to himself, Kit took careful aim at the rider heading the charging line. "Hold fire till I call it!" he roared. "Every shot's gotta count! Three and three we fire. Bill, Tuttle, Tom, you shoot first!"

The Indians came faster now, seeming to level out as they neared. Leading the attack was a war chief, his head topped with a single feather and his locks wrapped in otter fur, as befitted a man of his station.

"Now!" Kit thundered.

The crack of three rifles split the air. Kit could only fire at the place where he supposed his target would be. The combination of dust and rifle-smoke had momentarily blinded him. He was pleased to hear a horse-squeal, followed by the outraged cry of the Comanche warriors. Then the sky darkened to the flight of a hundred arrows. They arched through the air, striking the ground in deadly patterns.

One of the men grunted, but Kit was reloading at the time. It would have been too risky for him to find out who had been wounded and how badly.

Gradually he saw that the Indians had divided and gone around to the other side of the barricade. "Change over!" he yelled, suddenly realizing that the enemy was behind them.

The six men leaped over the mule carcasses and landed on their bellies in the dust. They waited. Several minutes passed before the warriors regrouped and once again began their charge. Kit squeezed off a shot, and, seeing a Comanche topple from his saddle, let loose with a cry of delight.

The Indians did not wait to gather for the third attack. They turned at once, knowing it took time to reload rifles. Swirling their rearing mounts in the dust, they came screaming back.

Once more Kit and the others jumped the barrier of mules. But this time, each man felt it would be the last. Angry and frustrated, Kit jammed a ball into his barrel and thumped the butt against the ground. There was no time to set it properly with his wiping stick, and no Indian was going to lift *his* hair without a rifle ball to show for his efforts.

"Here's for Taos!" Kit cried, leveling his rifle for a final shot. The air was so thick with dust and rifle-smoke and the swarm of flies over the mules' blood that he could hardly make out the figures riding toward them.

They came in fast. Their shrieks must be a frightful sound to die to, Kit thought grimly. But he held his shot. Wait, Kit. One more. Take one more. His body tensed, muscles flexed tight against bone in hopes of turning the deadly steel arrowheads.

Amos whimpered, and though Kit's eyes never left the enemy, he heard the whimper and cursed himself. Amos' was the only death he would have on his conscience in hell. The Tuttle boy should have stayed with Fitzpatrick.

The riders came within fifty feet before the first pony reared in defiance, whinnying and turning back. The unexpected resistance spread through the Indian cavalry like wildfire. Horses bucked, unseating one or two astonished riders. Others stumbled, unwilling to be forced forward even under the punishment of their riders' digging and whippings.

"What the hell's the matter?" Royce yelled in a voice that was a strange mixture of complaint and celebration. If he was going to die, he wanted it to be quick, but if he wasn't—whoopee!

When Kit raised himself to his knees, he saw that he was smeared with mule's blood. It was everywhere, pools of it seeping through the sandy soil around the men. "It's the mule blood that got 'em!" he cried in triumph. "Spooked the horses! Lord Almighty! Looks to me we won this round!"

The possibility of even such a temporary victory spurred the six men to rise and fire into the stampeding melee of riders and mounts.

"There's for Long Nose!" Bill Mitchell roared as a rider bounced loosely from his saddle and landed beneath the storm of hooves. He looked over at Kit. "Been owin' that bastard a rifle ball since the time he trapped my squaw back on the Gila. Makes the whole mad fight worth it!"

Kit didn't agree. He knew that as soon as the routed Indians claimed control of their animals, they would be back. If not in five minutes, then in ten, or in a hour. Whenever, they would be back. "You got the canteens, Amos?"

For the first time the youngest member of the band spoke. "I think I killed a man, Mr. Carson," he said shakily.

"Good work," his idol answered, clapping Amos heartily on the back and ignoring the boy's discomfort. "Now get out the shovels. We got some diggin' to do."

Kit and his men had shaken the power of the Comanche medicine in the first three passes. When the riders did not return immediately, they began digging a pit behind a row of dead mules and pulling the other bodies in around them to form a closed circle. Only the most accurate lance or arrow would have a chance of finding a hole in their barricade when they were done. And when they were done, there was nothing to do but wait.

Three hours passed. Still the Comanches did not

return. The trappers had dug down deep. In that way, they could stand and lay their rifles over the top of a carcass to steady their shots. But there was no shade from the sun. There was nothing to get rid of the stinging sand flies that were crawling all over them. And they didn't dare move.

"Hellfire! It stinks something fierce!" Bill swatted one of the many insects that had been drawn to the attraction of live flesh.

Kit tore a section of calico from his shirt and tied it around his face to protect him from the flies; then he offered the rest of the cloth to the other men.

"We can expect 'em to come back," Kit cautioned. "In fact, they'll keep coming till nightfall, most likely."

"Then what?" Royce asked, looking up from his slumped position. "What are we holding them off for? Sooner or later they'll get us, if the heat and thirst don't kill us first."

Kit knew exactly how much water they had in their pouches and just how much food: two or three days' worth. After that, they would be out of lead and powder too. "You got any better suggestions?" he challenged.

"Bent's Fort is right pretty this time of year," Bill offered with a wicked grin. "Them cactus-topped walls is a mighty lovely sight, them pink and yellow blossoms. Makes a man think of other pretty soft things."

Kit gave Brant a hard look. He knew then that Royce had been mouthing off behind his back. He would settle with him if he got the chance.

Royce was not disturbed by the vengeful glance.

"If we could sneak out of here come nightfall, we might have a chance of reachin' safety. How far you figure the nearest settlement is, Bill?"

"Sixty, seventy miles," Bill replied with a shrug.

"Ought to be a nice night for a stroll," Royce spoke confidently. "Sixty, seventy miles isn't as far as it sounds."

"What about Manhead?" Amos stuck in. "Arrow got him on the first pass."

Kit looked over to where the big Delaware lay, his body covered to the knees in his long black hair. Manhead grinned at him. "Not hurt. Small head." Without complaint, he held up the arrow he had dug out of his left thigh. "Manhead travel swifter than anyone."

Kit believed him. "Okay," he began. "So we wait till two hours after sunset. Take only what you can carry. Besides rifles and powder and lead, we'll need blankets, Amos. And a little food."

"But what about the pelts?" Amos cried. "We gonna leave 'em?"

Kit turned to the bales of beaver pelts lying in the bloody sand. His muscles contracted in frustration. Two years' work, all for nothing. Two years and nothing to show for it.

"Business is business, Amos. War is war. And this here is war. You just be mighty glad you got a head left to talk with. You come away with your life, and you're way ahead of all them who don't. Beaver ain't gonna dry up next week. We'll get another chance. Damn me if we don't!"

Still, as they settled down to wait for sunset with only the flies, the desert sun and the faraway whoops of their enemies as company, Kit could not stop the sick, helpless feeling that made him want to fling himself in the dust and cry like a child. Two years wasted! Two years!

Chapter 11

Kit inhaled deeply. Thin mountain air slid soothingly down his throat. Absent was the painful sting of alkali.

For four days, Kit had lain inside the adobe walls of American House. When he and the others had been brought in, they could hardly speak. The scab-encrusted blisters that had once been their lips would not separate.

Two days before, when the delirium had receded for good, Kit could neither lift his head nor control his bodily functions. Now he could move his head from left to right and the insistent pressure in his intestines had subsided. He rolled to his side and swung his feet to the floor to sit up. The world seemed to turn over. He swayed dizzily. But the dizziness, too, he controlled.

His feet were bare and still tender from days spent crossing prairies. His moccasins had given out after the third day. Every day after that, he had been forced to cut at his buckskins to make crude replacements.

For a time Kit had begrudged Amos his preference for boots. On the last day, though, Amos had dropped to the ground begging to be left behind. The boy couldn't walk. When they pried his boots off, they discovered why. Although the heavy leather soles had protected Amos from the sharp rocks and cactus thorns, his feet had swelled in the heat and turned to a bloody pulp. Kit groaned at the thought. He and Royce had carried the boy between them, each too tired to care that Amos' weight added extra pain to their own crossing.

When riders had appeared on the horizon, Kit and his men had not even attempted to resist. They had no more water. Their rifles were so clogged with dust that the men doubted they would fire. Then, almost swooning, Kit had heard the familiar, gruff voice of Ewing Young. He had ridden out to greet the William Bent caravan from Bent's Fort and had met instead the half-crazy trappers led by Kit Carson.

Now, putting one foot slowly in front of the other, Kit walked to the other side of the room where he found a pot he could use for relieving himself. His feet ached as he made his way back to the corn-shuck mattress. He was sore, but at the same time pleased that no part of his body had been damaged beyond recovery.

"Should have known you'd do it your own way."

Kit had just stretched out. He lifted his head and saw Ewing Young standing inside the doorway.

"Don't be a damn fool," Young ordered briskly as

Kit murmured Young's name and tried to sit up. "You ain't gotta get up for me." Young came over and sat down on the edge of the bed. "You seein' things properly?"

Kit nodded.

"You're lucky. Damn lucky. Six days without food, three without water. You been tryin' to shame the majority of us who believe a canteen and a possible sack ain't sissy doin's for a man that figures to cross the desert?"

Kit didn't jump at the bait. "I left my life's work on the Cimarron desert. Two years' worth of pelts." He turned to face Young, his still-sore eyes flaming with emotion. "I done it, Ewing. I trapped myself a king's ransom in fur. Was coming to Taos to show you in particular." His voice cracked under the effort of speech. "I . . . I got nothing now. Nothing!"

In an oddly gentle gesture for the big man, Young put a hand on the younger man's shoulder. "I heard all about it, Kit. You was ravin' fit to beat the devil about beaver and secret streams and Comanches. Hey!" His features brightened. "They tellin' the truth about how you held off over a hundred of them Indians?" He winked. "You can tell me, son."

Kit moved his head impatiently. "Ain't got nothin' to say. We lost, that's the end of it. We lost."

Young had pressed the other members of Kit's party for details of their ordeal and had learned an earful. Not that he really believed a half dozen men had held off one hundred warriors in the midst of the sandy dunes near the Cimarron River. That was the sort of tale any trapper might spin when he sat in front of a warm fire with a belly full of buffalo rump and whiskey. And yet . . .

Kit had fallen asleep. Young stood up and gazed down at him. He studied the deep lines in the young man's once-smooth brow. The blue eyes hadn't changed. But he sensed that Christopher Carson *had* since he'd seen him two years ago. And the changes appeared to be all for the better.

No matter what else those delirious trappers had told Young, they had sworn to him that it was Kit Carson's quick thinking and determination in the face of overwhelming odds that had brought them in alive. In territory like this, there could be no finer praise.

When Miguel Lopez ducked inside the door of his home, his sister, Renata, ignored him and focused her eyes on the work in front of her. Her fingers worked expertly, forming the corn *masa* into small balls of dough, then patting them into flat, thin pancakes between her palms.

"Hello, Renata," Miguel called over his shoulder. He did not bother to wait for a reply.

Renata followed him with her eyes as he hurled his ropes and leather gloves into a corner. Miguel was a herdsman, and good at his work, but his drinking was taking its toll.

"Where is my tequila?" he asked.

Renata pointed to a cask-shaped gourd on the table. She had long since given up trying to stop her brother from drinking. But her hands worked faster. Hopefully, she would have the meal complete before Miguel had drunk too much to be interested in it.

Once she had been very proud of her brother, admiring his handsome face and strong physique. She had even vowed to marry no man who could not measure up to him.

Miguel's descent into a whoring, drunken brawler had begun two years before that summer. He had taken to the wrong sort of women, spending the money he earned freely upon them while she and their mother were forced to make do. Only Miguel's moments of guilty conscience made him occasionally turn over his pay untouched. Now there were just the two of them and her baby. Their mother had died over a year ago.

The wail of the child startled Renata so badly that she cut her finger on the knife she was using. Even Miguel's attention turned to the doorway of the room the cry had come from.

"I thought I told you no one is allowed in this house but you," he hissed.

Renata drew back from the hatred in his gaze. "I . . . I did not expect you so soon." The excuse, a poor one she often used, seemed to appease Miguel for the moment. He tilted back the jug and took a long swallow as Renata wiped at the blood pulsing from her cut finger. Should she go to the child or attempt to finish the meal?

Miguel decided for her. "My meal is served to me before you bare your breasts for that damned child," he roared, pounding the tabletop with his fist. "*Caramba!* A man deserves some service in his own home."

He rose, and Renata noted that his gait already was unsteady. That meant she would suffer verbal abuse, and hopefully nothing worse.

Only once had Miguel actually hit her. That was the night her mother had told him she was pregnant. Renata did not know if he'd hoped to make her lose the child. Whatever his reasons, he had been unsuccessful. The child had continued to grow while, until its birth the father's name had remained a secret.

Renata shuddered. She hated remembering that night, remembering the fixed look of hatred that had come into Miguel's eyes when he bent over her. He would wait, he had said, and deal with the gringo first, using her as bait to bring the man back. Then he would deal with her.

Miguel took his seat, and Renata emptied her chili and onions into the pot of bubbling stew. For all of the first year, carrying Royce's child and the happy feeling of love for Royce that she had finally surrendered to, she had been certain he would return. Deep in the quiet of the fall nights, she had relived his touch. As she lay in bed, she could almost feel the hot pressure of his lips, the insistent caresses, the pleasure of his body as he made love to her.

But he did not return to her. And, while her fear for his life was somewhat eased by his absence, the realization of her loss caused her to suffer unbearably. Miguel's threats to throw her out did not upset her nearly so much as the thought that she would never see Royce again, would never be able to introduce him to his child. Most painful of all, she would never be able to tell him of her love.

"You are going into town to the fandango tonight?" Miguel asked in a mocking tone.

Renata looked up from the skillet where she had begun to fry the tortillas. "Don't tease me. You know you never allow me out of the house. Besides . . ." She let her voice trail off as she glanced at the bedroom doorway.

"Ah, yes, the kid." Miguel's tone grew gleeful. "All the better reason you must paint your face and go whoring tonight." He paused, tilting his head to one side so that his black, shiny hair swung across his brow into his eyes. "You do not know, do you?"

Renata took a deep breath, struggling with the best answer to give him. "No," she said finally and turned her tortillas, but her eyes refused to focus as she waited for his next words.

"Well, then you will go with me to the fandango tonight." Miguel bounded to his feet and came straight over to his sister. "You will wash the color from your cheeks. I want to see your lovely complexion. You will put on your red *enaguas* and the *camiseta* of fine linen you hid away. Then you will come with me."

Renata shook her head violently, her eyes never leaving her work. "I have told you before. I will not whore for you."

So quickly did Miguel grab her by the wrist that Renata did not have time to release the skillet; it was knocked off the flame onto the floor. He pulled her around to face him, his breath heavy with tequila. "You *will* whore tonight, Renata, and for the best of reasons. You do not want your gringo lover to waste his money on another." He released her arm. "You *will* come with me tonight, *hermana mio*. I want to see you embrace the man I must kill tonight."

"Do you hear me, son? There's fine doin's tonight."

Kit shifted his shoulders uncomfortably. He was dressed in a calico shirt, a gift from Young. The fandango at American House had been planned especially in his honor, but he could hardly believe it.

"Here's the meanest, fightingest, finest young cur to ever come all the way to this greaser hole of Taos!" Gibbon, Ewing Young's right-hand man, clapped a heavy hand on Kit's shoulder. "Make way! Make way!"

The *sala* of Young's rooming house had filled hours before, as soon as the day's work had ended. The inhabitants of Taos loved nothing better than a chance to celebrate. This time, though Kit and his men had come in with their hands empty, they could celebrate a great victory against the scourge of the Taos Trail—the Comanches.

Kit hung back in the doorway, embarrassed by the strangers' cheers that greeted him. Along the narrow end of the room, the orchestra had assembled. There were Indian drums, a guitar, a fiddle brought all the way from Missouri, and a mandolin. Lining the bar and filling the chairs were the men and women of the town. With an appreciative glance, Kit studied the many rebozo-clad females, their cigarettes hanging suggestively from their pouting lips. Lord, he thought wistfully, he could sure use a few pesos.

Gibbon shoved Kit into the room. "Where's the music? Ain't a proper fandango without there bein' music!"

Obediently the orchestra struck up a Spanish tune, and the milling crowd separated into couples.

Kit walked over to the table occupied by Royce and Bill Mitchell. "Where's Amos?"

Royce pointed, and Kit turned. Near the middle of the dance floor Amos stood, his right arm wrapped tentatively about the waist of a sultry beauty who was smiling provocatively at him.

Kit smiled. Amos deserved much more for his pains on the Cimarron Desert. But the winning of his first woman would have to do. "What are you drinkin', Royce?"

"*Aguardiente*. Young's good stuff, too." Royce held out a cup. "Put a few hairs on your chest." He grinned. "Spanish women like a man with hair on his chest, not like those hairless boys they usually lie with. That's why they call them *pelados*."

Kit accepted the drink and seated himself. "You appear to be mendin'."

Royce nodded. "Sure thing. A little too much sun, that's all. Damned if I'm not as dark as an Indian."

"Plenty dark enough, but too much mouth," Manhead offered in his deep, flat voice. Then, turning toward Kit, he grew the closest thing to a smile that he could muster.

Kit eyed Bill Mitchell with interest. The scanty clothing had been traded for buckskin leggings and a breechcloth. Mitchell's chest was bare except for the meager covering of a skimpy leather vest.

"Young's orders," Bill explained, seeing Kit gazing at him. "Said we was to come prettied up for the townsfolk. These is my best duds."

Kit's laughter was genuine as he settled back to enjoy himself. The bitter disappointment at the loss of his pelts had not disappeared entirely, but for one evening it could be tempered by the easy flow of whiskey and the rhythm of wailing guitars and swirling skirts.

The dancing began with the more formal strains of *Malagueña*, but the mountain men—and there were many in Taos after a spring on the trail, did not care much about dance steps. Soon they were pushing aside the Mexican men. Grabbing their partners around the waist, they whirled them in time to the beat. Indian steps they had witnessed were added, as well as their own brand of polkas and jigs remembered from the barn-raising socials of their formative years back East.

"You like to dance with me, señor?" The liquid voice broke over Kit's inebriated thoughts like rain on a dusty trail. At once he looked up. Flashing at him were the eyes of the most beautiful woman he had ever seen. She was not dressed like the other girls, in skirts and white blouses. Black lace covered every inch of her from neck to toe, yet it still revealed every curve and indentation of her exquisitely proportioned body. Around her throat hung a heavy gold cross, and in her thick hair was a tortoiseshell comb inlaid with precious stones.

"You do not speak, señor?" the woman asked coyly.

"Before beauty every man should be silent," he answered promptly in Spanish, and received a luscious smile for his trouble.

"Come." She held out a hand to him. Kit rose, bowed over the petal-soft skin just as he had seen the wealthy Mexican ranchers do, and then followed her out onto the dance floor.

"Phew! That Carson fella sure is lucky. Just look how that señorita is battin' them fine black eyes at our boy," Bill commented with glee.

"Señora," Royce corrected glumly. "Her husband

is Don Carlos Estoban. That little lady is jist askin' for
trouble!" He looked over toward the door. A man with
aquiline features stood conversing with Ewing Young.
The aristocratic face revealed no anger, but the man
played nervously with the brim of his intricately
designed hat.

Royce noted other clutches of Mexicans—herdsmen and tradesmen—watching and smoking while their
eyes jealously followed the movements of their women
in the arms of the Americanos. A little more whiskey,
an indiscreet remark, and . . .

The sight of Renata Lopez standing in the doorway sent the front legs of Royce's chair crashing to the
floor. He sucked in a long, slow breath and held it.

Renata had prayed that Royce would not be near
the door. Her eyes had searched for and found him almost at once. At the moment his gaze found hers, they
each read the answer to their own questions. Nothing
had changed. Renata took a deep breath, the effort
causing her shoulders to tremble.

"You see him too, don't you, *puta*? The gringo
they call Brant?" Miguel whispered in an ugly voice.
"Go to him, Renata. You think I do not remember you
dancing with him against my orders? I do. Go to him
now, put your arms around him, make him remember
what he took against your brother's command. Make
him remember so that when I kill him, he will know
why." He pushed her forward.

Royce rose slowly to his feet as Renata came
closer. Had she always been this beautiful? Her red
petticoat swayed becomingly as she walked. He followed the movement of her hips, and his breathing
quickened.

Renata's blouse was thin and finely woven. Beneath it she wore nothing, drawing more than a few eyes to the smooth curves of her breasts.

At last Royce gazed at Renata's face. Her lips had been carmined, but the blush on her flawless complexion was natural. Renata wore her hair free, not plaited like the other girls, and it fell in soft waves to her waist. Royce shook his head in disbelief. Renata was different, and yet she was the same. And his desire? Yes, that was the same, too. Without a word, he reached out to slowly encircle her waist, and in a moment they were swept into the music and wild dancing.

"Damn Mexican! Here's for foofaraw!"

It happened quickly, and yet it could have been expected. The mountain man who had spoken picked up the man beside him, heaved him to his shoulder, then swung him around several times before flinging him into a crowd of other Mexicans who were standing to one side.

A roar went up. Dozens of knives flashed as they were whipped from the waistbands of both Americans and Mexicans alike.

"That's Bill Mitchell!" Kit heard a man exclaim. He pushed through the crowd in time to see four men charging the American who was stationed in the middle of the floor. Women shrieked as Bill pulled his knife to defend himself and jabbed into the first man's belly. Even louder was Kit's battle cry as he charged into the fight to help his companion.

"Tonight," Royce whispered urgently to Renata. "By the pueblos. Please!" He planted a hurried but forceful kiss on Renata's astonished face, while at the same time drawing his Green River. In an instant, he too, had joined the brawl.

The three comrades stood shoulder to shoulder, lamplight reflecting from the lethal blades in their hands. Twenty Mexicans had formed a circle around the Americans. Kit didn't like the odds, but he knew it was their fight. No one else would join them unless they were drawn into it by a careless punch or jab.

Bill was grinning like a hyena, his lips drawn back. His Comanche war cry startled more than a few of the Mexicans. It was the most feared sound in the entire New Mexico Territory. More important, the shock of it gave the Americans the edge as they rushed the natives, smashing with their fists and thrusting their weapons forward to force the Mexicans back.

Grabbing up an empty stool, Kit hoisted it high, then brought it crashing down on the floor. The legs separated into three stout poles, just the right size for weapons, but less likely to deal out deathblows. Kit knew that if too many men died that night, Taos would be off limits to mountain men for quite a while.

The clubs proved to be good weapons. Many of the locals went down under them before the dance floor had been cleared. The brawl ended quickly.

"Here's for mountain doin's!" Bill shouted, letting loose with a final, hair-raising whoop as he flung his club away.

"He will meet you *where*?" Miguel asked, his anger increasing.

"I did not promise to meet him! The fight—it ruined everything!" she cried desperately.

Miguel wiped his mouth with his right sleeve. "Then we will go to him."

"No! Please! Miguel!" Renata exclaimed as he grabbed her arm and began dragging her with him. "No! Think of my child! Please, Miguel. I beg of you, Miguel!"

But Miguel was not listening. Renata knew that he would kill Royce, or that Royce would kill him. Either way, she stood to lose, and nothing could stop it. Unless . . . unless Royce refused to fight Miguel. Passionately, she prayed for him to have the strength to refuse the challenge.

After the fighting, Royce, Kit and a few other Americans had retired to a clearing just outside the city's limits. Ewing had sent them out with blankets and half a barbecued buffalo to keep them occupied. With plenty of whiskey as an addition to their feast, the men had settled comfortably around a hastily built campfire when a scream drove them all to their feet again. A man was coming toward them, dragging a woman behind him.

"What the hell!" Bill exclaimed.

"Maybe Carson's little filly got her husband in a fit," Gibbon snickered.

Royce did not join in the speculation. He knew that it was Renata who had screamed. He also knew that it was her brother who had provoked the scream. Miguel must have seen her sneaking away from home.

Royce reddened in anger. He wanted to take Renata as his wife. He had known that the moment he had seen her in the doorway of American House. She was his woman.

Miguel pushed Renata into the circle of men.

Their faces glowed in the dim light of the campfire. She whimpered involuntarily.

"I want the man who calls my sister his woman!" Miguel demanded in English tainted with a Spanish accent.

The cold, expressionless look in Royce's eyes as he stared at the Mexican told Kit everything he did not already know about his friend's feelings for the girl. Kit fingered his rifle. It had been in his hand ever since they'd left Young's place.

Royce stared at Renata's swollen cheek. "Did this man do that to you?"

"He is my brother—Miguel," Renata managed faintly.

Royce stiffened. "Not even a Comanche hits his own kin," he whispered contemptuously. Deliberately he spat, just missing the tip of Miguel's boot. "You will not dare touch her again after tonight, Lopez, or I will kill you."

Miguel snarled, but didn't move. "You made my sister your *puta*, gringo, but that does not give you the right to tell her brother how she is to be treated. I will hit her if I wish it, and also that *niño* you put in her belly two summers ago."

If Royce understood the words, there was no sign. He merely reached out his hand to the woman in front of him and drew her close.

"You will not fight him, Royce. You must promise," Renata pleaded.

At first Royce said nothing. He wanted nothing better than to smear Miguel all over the ground, from here to Juarez. "Won't touch him unless I have to," he murmured finally.

Reaching behind his back, Miguel produced a long skinning knife. "Be witness to your own death, gringo. Miguel Lopez will have your heart to give your *puta* before the night is finished."

Royce's reaction was swift. Pushing Renata into the waiting arms of Kit, he drew his own blade.

"No, Royce!"

"You mustn't interfere, señorita," Kit admonished gently. "Ain't no longer up to you. It's the way of things. Royce won't kill him if he can help it," he assured her.

The two men had squared off silently. The fight was vicious and quick, and the only sound around the campfire was the harsh breathing of the opponents.

Holding Renata away from the fighting, Kit swore angrily under his breath when he saw Royce slip, stopping the thrust of his knife just short of the Mexican. Royce wanted to best the man, yet spare him. Kit sensed that would be impossible. Regardless of Royce's intention, Kit knew his friend would not be able to walk away from this fight until he had killed the man who faced him.

Suddenly Miguel threw himself at Royce's knife, taking it high in his right shoulder. The contact sent the two men sprawling. Almost too late, Royce saw the cunning of the maneuver. As his Green River had connected with Miguel's shoulder, Lopez was bringing his own blade down in a swift arc toward Royce's unprotected back.

Royce released his blade. He kicked himself away, but not soon enough. He felt the knife cut into his back, then he broke free as he fell away. Searing pain made him groan, but at once he was on his feet, completely devoid of his intention of keeping Renata's brother alive. As the Mexican rolled to his feet, Royce's blade was still sticking out of Miguel's shoulder. Decisively, Royce knelt to pick up a handful of dirt. Then he flung it at Miguel. Lopez staggered, cursing, and Royce jumped him. Yanking his blade from the Mexican's shoulder, he buried it again, this time lower, where it could do more damage.

"Royce! Miguel!" Renata broke free from Kit, and they both rushed to the fallen men.

Kit reached Royce first. "He's hurt, but he'll live," Gibbon commented as they began the task of stopping the bleeding.

"And Miguel?" Renata asked.

Gibbon shook his head. "Afraid your brother's dead."

Chapter 12

"Shouldn't be messin' where it ain't my business," Kit grumbled to himself as he walked along, tugging at the confining shirt collar that squeezed his neck.

Two weeks had passed. Royce did not appear to be recovering well, even though Ewing Young had stitched him up properly. It was Brant's spirit that had Kit worried.

He kicked halfheartedly at the gang of dogs that came racing up to greet him. Their barks and yips were in warning, and at the same time in curiosity. This was the poor side of town. Kit smirked. Hell, the whole damn town was on the poor side, except for a few haciendas like the one owned by Señor and Señora Estoban. Now *there* was a house. Red-tiled, with large rooms, it boasted the finest, softest beds he had ever felt.

Kit counted the number of times he had been invited up to the house during the past ten days. Three, and each time, his hosts insisted that he spend the night. And each time, Señora Estoban had found a moment to linger in his doorway. Once, though she had merely talked with him, her black-eyed stare followed him hungrily. What was it that Sweet Blossoms had said about a dog and a bone? Señora Estoban did not need to be shown that he was a man.

The second night she had lingered until he'd begun to undress. At first she thought he was trying to frighten her away. But she stayed. And soon he had stripped until he was wearing only his moccasins. It was then that she vanished without a word.

The third time, only the night before, the señora had joined him in the undressing, reaching out to take him into her arms. She had called him her billy goat, saying his beard and whiskers reminded her of the randiest thing in the barnyard. After that, her wildness made him forget her words.

"Wild woman. She nearly got me killed!" Kit voiced, without much conviction. With Señora Estoban, he had discovered that he still had a few things to learn where women were concerned.

Finally he came to his destination. Hesitating outside the hut belonging to Renata Lopez, Kit felt ill at ease. He knew where the girl lived, because when Royce's messages had failed to bring her to him, Royce had insisted on Kit coming with him to see her the day before. But she would not let them in. They stood in the heat until Royce grew weak and dizzy.

This time Kit came alone. He noticed that, since the day before, someone had swept the dirt from the doorway. Even the single window, small as it was, had been filled in with mica and grilled with wrought iron. Kit took a deep breath and knocked.

"Who is there?" Kit heard finally, after moments of waiting in the heat.

"Christopher Carson, come to pay my respects, señorita," he said in careful Spanish. Then he removed his hat, remembering that this was a house of mourning.

"You are alone?"

"Yes."

Slowly the door was dragged open, and Kit was ushered into a dark room where the smoky offering of incense tinged the air with a blue-grey haze. Strings of red peppers flanked the small fireplace, and piles of Navaho blankets lined the walls for seating. Kit's attention was drawn particularly to the flickering mass of candles that had been set in front of the tinsel icon of the Holy Mother. A mat lay on the floor nearby.

Kit had interrupted Renata in the midst of her prayers. He turned to her with a sad smile. "I come to tell you on behalf of my friends that we are truly sorry about the death of your brother."

Renata made a tiny movement with her shoulders, but did not reply. Her eyes were puffy. She's been crying for a long time, Kit realized. Why should she suffer so much for a brother like Miguel Lopez? If the girl had tears to spare, they should be for Royce.

"I come to ask a favor of you," Kit began. Renata looked up at him, and Kit was seized with pity. She was pale. Her face seemed ashen against the stark black of her mantilla. "My friend Royce, he's not mending like he should."

Renata turned away at the mention of Royce's

name, but Kit continued. She had to hear what he was
going to say. "Royce Brant is a friend of mine, and I'd
like it if you was to say a prayer or two for his recovery."

Renata turned back to him so resolutely that Kit
had no time to prepare for her fury. "*Estúpido Americano!*" she cried. "Do you not know that I pray for
him every hour of the day and curse myself for the
disloyalty?" Sobbing, she drew her hands to her face.

"I'm sorry," Kit muttered, reaching out uncer-
tainly to console her. Instinctively, Renata leaned
toward the source of that comfort, and Kit held the
woman in his arms.

Giving comfort to weeping women was not Kit's
specialty. He was very much relieved when Renata finally quieted and pulled away to dab at her eyes with
the edge of her mantilla. Yet when he released this
lovely Mexican girl, he understood even more why
Royce had remained loyal to her memory. She was as
soft and slight as feather down, but womanly as well.

"Coffee, señor?" she asked quickly, as if the verbal attack had never happened.

"Yes, please," Kit replied, feeling confused. The
reasoning of women—he never would understand it.

"Señorita," Kit began again, "I gotta tell you that
I came on account of Royce. He wants to talk to you
somethin' fierce. He . . . well, I guess he can speak for
himself."

"He wants to marry me," Renata said lifelessly.

"That's right," Kit conceded. "To tell the truth,
it's what he's been wantin' to do ever since he left two
summers ago. I know that for a fact." Kit held up his
hand to forestall any interruption. "I realize he took

the devil's own time getting back to you. But maybe you know more about why he might have done that than I do."

Kit paused to sip his coffee. What could he say that would be reassuring? "Royce don't talk about his women like most men," he blurted, surprising himself. "He never said a word to me about you till he was delirious with fever."

"You do not understand, Mr. Carson."

"You're right. I don't," Kit announced. "And I'm not sayin' you should tell me either—ain't none of my business. But you owe some kind of explanation to Royce. He's the one . . ."

The sound of a child's cry cut Kit short. He turned to find a little boy, about fifteen months of age, wobbling in the doorway on unsteady legs. Renata rose and went to kneel in front of the child, whispering Spanish endearments. The boy bent his head shyly against his mother's shoulder. Quickly she scooped him up and returned to her chair.

"This is Jaime," she announced, shifting the boy in her lap so that his face was clearly visible.

"Howdy, James," Kit greeted cheerfully. "Fine boy," he told Renata. "Any man would be proud to claim a boy like that as his own. Don't take much lookin' to know he's Royce's son."

For a moment Renata smiled. Then her eyes were clouded once again with worry. Was she afraid that Royce would not claim the boy? Is that why she was reluctant to see him? Kit studied her face. She was pretty, as pretty then as the night she had come to the fandango in her striking outfit. There was nothing forward about this woman. Her eyes held a faraway look that could keep all but the most determined man in his place. Somehow, Royce had overcome that distance. Kit sensed that no other man would.

"Ain't fair to your boy, you keepin' him from havin' his father," Kit let out again, without thinking.

Renata tensed. "How will I ever explain to my son that his father killed his uncle?" she demanded. "How will I explain that Miguel wanted Royce dead because he had taken and dishonored a woman of his household? How will I explain my desire to marry an Americano when it was Americanos who murdered his grandfather?"

So that was it. Kit took a deep breath. "Americans murdered your father? When?"

Renata rested her cheek against her son's, then kissed him. "It was ten years ago," she began. "We had just arrived in the New Mexico Territory. My father owned a small ranch near Mexico City, but the opportunity came to own even more property in this new territory. We came and settled just north of Fernandez de Taos, the ranch we still own. One day five gringo trappers came riding to our door. They demanded the horses my father had just bought from the Navahos. The men said the horses were theirs, stolen a few weeks back. My father refused to give the animals up. He said he had paid for them." Renata shook her head wearily. "We were alone: my mother, Miguel just twelve at the time, and I. When the men grabbed my father, we did not know what they intended to do. Even if we had known, we couldn't have stopped them. What we hoped was that the trappers were only going to force my father to give them the horses. We did not

suspect they would hang him from his own gatepost."
She began to weep.

Pretty strong stuff to be thrown at a young girl,
Kit thought. But Renata and the boy and Royce were
alive. It didn't make sense for them to be separated because of past circumstances.

"Do you love Royce?" Kit asked when the silence
became uncomfortable.

"Love him? I will never love anyone else!"

"Then talk to him. Work this out together."

Kit did not stay too much longer, just time
enough to coax Renata's child from her lap into his
own. The feel of the boy in his arms made Kit keenly
aware that he was now twenty-two, and at the age
when he, too, could be a parent. Nervously shaking off
the thought, he said good-bye and left the house.

That's what being around women did for a man,
Kit thought as he walked along. Made him believe he
should settle down, start raising kids of his own so they
could grow up and head out for new territory while
their papa broke his back and forgot how to dream—
just like his own father had. No, sir! Not him! He
would keep to women like Señora Estoban. All she
wanted from him was a little fun. That's all he wanted,
too.

When Renata did not appear at American House
during the next two days, Kit spent much time thinking
that his meddling might have made things worse. Not
having the nerve to tell Royce what he had done, he
merely sat in a corner of the *sala* talking with every
new trapper that came in. He was trying to plan where

and how to begin a fall hunt without traps or pelts to buy their needs.

When Renata finally appeared at the door of the boardinghouse on that third night, Kit was not certain who was more pleased—he or Royce. "*Bienvenida, señorita,*" Kit offered in greeting as he ushered Renata past the undisguised leers of the other men in the room.

Renata paused just before reaching the table where Royce stood. She looked into the gentle, smiling face of the blond American. "My son, he waits for me outside. You will see to him for me?"

"Sure thing," Kit returned promptly, only to grimace when she turned away. So he had been relegated to being a "nana." Next time he'd keep his nose out of other people's business. Yet as he walked out to retrieve the child, he sneaked another look at the couple he had reunited. Royce's face had brightened as Renata reached out to touch his cheek.

I guess everything turned out in a way that was worth my trouble, Kit thought.

The next day, the announcement of the wedding came as no surprise.

"Do you know what you will do come fall season?" Gibbon asked when the last members of the wedding party had dragged themselves from the three-day bash.

Although Kit made a great effort and opened his eyes, the sight he saw snapped them shut. "Do you get uglier ever time I look on you, Gibbon, or is it just that your original bad looks are such a shock that a body can't record them proper every time?"

Gibbon cackled with glee. "These looks of mine are my protection," he offered, continuing the spirit of the gibe. "I'm so bad-lookin', any Indian would think twice about liftin' this old coon's hair. Thank heaven beaver ain't afraid of me much."

Beaver! Kit groaned and slid farther into his chair. He had given up thinking about trapping these last few days. Drinking enough Mexican brandy and Taos Lightning to fill a beaver pond—that had been his only activity. But he had noticed that the nights were becoming cooler. In a few weeks the aspens in the mountains north of town would begin to turn gold. He had to have a plan for the fall hunt.

"Reckon you might take to lookin' up north like a few of us fellas is set on doin'," Gibbon suggested. "Bent's Fort, that's where we're headed come first light. Ride along, you're welcome."

Kit pondered the idea. In spite of his own prejudices against the merchant from back East, he had to admit that the Bent fellow was doing something right. He had been too ill from his desert crossing to actually talk to Bent when he arrived in Taos with Ewing Young's party. But Young was trading with Bent and, therefore, must have thought Bent was a good man. Kit had asked his friend about him and Young had told him that Bent liked to be in the wilderness, liked doing his own trading, and was looking for new men.

Of course, Kit thought, I still want to make my own way. But maybe, just maybe, Rube and Wooten hadn't left Bent's Fort and were waiting for the chance to join up with him again. They were good men. A little skittish maybe, but good men all around. He could not begrudge them their prudence in heading for the safety of the fort. If he had done the same himself, he would be sitting pretty with more money in his pockets than a St. Louis banker.

"When do we leave?" Kit asked enthusiastically.

"Now you're talkin'! First thing tomorrow," Gibbon grinned. "Ain't much left here for us anyway, what with Royce bedded down for a spell. Got to get me another squaw, though. That's a fact."

Kit wasn't listening. Another reason for riding up to Bent's Fort had suddenly sprung into his mind. The reason had more to do with a red silk bandanna he had been packing around for more than a year than with trapping and trading. Rumor was that St. Nair still worked as a hunter for Bent.

"That Frenchman deserves a visit," Kit declared.

The adobe walls of the massive fort shone like fool's gold in the late afternoon sunshine. The cacti atop the walls featured bright yellow blossoms and provided as fine a protection against intruders as barbed wire.

"Looks like royalty's expected, the place is so fancied up," Kit quipped to the man nearest him. "Reckon they serve tea, too?"

As they rode in, Kit studied the tepees that seemed to dot the banks of the river. Cheyennes made up the major portion of the encampments, but he saw Arapahos as well, their tepees more imaginatively decorated than those of the other tribes.

Memories of the Arapaho girl flitted across his mind, then were dismissed. "Comes from too much time hangin' around that lovesick calf, Brant," Kit told himself. "Let's see if the storekeeper's home!" he yelled over his shoulder and raced up the slope toward the fort.

To his irritation, Kit found that William Bent was not at home, and that the sentry on duty had strict orders not to allow any man in he did not recognize.

"If that don't beat all," Gibbon said, snorting derisively.

Swinging a leg over his saddle to dismount, Kit agreed.

"What you expect we ought to do?" Gibbon asked.

"Beats me!" Kit shrugged, snatching his hat from his head. "Sure as hell didn't expect to waste my time beggin' at the front door of this overgrown beaver lodge. I'll be goin' back to Taos, I guess."

An Indian cry set both men gearing for possible trouble. Coming toward them at a full gallop was a scarecrow in buckskin. His long, grey beard flew like a banner over his shoulders. The character didn't pull in rein until the last moment. Then he flashed an Indian sign of greeting and, dipping down from his saddle, scooped Kit off his feet. Amazingly strong for his brittle appearance, the rider swung Kit up over his saddle horn and let him drop gently to the ground on the other side. "Whoa! Well, if it ain't my favorite beaver kitten, Christopher Carson himself!"

Only a few men knew Kit's full name, so it did not take Kit long to figure out the outlandish fellow's identity.

"Blackfoot Smith!"

"None other," the man acknowledged as he lowered himself to the ground. He swung out two long, skinny arms and encircled the younger man in a viselike hug. "Growed up a mite, you have, though not an inch in height," the man teased.

Kit took a playful swing at Smith's head and missed. "Growed up enough to learn you a trick or two, old-timer. I haven't forgotten how you made me eat a whole side of elk I massacred while trying to learn to cook for Ewing Young a few years back."

"Massacred? Boy, that elk was burnt past use as coyote bait." Blackfoot bent down and whispered, "You still havin' it come back on you now and then?"

Kit imitated a huge belch, and his friend howled.

"What brings you to the Arkansas?" Blackfoot asked when he caught his breath.

Kit sent a sour look at the closed gates of the fort. "Had some business with Will Bent. Guess I don't need to see him that badly, howsomever."

"Sentry won't let you in?"

Kit nodded.

"They've got their orders. Cap'n Bent, he makes 'em tow the mark or makes 'em leave a few scraps of their hides behind."

"The Bents use the whip on a man?"

"Pure truth," Blackfoot answered. "Don't have much traffic with shirkers and riffraff. A man does his job or else. Can't expect 'em to do otherwise, not with the sort they deal with."

Kit stared directly at the old man. "Bent got a man by the name of St. Nair workin' for him?"

Blackfoot scratched at his beard. "That'd be that long wad of tobacco Will's been learnin' to chaw. Mean cuss. Never seen eyes like his 'cept in a mountain cougar." He spat on the ground and shivered. "You after him?"

Kit nodded.

"Then you might as well make yourself a home in my digs till Bent gets back. Got me a fine old gal keepin' me warm these days. She's *some*, she is."

An hour later, Kit had a chance to see for himself why the mountain man was so fond of his woman. Blackfoot called her by the English name "Sal," but she was full-blooded Crow—and a first-class cook, as Kit's protruding belly attested.

"Ain't the most pretty woman in the world," Blackfoot told his guests as they sat around his fire and smoked his special blend of tobacco, mixed with red willow bark. "But she does me proud.

"You got yourself a woman, Kit? No? Let me tell you, a man's got to get himself a helpmate. Strappin' young fella like you will run himself ragged over every woman between here and Canada if he don't trap one for his own. That Sal of mine, she knows how to keep a man from painin' himself. And it don't take nothin' much to keep her happy. A bit of beads, a mirror, and a pretty blanket, that's all she wants. Ain't like city gals, needin' a permanent roof over their heads and goose-down pillows and all sorts of foofaraw. Tarnation! This fella don't need no citified white lady that weeps at a blister and can't carry half her weight on her own back. Get yourself a Indian gal, Kit! She'll keep your lodge clean, your stew pot full, and make your bedroll the only place in the world worth curlin' up in. You come home tired, gut-sore for meat and sleep, and she'll be there to calm the fret, boy, to calm the fret."

Kit rolled his eyes at Gibbon. It looked like the whole frontier had decided it was time he settled down.

"Give me a spell yet, Blackfoot. You was young once. When I get rheumatism so bad I can't collect my own wood for fire, that's when I'll pack a squaw."

Blackfoot chuckled. "You ain't been to the Arapaho camp yet, have you? You just wait. If you ain't fit to bust your britches over them little gals above a hour in their company, you might as well take up with a billy goat."

Kit had had enough of marriage talk. "What you hear about Bridger and Fitzpatrick? They win their feud with them eastern fur company boys?"

Blackfoot perked up, a new tale rolling onto his tongue. "Mean you ain't heard how the Crows is now callin' Fitzpatrick 'Whitehead' instead of 'Broken Hand'? No? Lord! He nearly lost his scalp a dozen different times last summer. Chased by Blackfeet over a hundred miles. But let me—as they say—commence at the beginning . . ."

And the night was passed by swapping stories.

William Bent lowered himself from his saddle with a satisfied grunt. Summer was not the best time for trading, but he had heard of a band of Crow Indians camped a hundred miles to the northwest of the fort—a range pretty far south for them, and the sort of opportunity he didn't want to miss.

The Crows were known throughout the territory for their superb horseflesh, and with good reason. William looked over at the herdsmen working in the corral. One-eyed Juan, the best of the New Mexico cowboys he had hired, was eyeing with partiality the new breed they had brought in. It was the Crows' own breed, called palouse. William knew that Juan would soon have the unbroken mare eating out of his hand.

"Wish I had that much faith in the rest of this crew." William let the words slip softly from his lips as his gaze swung back to the men riding in behind him. The hunters were the worst of the lot. They were indifferent, never straining themselves when they could sit and wait for the next herd of buffalo to cross the plains. And that St. Nair! If he crippled another man, William knew he would have to run him off—if he could.

"Cap'n Bent, sir?" One of the men hired to guard the fort came running across the corral as William handed the reins of his mount to a cowhand. "There's a man down in the Cheyenne camp looking for you, sir. Says his name's Carson."

William's black brows shot up. "Carson? Blond hair and whiskers? Short man, sort of scrappy-looking?"

The sentry nodded. "That's the one."

There was no reason in the world William could think of that would bring Carson to see him, and it made him curious. "Send a man for Carson, boy," he ordered. "Oh, and send St. Nair to me first."

Kit took his time acting on Bent's invitation. It was a full day later when he ambled up to the fort. And when he entered, he was met with such deferential treatment that he began to wonder if the invitation had been a trap. The iron-studded doors hid a long, wide tunnel that had been built into the fort's eighteen-foot wall. Beyond the tunnel lay the huge courtyard. Children of the fort's employees played there, while Indian women lounged in the shade of blanket awnings. From

the blacksmith's shop came the sharp scent of hot
metal and oil mingled with the odors of horseflesh and
dry goods. The surroundings were reminiscent of a
country main street.

"Merchant doin's!" Kit muttered as he allowed
himself to be shown to the main office. He entered with
shoulders squared and head high. He had come for two
reasons.

William looked up from his paperwork as Kit's
shadow crossed his desk. "Kit Carson," he said in
greeting, extending his hand. "Don't believe we've met
before."

Kit looked at the black-bearded, hawk-nosed
man, but did not extend his own hand. "We've met,"
he snapped.

A frown creased William's brow. He had not
meant to bring up the past, but now that Carson had,
he would speak his mind. "You slapped me with a Indian scalp, as I recall."

"You called me a bloodthirsty savage in a white
skin with no morals a second before that," Kit countered, controlling his tone.

William spread his fingers across the papers on his
desk and took a deep breath. "One thing a man learns
in this land: he can make few mistakes that don't come
back to haunt him."

Kit let the silence drag. Then he said, "That's so."

Closest thing he's gonna get to an apology from
me, William thought. "Welcome to Bent's Fort, Carson," he said aloud. "Have a seat."

"Don't mind if I do." Kit lowered himself into a
well-made oak chair, the likes of which he had not
seen since leaving Missouri. The whitewashed adobe

walls seemed to be the only concession to the wilderness. Mirrors, pictures, oil lamps and imported carpets provided a formality that, to Kit, seemed out of place. He could barely keep the contempt from his face.

Noting Kit's reaction, William checked his inclination to smile. More than likely, the man had never seen so much finery in one place before.

"We've been hearing about you, Kit," he began finally. "Rube and Wooten were mighty carefully courted when they showed up with all those top-quality furs a few months back, I can tell you. Of course, they kept their mouths shut." William did smile now. "You weren't so lucky, were you?"

Kit shrugged. "Had Comanche trouble. We lost a few pelts, a few mules."

William sat back in his chair, a bit bewildered. Any other trapper would have launched into an hour's narration about the desperate experience he'd had with the Comanches, and how only his own cunning and bravery had saved the day.

"Care for a cigar?" William reached for his favorite box. "Got a newspaper from St. Louis yesterday. Would you like to read about President Jackson's latest altercation with Congress?"

Kit picked up the paper and deliberately began to read aloud, " 'Notice. To whom it may concern: That Hesperus Jones, indentured servant of sixteen years . . .' "

William waved him to silence. "Okay. You made your point. You can read. I apologize for putting you to the test." William cleared his throat. "But tell me, if I'm wrong in my estimation of you, why are you bouncing around the territory when you could be putting that wit and wisdom to useful purpose?"

Kit smiled for the first time. "Why did *you* come West?" he asked. "Wasn't it because you heard about a place where life was lived free, where adventure could be had just by steppin' a toe across a border, where the thirst to be the first and best was always bein' whetted by the next bend in the river? That's why I'm here. I aim to carve myself a name in this territory. Don't need no towns hemmin' me in. Got to be on the front edge of life. Got to be where a man is as good as his word, and brave as his strength can make him."

William whistled. "That's quite a speech for a man who doesn't talk about himself." Kit's blush made him relax. "Have some brandy—the real thing, from France—then tell me why you've come to me."

Enjoying the smooth fire of the liquor sliding down his throat, Kit was quiet a moment. Then he sat forward, an earnest expression on his face. "Fact is, Ewing Young suggested I come to deal with you." Kit watched the man across from him for any reaction. There was none. "I lost everything but my life on the Cimarron this summer," Kit continued. "Now I've got no traps, no possibles, no money. I'm flat busted."

It was all William could do to keep from jumping into the pause with an offer of a job, but he held off. The young man was eating his innards to keep from asking for work. He would have to come to it in his own time.

Kit licked his lips. "I could use an advance, signed legal and all. I'll pay you back before two months."

"Why didn't you ask Young?"

Kit's chin shot out. "Ewing Young is a particular friend of mine. Anything I ask of him he'd do for me. I don't want no favors. I made a stupid mistake. I'll pay for it in my own way.

"Now you and me," Kit smiled, "we don't waste no time thinkin' on our love for one another. You make me a loan, you'll expect to collect or have my hide. I like that. I can owe you because you don't owe me nothin' or care one tiny bit whether I make it or not. You understand?"

William did understand. And he knew it took a certain kind of cussed contrariness to inspire a man to turn to his detractors for aid. "So, you and me, we'll be going into business together, so to speak?"

Kit shook his head vigorously. "Not a word of it. You and me, we'll have a debt between us, if you're agreeable. I pay you in pelts, owe you nothin' else."

"What if I want a provision included that you'll trade your entire fall catch to me—for a fair price, of course."

Again Kit gave his shaggy head a shake. "No deal. I got to be free to trade where I will." He rose to his feet. "Guess we got no more to discuss."

"Wait a minute, you hotheaded young fool!" William shouted, his face flushing. "I didn't say no! Don't you know the first thing about trading, Indian-style? A good trader never takes the first offer made to him. Maybe not even the tenth, if he thinks he can get a better deal. I'll see you your traps and gear for the fall hunt. As for you and me, there'll be a better time to strike another deal between us."

Not so much as a muscle twitched in Kit's face as he listened to Bent's words, but inside he was singing.

"You ain't a half-bad man, Bent. I thank you. One thing more." His expression hardened. "You got a man named St. Nair workin' for you? I want to talk with him."

William hesitated. He had not just come through one of the toughest moments of his trading career to lose his newfound trapper to the likes of St. Nair. "Sent him out of the fort yesterday," he admitted. "Heard about your run-in with him in Taos two years back. Why are you looking for him, anyway?"

Kit pulled the red silk bandanna out from under his leather shirt. "St. Nair was wearing one of these last time I saw him in Taos. I found this in our camp the fall after it was shot up real bad by a band of peculiar-lookin' Indians. You know anything about that?"

"I'll be honest with you, Kit," Bent replied. "Some of my hunters were joking amongst themselves that winter about raiding a Rocky Mountain Fur brigade. Thought they were lying or stretching the truth. Was anybody killed?"

Kit nodded.

"Want you to know that the raid wasn't by my orders. That's a fact," Bent assured him.

Kit gave Bent a long stare. Then he shrugged. "If that's true, then my business is with St. Nair. Thanks for your time."

As Kit turned to go, he saw Grass Singing standing in the doorway. She wore moccasins and tight leggings that showed off the curves of her calves. Around her waist was a hairless doeskin robe. Silver bracelets dangled from her arms, and she wore turquoise earrings. Tangled in the glossy-black fall of her hair was a deer's tail. From the waist up, the girl was naked. Arapaho girls did not believe in overdressing in hot weather. Her firm young breasts made Kit swell with desire.

"Come in," William coaxed, missing nothing of the young man's reaction to the beautiful girl. "Have you met Mr. Carson? Kit, this is Waa-nibe. We call her Grass Singing."

Kit swallowed. It was his heart that was singing, and shouting, and beating in his chest. Kit heard himself stammer something. Then, embarrassed, he hurried by the girl and through the doorway.

William laughed and patted the girl's arm when Carson had gone. So, the taciturn young man had a weakness after all. "You know what?" Bent confided to Grass Singing. "I think I just figured out a foolproof plan to get that scrappy youngster to stick around and work for me."

Grass Singing did not understand much English. Even if she had, she would not have heard the Black Beard's words. Every thought was focused on Turquoise Eyes. She reached up shyly and touched her love charm—the deer's tail. It had worked just as Turtle Eye had promised. It had brought her man back from the Shining Ones!

Chapter 13

"Sorry, Kit," Royce said, shaking his head. "I tried to tell you before. I've been lookin' for something permanent ever since I left Kentucky. Never thought I'd find it." He looked lovingly through the doorway of the next room where Renata was putting their son to sleep. "Well, I did find it," he went on, "better than I could've dreamed. Got me a wife and son, got a farm in the Lopez place, too. Did I ever tell you I was a farmer before turnin' trapper? It's gonna be a good life for me and my family."

"Farmin'?" Kit repeated incredulously. "Diggin' in the dirt like you was a Mohave? What kind of work is that for a grown man?"

"Sorry you feel that way," Royce replied, concerned for his friend, and too, not looking forward to separation from him. "A man's got to do what his conscience tells him. I've been lucky a second time, found the right woman. I'm not giving it up for nothin'. You'll understand why one day."

"The hell I will!" Kit thundered, bounding to his feet. "So, you can't drag yourself away from your woman's side long enough to take a stroll through the Rockies this year. I feel for you, Royce, I most certainly do. Any man that's got his head so addled on account of love he can't think straight has got my sympathy."

Hearing the insult, Royce merely laughed. "Like I once told you, Kit, when you fall in love, you can talk to me about women." Then, changing the subject, he said, "You get all the supplies you needed up at Bent's Fort?"

Kit opened his mouth to continue his argument, then decided it was not worth it. He answered, "Everythin' but a new horse. Ewing Young loaned me one of his. Gonna take me most of the season just to pay off what I owe Bent, especially since I went into debt for Tuttle, too."

Royce made no comment on Kit's generosity. "I'm glad to hear you got Rube and Wooten, too. But what about Bill Mitchell? Manhead? Tom? With all them collected, it sounds to me like you're ready to ride."

"I am." Kit's voice was wooden.

"I'm gonna miss you too, Kit." Royce smiled, but his eyes were clouded with emotion. "You and me, we're like brothers. Don't forget to come back to Taos."

Kit gathered up his things. "I'll be back."

"Don't like it above half," Kit said to Tuttle dur-

ing their second week out. He had been leading his
men in and out of the narrow gorges of the lower
Sangre de Cristo Range, up into southern Colorado.
The ground crackled beneath their feet, the once-blue
gama grass wheat-brown and dry. "Ain't often the heat
hangs in the air past September. Must be a terrible
spell of weather ahead."

Amos pushed a handful of hair from his eyes to
search the cloudless sky. Other than the call of jays
and nuthatches to keep them company, their surroundings were quiet.

"Speakin' for myself, I like this weather, Cap'n
Carson," Amos admitted.

"Told you about that cap'n stuff. Don't like it,"
Kit grumbled, but as usual he knew it would do no
good. Ever since the story about his adventurous ex-
ploit on the Cimarron had made the rounds of the
trappers' campfires, the label of "Captain" had stuck.
"How's your feet?"

"Better than ever." Amos held up one large moc-
casined foot. "Mr. Bent's Cheyenne wife cut 'em for
me special. Lots of parfleche on the soles."

Kit nodded. "We'll make camp early. Looks to
me the weather won't hold much past dark."

He moved on, leaving Amos behind. The tender-
foot hadn't noticed the smoky mist sliding down the
eastward slope of the mountains to the west. And he
hadn't sensed the pregnant stillness in the underbrush,
or heard the hectic chirping of birds in the trees overhead. The twitching of his mule's tail he attributed to
restless hunger. "Beats me how Cap'n Carson expects
the squeeze of one tiny drop of water out of that blue
sky," he murmured with a shrug.

By nightfall, Kit was pacing the camp. They had set up on the bank of a narrow stream beneath a stand of cottonwoods. He made the rounds of the pack animals that were picketed nearby, retying a knot now and then and patting each rump with a whispered Spanish word of comfort. The animals were little grey burros from Taos, unaccustomed to the harshness of an American trapper's tongue. Heads lowered, ears hitched forward in nervous inquiry, they snatched hungry mouthfuls of green grass that they had found at the base of the trees.

Along the edge of the camp, just out of range of the firelight, Kit heard the scuttle and scurry of padded feet. Prairie wolves. They were a constant companion, sneaking along the fringes of the camp until a turned back or head nodding in sleep made them bold enough to dash in and dart off with food.

"They're looking for trouble tonight," Kit said softly. He didn't even bother to draw a bead on the scrawny animal that darted momentarily into his view. A man could waste his entire supply of galena on the nuisances and still be hounded from one end of the territory to the other.

Only the day before, Kit recalled, he had just slaughtered the elk he'd killed when a whole party of little coyotes had formed a gallery of onlookers a short distance from him. There they'd sat—tawny-faced, yellow-eyed, their black-tipped tails swishing—patient as ladies at a church meeting waiting for him to finish up. He'd heaved a section of meat at his audience. One wolf had snatched it up, only to be blocked by a much larger white one that had been lying in the tall buffalo grass. Outsized, the smaller beast had dropped his bounty and fled back to the safety of his comrades.

But tonight, the wolves seemed not so much interested in running off with skin ropes or saddle leather as in seeking the comfort of the fires. Kit hitched his rifle to his shoulder. He felt as frisky as they did, watching and waiting—he didn't know for what. Once again he stared at the sky. A milky moon had risen shortly after sunset, but his gaze was caught by one of the silver-white flashes that had begun soon after. Lightning. There was no sound yet, just the stillness and spooky light. To the west, the mist had turned solid. Before it a lacy veil was spreading across the night, shielding the stars. The weather was turning.

The perishable portion of their supplies—including the pelts they had just begun to collect—the trappers placed under skin robes in case of rain. Then they made themselves comfortable. Bill Mitchell, Wooten and Rube used cottonwood branches to hold up their makeshift tents while Manhead and Tom merely rolled up tightly in their buffalo robes in high ground. Kit showed Amos how to dig a pit around the place where he laid his blankets in order to drain away any rain that might fall.

"Sure goin' to a heap of trouble for chancy weather," Amos commented when he'd finished the work.

Instead of answering, Kit dragged up a Navaho blanket Royce had given him and wrapped it around his shoulders. "Them Navahos have a way with thread," he told Amos. "Weave it so tight even a gully-washer won't seep through it. Rest up, son. Come the fireworks, you're gonna be bug-eyed awake."

Kit had first watch. It was just as well with him. He sat with his back to the mountains, his attention on the open prairie in front of him. As the night wore on, the strangely mournful cry of a distant wolf broke through the stillness. Nothing beneath the sky would rest easy this night.

Kit shifted position. The Hawken lay across his knees, his finger still resting on the trigger. If it were a bad enough storm, many animals might be driven against their natural fear of man and try to keep shelter with him.

It wasn't long before the first crack of thunder shook the leaves from the cottonwood canopy overhead. Soon the flashes increased in frequency and intensity until the earth was bathed in light.

Kit wasn't sure when he first became aware of the subtle change on the open land. Crystal-bright zigzags of white flame had been striking a pattern all around them for more than an hour, but now, accompanying the increase of smoke in the black sky, there was a gradual emergence of a new light at the farthest edge of the horizon.

"The prairie's afire!" The realization stunned Kit. He gave the signal even as he ran to jump on his mount's bare back. One slice of the Green River and the picket line was severed. Kit grabbed up the loose end and headed his horse toward the faint glow on the distant plain.

The horse protested, the crack and snap of lightning maddening it, but Kit dug his heels in, viciously urging the animal against its will. A moment later he was galloping across the valley floor.

The first gust of wind brought the acrid smell of

burning sagebrush. The wind rose quickly after that, moaning in Kit's ears and dragging at his hat and hair. It was blowing up from the east, where lightning had set fire to the dry grasses.

Kit swore under his breath. Prairie fires were one of the most dangerous and unpredictable natural disasters that could hit the plains.

Fanning out on the open ground and driven by the wind was a wall of flame perhaps a quarter of a mile wide and growing. Kit kept his shivering mount clamped tightly between his legs. The horse smelled the fire, too, the scent of death on racing tongues of flame.

Suddenly the animal reared, whinnying in fright. Kit tugged at the rope looped about its neck and calmed the horse's skittishness.

The fire was less than ten miles away. Between it and the stream where his men were camped was the herd of grazing buffalo they had passed around noontime. In the dull glow of the flames, Kit could pick out dozens of the black, humped beasts moving now like thundering mountains.

"Stampede!" he exclaimed, hearing the rumble ahead during a lull. Fire and stampede at night!

Wheeling his horse, Kit raced flat out back the way he had come. A heartening sight greeted him when he reached his camp. Bill Mitchell and Manhead were already slinging blankets soaked in water over the backs of the pack animals. The rest of the group had moved most of the gear to the edge of the stream. At least his men had not made the mistake of thinking they could outrun the fire.

Kit leaped from his mount. "Buffalo stampede!" he yelled hoarsely. "They'll head for water, sure!"

The news momentarily stopped the men cold. They knew they could soak themselves in the stream; it was wide enough that the fire could not reach them if they waded to the middle. But a thousand tons of fire-crazed buffalo at full gallop would not stop at the water's edge.

"The trees," Wooten suggested anxiously, gesturing toward the cottonwoods.

Kit shook his head, remembering how he had once been trapped in a tree by a grizzly. He would just as soon take his chances on the ground this time. It would be the water or nothing.

Suddenly a blinding flash struck the tree nearest Kit, and he was thrown to the ground ten feet away. The cottonwood trembled as a great cracking sound was heard. Then the tree split in two, falling away from its own center as cleanly as if a giant axe had been swung through it.

Kit scrambled to his feet. He had his answer. Gather up what'll burn. We'll start our own fire!"

The men didn't balk at the suggestion; they simply threw themselves into the work that had to be done. Axes hacked at the felled tree while Kit coaxed some of the smaller branches to flame and dragged them out into the dry grass.

Buffalo were afraid of fire. Kit knew that if he and his men could make theirs big enough—and make it last long enough—the herd just might be turned aside.

Within minutes, the section of surrounding prairie was on fire. While his men herded the stock into the shallow water of the stream, Kit grabbed up the last of the equipment.

Soon they could feel the thunder of the stampede. The buffalos' path was illuminated by lightning, and in the midst of the tumult, Kit felt his blood begin to race. What he was experiencing was an emotion very different from fear. Even though the scene unfolding before him meant terror and possible death, it was also one that few men would ever witness. Kit wouldn't trade the moment for anything in the world.

The burros were braying, their sensitive nostrils picking up the scents of both the musky odor of the buffalo and the fire. Kit tugged hard at the lines in his hand, but his eyes never left the prairie. For what seemed like hours, the trappers waited. The sky grew red. The stampede drowned out the pounding of their own hearts.

"They're turnin'! I can tell!"

It was Wooten's voice that rang out. Unable to stay put, he had left the stream to climb one of the cottonwoods nearest the bank. "Goin' north, they are!"

Leaving the burros churning in the stream, Kit leaped onto the bank. A moment later a raindrop hit his left cheek. The crackling and hissing of the flames increased as more drops fell. Then a new bolt of lightning, followed by a roar of thunder, seemed to rip open the purple underbelly of the heavens, and sheets of rain emptied onto the midnight prairie. Within minutes, the rain transformed the dusty earth into a quagmire.

"Whew! Damndest thing I ever saw!" Rube yelled.

By sunrise, the entire band of men had managed to put the camp back in order. Only the dull-grey smoke of the dying fires and the black, muddy earth reminded them how closely they had come to death.

"How many packs did we lose?" Kit asked the men assembled before him.

"There's the one Wooten lost when Bess bolted," Rube offered with a snicker at his friend's misfortune. "But, more'n not, lil' Bess will be waitin' over the other side of the hills." Rube paused a moment, then said, "Damndest thing—your luck, Cap'n Carson. Ain't a man here ever gonna question your orders again."

Kit eyed the big man closely for any sign of sarcasm, but didn't find it. Deliberately he spat near his own foot, then with his moccasin toe covered over the damp spot. The Indian custom of burying old grievances made Rube smile. Kit had not been unfriendly since he and Wooten had chosen to ride with him again, but the fact remained that the two men had once demanded to go their own way. Now any bad feelings attached to that decision would be forgotten.

"What the hell we standin' around for? The mountains is waitin'!"

Kit's men heeded his words, and within moments, they were eagerly crossing the last short distance between them and the best trapping grounds south of Montana.

Winter was approaching quickly in this region of the northern Rockies. Already the ground crunched as ice broke under the hooves of the animals. To the west, the majestic mountain peaks wore heavy mantles of white.

Kit tugged the brim of his hat down lower and sighed. Three weeks before, he had run into "Gabe" Bridger up on the headwaters of the Green River. They had been glad to see one another after nearly three years, and both groups had combined. The small band of six had ridden with Bridger's huge brigade numbering nearly two hundred.

"Too darn many folks!" Kit decided after ten days, and he went to announce to Bridger his intentions of taking off again on his own. Bridger had merely shrugged, wished him luck, and uttered a few cautionary words against the Blackfeet.

The number of Blackfeet raids was increasing, Kit thought, lifting his head to scan the ridge they were heading toward. The stories he had heard were told by men who made their living in this portion of the frontier.

By comparison, the fur war that existed among the different companies was of little interest to him. Perhaps he'd add his own cunning to the fracas if this year's trapping made the thought worthwhile. But what had convinced him of the ferocity of the Blackfeet was his first glimpse of Tom Fitzpatrick after nearly three years.

Kit shuddered, remembering his first sight of the man. He did not even recognize his former brigade leader. The flaming red hair had turned silver. Blackfeet doings, Fitzpatrick had told him, going on to explain how he had been trapped by an entire village of migrating Blackfeet two years earlier.

"My escape cost me everything," Bridger had reported. "My rifle, my horse, my saddle, my possibles—even the color of my hair."

Without being aware of it, Kit put a hand to his own scraggly locks. He understood enough of Fitzpatrick's character to appreciate that the Irishman's survival had depended primarily on his cool head. If

Fitz had been so scared that his hair turned white overnight, then the Blackfeet were a force to be reckoned with.

What Bridger had also mentioned was that the Blackfeet were being armed by the newest American Fur Company fort on the upper Missouri—Fort MacKenzie. Already an almost insurmountable enemy when armed only with arrows and tomahawks, now the Blackfeet had power at least equal to the trappers' own.

In spite of all the stories he had heard, Kit knew he had to have more freedom than Bridger's brigade allowed him. Besides, he was accustomed to being his own boss, and even Bridger's commands were difficult to swallow after having blazed his own path these past few years. So, he had packed up.

What surprised Kit was that four of Bridger's men wanted to join him. Bridger wished them well, yet reminded the four that they were bound by their signatures to trade their catch only with him. Kit agreed to make sure they honored the commitment.

A fresh pelting of sleet had fallen before noon, forcing Kit's party to find shelter in a pine grove.

"Think we're gonna reach the Big Snake?" Amos asked as the men squatted around the tiny fire for their midday meal.

Kit nodded. "We got another few days before the snow sets in proper. Time enough to reach winterin'."

"Don't know," Wooten said, shaking his head. "Sky's the color of a rifle barrel. Air's so thin I can't hardly draw breath. I'll bet there's heavy snow before mornin'."

"Might be right, after all," Kit replied after giving

the matter serious thought. "Leastways, it'll take a few days till the pass is plugged. We'll be through. Caching our pelts on the Wind River was a good move. We're light, able to move fast."

By nightfall, Kit had revised his opinion. It was doubtful that they would reach the relatively mild wintering grounds of the Snake River Valley before the blizzard set in. New snow had begun to fall less than an hour after they broke up at noon. Now the unmarked path before them swirled and danced with huge flakes that stuck as the temperature fell.

"Don't like the feel of things," Kit confided to Manhead when the others were bedded down for the night. Though he had not felt comfortable saying those words to the full brigade, there was something about the quiet self-assurance of the Delaware Indian that inspired Kit to tell him as they prepared to take the first watch.

Manhead said nothing, his black eyes like jasper in the campfire's light. "You've seen the same 'sign' I have," Kit continued. "There's Indians about. That flush of quail back in them timbers yesterday—nothin' but humans could've set them flyin' like that." He smiled suddenly, thinking of the shame that mistake must have cost the young brave who had spooked the birds. A veteran warrior would not have been so careless.

"Maybe they're just a band of braves lookin' for their first coup," Kit added without much conviction. Untried braves would not track ten mountain men through the Rockies. Most of them were warriors, all right. He would stake his cache on it.

"Indian 'sign' worry Little Chief." Manhead grinned, his teeth just showing through his lips.

Kit shrugged. Little Chief. The Cheyennes up at Bent's Fort had dubbed him that when they learned he was the leader of the six men who had held off the Comanches. It appeared now that he would be stuck with the name for the rest of his life.

"Be a fool not to keep my eyes open and my nose clear," Kit speculated, answering Manhead's teasing. He reached down to pull off the smooth, thick-soled moccasins he had worn during the fall, then moved to his possible sack to draw out the new thin-soled footwear he saved for the winter weather. "I think I'll be needin' these right about now so I can get a toehold on the ground. It's slippery."

The sight of the Arapaho-made moccasins sent his thoughts crashing back through the last months to that day in midsummer when he had seen Grass Singing standing in Bent's doorway. Even now his loins throbbed with the images he'd conjured up.

Bent had told him that Grass Singing was the daughter of the Arapaho Chief, Soaring Vulture. The chief belonged to the Crazy Lime Society, and that made him important in Arapaho circles.

"She comes to the fort to trade her buffalo robes," Bent had explained. "A lot of times she stays to watch the business of the white man's world. In fact, she seems to be fascinated by anything 'white.'"

"Anyway," Bent had continued, "I give Grass Singing the run of the fort because it pleases Owl Woman. My wife may be Cheyenne, but she has a special feeling for the Arapaho girl and enjoys her company. And," Bent had added, laughing, "when my wife's happy, I'm happy."

Kit's rising hopes had been shot down with the announcement that no man, under penalty of the whip, dared touch Grass Singing. She was Arapaho, a maiden untouched, and for the sake of everyone concerned, she had damn well better stay that way till some man made a proper offer for her.

Kit dismissed the possibility of marriage, but he sensed reluctantly that his conviction was weakening. "Must be getting old," he muttered to himself. There he was, in the middle of what would probably turn out to be a raging blizzard, and what was he wasting his time on? Thoughts of an unattainable Indian girl. What a fool he was!

"What do you mean, you didn't hear nothin'!"

Kit had sprung out of his snow-covered robes the moment he learned that their mounts had been stolen during the night. His angry blue stare raked first one man and then the other, as Rube and Tom Hill, a Delaware, stood sheepishly before him.

"Wasn't nothin' we could do," Rube began, faltering uncharacteristically under Carson's scrutiny. "That's a fact, Cap'n Carson," he continued. "Me and Tom, we figure they must have snuck up on us when the blizzard was at its worst. Didn't hear nothin' but wind howlin' down the valley. Snow was so thick it looked like a wall."

"How many lost?" Kit looked to Tom for the answer.

The big red man made the hand sign for twenty.

Kit swore under his breath. That was every one of

their mules and horses. "Get your gear hitched up," he ordered angrily. "We're movin' out!"

"Gear? Movin'? Where?"

Impatiently, Kit turned to Amos Tuttle. "Son, you got to do somethin' about that hoot-owl tone of yours. We're goin' after our horseflesh, of course. Can't walk all the way to the Snake Valley. As for the gear," Kit continued, smiling with fake sweetness, "seems to me all along we had more two-legged mules in this brigade than the four-legged kind. What you can't carry, you lose!"

The blizzard had dumped a foot of snow into the valley where they were camped. The snow meant hard travel over treacherous ground in the aching cold. But at least it would slow the thieves. Men on horseback could not move any faster than men on foot in this damn weather. Still, Kit thought resentfully, it was no way to end up the season

Five days of pursuit—fifty miles of dogged travel through snow-choked ground that sometimes left a man floundering up to his waist in a drift—was the time it took for Kit's band to locate the raiding party.

The Blackfeet's trail had been easy enough to follow. The Indians hadn't even attempted to cover their tracks, and the huge imprints that their snowshoes had made were taunting reminders that they were still out of reach.

But the weather had given the Indians little leeway to escape. The snow continued piling up. Soon the icy crust was so hard that it cut the legs of the animals, leaving a bloody trail when the Indians had stopped to hack out a path through the drifts.

The Blackfeet were sighted, finally, at the edge of a valley on the eastern slope of the Rockies. Kit and Manhead had moved on half a mile ahead of the rest, realizing that if the Indians reached the break called Union Pass, he and his men would lose any chance of recapturing their herd. But nightfall on the fifth day revealed that the Blackfeet had camped on the rocky slope on the near side of the pass, tethering their animals higher up where the ground had been swept clean of snow by the icy blast of the northern winds.

"What now?" Kit asked himself as he and the Delaware lay in the snow fifty yards from the Blackfeet tepees. Two men could not successfully steal back all twenty animals. The odds were two to thirty-five, according to Kit's count. "We'll have to parley," he announced to his companion.

"Better we wait for the others," Manhead advised, staring out over the frozen land. "Two men don't make good parley. Ten men are better."

Kit had to agree. But as he lay belly-down in the snow, waiting for the rest of his men, he did not like either the looks of the sky or the sense he had of the Blackfeet's intentions. The Indians were quiet; raiding parties were more exuberant, customarily. It was almost as if the Indians were not convinced that their dealings with the whites were completely over. And because they seemed this way, Kit, in turn, was not content with his success in tracking them down.

The wind nipped at his face, and bits of sleet made his skin numb and his eyes watery. Uncomfortable, smelling trouble in the air, Kit suddenly felt very much alone.

"Must be missing Royce," he grouched. It had not

been the same this season without Brant. There had
been no one he could really trust, no one to help him
watch his step or ease his temper. It was not that he
needed Royce to nursemaid him, or do anything for
him, Kit thought. That would have been sentimental
foolishness. But, he reflected, Royce had always been
there to back up his decisions, to make him feel that he
had come by his judgments properly.

Two hours later the rest of the trappers arrived.
Kit waved the sign for a parley. The Blackfeet did not
seem particularly surprised by this announcement, and
this wasn't encouraging.

"Must have spied us a while back," Amos ventured.

"Right. So why didn't they do somethin' about
it?" Kit replied. "Must be they know we ain't gonna let
'em go through that pass without a fight. Guess they'd
just as soon fight us where they can see us."

"Ain't powerful smart, us showin' our number," Bill
complained.

Kit ignored the remark, looking toward the mountainside where the Indians' discussions had broken off.
"Looks like we get to talk one-on-one."

He pointed to the single warrior who had stepped
out from behind the rocky debris that sheltered the Indian camp. Kit adjusted his Green River and pulled his
hat down tight. He propped his Hawken up against a
tree trunk. The rules for parleying required that there
be no weapons in sight.

Kit and the young war chief met on the open
ground between the two camps. It immediately became
clear to Kit that the Blackfeet hoped for nothing more
than learning the trappers' number and strength. Their

ambassador refused adamantly to admit any part in the theft.

"We are Blackfeet," the warrior, Yellow Coyote, said in Indian hand sign. "Blackfeet no steal from whites. Horses stolen from the Snake Indians, our sworn enemies. No want fight with white man over Indian horses."

Kit's gaze was sharp as, in sign, he replied to the Indian's assertion of innocence. "Blackfeet no want war. Whites no want war. Come. Together we smoke pipe."

"I ain't goin' out there!" Bill Mitchell sat cross-legged in the snow, his flesh bare beneath his breechcloth. "Plumb crazy, us leavin' our weapons for them to sneak up and steal."

The other men agreed with Mitchell, yet none of them were ready to undercut the orders of their leader. "Okay, Bill. You wait and watch," Kit compromised, sensing tension. "First sign of trouble, you plant a ball in the nearest Blackfoot."

More at ease after hearing this, the other men stacked their Hawkens and strolled out into the open behind Kit. At the same time, most of the Blackfeet warriors emerged from their places on the hillside.

The pipe-smoking ceremony was long and tedious as every man squatted in the snow and had a chance to smoke the sacred pipe twice. Then Kit began again to speak about the stolen horses.

"We want back the horses you have taken," he told them. But glancing around the ring of painted faces, Kit realized instinctively that the matter would come to war. Still he persisted with his demand through every evasion the Blackfoot spokesman offered.

Finally, two warriors were sent back to their camp. They returned with six half-starved pack mules, their ankles bleeding where the icy snowbanks had cut them.

Yellow Coyote smiled broadly as the animals were presented. "These the Blackfeet offer the poor whites who have no business in our lands. They will help you cross the mountains."

The mules were accepted, reluctantly, and returned to the trappers' camp. Afterward, the discussion between Indians and trappers was resumed, the Indians becoming increasingly belligerent. Finally, after sitting for three hours in the frigid evening air, Kit was in no mood for more insults. Something snapped inside him.

"Get back and grab your guns, boys!" He jumped to his feet and, to the astonishment of Indians and trappers alike, ran back to the pines where he had left his Hawken. It was war!

The first shots rang out almost simultaneously from both camps.

"Damnit! Bridger was right!" Rube yelled as the sound of two dozen rifles cracked on the Blackfoot side of the clearing.

As Kit reloaded, he made some quick calculations. There were thirty-five warriors by his count, most of them with rifles, by the sound of things. His ten men would have to be very careful, and very lucky, if they hoped to rush the camp and steal back their horseflesh. "Damn them," he muttered. "Damn them."

For more than an hour, deadly lead fire crisscrossed the area between the two camps. Then Kit signaled his men to cease firing. "We ain't got enough lead and powder left to spend the next week plunkin' away at the side of that hill. More snow, I'm thinkin' before morning. They'll try to keep us nailed down till it's too late. Got to rush 'em."

"Now you're talkin'!" Rube nodded his big head. "Rush 'em. Scare the hell out of 'em."

"Them Blackfeet is poor shots," Wooten offered.

"Them Blackfeet got three times our rifles," Amos shot back.

Kit's attention swept to the youngest member of their party. Damn! There was no way Amos would ever have the eagle's heart of a real trapper. He just never would.

"It's our only chance," Kit responded at last. "We'll freeze out here in the open. Now get set to jump 'em!"

It was a desperate act, and Kit knew it. His men knew it, too. But there was no other choice. Without mounts, they would be on foot and easy prey for everything that prowled the mountains.

Kit and Manhead went first. The battle cry ripped out, giving them the courage necessary to move out in the open. Shots rained in. Kit was brought up short behind a small bush. He spat a ball into his barrel after pouring in powder. Then he rammed his wiping stick down to seat his ammunition. A quick look at Manhead revealed him doing the same.

The two did not speak. They knew that one man kept his rifle loaded while the other spent his ball. So did the rest of the trappers. That way everyone was covered.

Manhead raised himself from the snowdrift. Exposing his long torso to the Blackfeet's fire, he took careful aim at a warrior. At that instant, Kit saw a second warrior rise up, his rifle aimed at the Delaware's chest.

"Damn fool!" Kit grumbled, leaping up to fire against the second man.

Two shots cracked at the same moment, bringing down two Blackfeet. Almost at once, Kit realized that he had left himself open. Manhead's shot was spent. So was his.

Kit saw another Indian move in. In the same split second he heard the shot, he flung himself headfirst into the snow, but not quickly enough.

On his left side, scorching pain raked his neck and shoulder. The heat blazed against his skin. Reaching a hand up, he felt the wound from the Blackfoot's rifle ball. Warm blood flowed freely from it, sticking to his clothes. Kit took a deep breath and tore away the shirt. Gasping at the pain the action caused, he rolled onto his back in the crunching snow, his Green River pulled in defense. He would not go quietly, by damn. Not even now.

"You hurt?" Manhead had crawled from safety to reach him. He pushed Kit's hand away from the wound, his usually blank features grim. "Plenty bad hurt. Take this. I kill, count coup for you." With that he was gone, wriggling on his belly in the snow as the rifle fire continued.

Kit looked at what the Delaware had pressed into his hand. It was one of the beaver pelts Manhead had been using as a head covering. Slapping it against his shoulder, Kit hoped that the thick fur would stop the flow of blood.

The minutes dragged on, seeming to pull the last bit of daylight from the sky. Kit knew the bleeding had not stopped. He knew that there would be no one to come to his aid. His men were fighting for their lives. There would be no help for them either. The thought released in him a grim awareness. He had never asked very much of others. He had few regrets. Now, if he was going to die, he would do it alone.

"Hate like hell though," Kit said, trying in the midst of his pain to keep his spirits up, "to go under owin' that shopkeeper, Bent."

Chapter 14

The sensation of awakening was painful. Kit's eyes remained slits against the dawn light. He was not dead, although the knowledge was not much comfort at that moment. The effort to breathe was as painful as if his lungs had been jammed with ice. His face ached with cold and his fingers and feet seemed to be disconnected from the rest of his body. They would not move.

After a minute or two of struggling to maintain consciousness, Kit realized why he felt paralyzed. Turning his head ever so slightly to the right and left, he discovered that he was encased in snow. A second snowfall, the one he'd dreaded, had unleashed itself during the night and covered him. He shook himself as much as he could, and the dusting fell away from his face.

"Cap'n Carson?" Amos' anxious face was a blur

through Kit's eyes. "You're alive! Lord! Thought you was gone under for certain."

Kit tried to be reassuring. "Hell, son. Takes more than Blackfeet to stop me." The pain the speech triggered made him groan in spite of himself.

A moment later he felt hands brushing away the snow, then gently probing his injured neck. "Froze up solid!" he heard Bill Mitchell exclaim. "The blood done froze up and plugged the wound. Snow saved your life!"

Kit swallowed, stretching the injured muscles. The pain was excruciating. "How many . . . we lose? Blackfeet?"

Bill Mitchell bent over him. "Blackfeet took two of our boys—Bridger's boys, that is. Wooten took a ball. That's all. Damn Blackfeet haven't gone one foot toward them hills. Expect they're just waitin' for full daylight to commence the war again."

"No." Kit's command was a mere breath of sound. "Retreat."

"What'd he say?" Amos' voice was hollow.

"Cap'n Carson says get the hell out of here," Mitchell told the younger man. "Well, you got ears. Get me a couple of saplings, strip 'em, and bring 'em here. Got to make a travois to carry the cap'n. Looks to me them wolf-bit mules the Indians gave us for spite yesterday is gonna come in handy."

"What about our equipment? Can we reach the pass?"

Bill spat on the ground. "Ask too many questions, you make for hard feelin's. Now get them poles!"

"Goddamn, but I'm sick of lookin' on your ugly

face!" Rube drew his Green River as tempers flared. For more than a month, the Carson brigade had been holed up in a tiny cave.

"Put that weapon down!" Kit sat propped up on his saddle and bedroll. Deliberately he reached for his rifle and placed it across his legs. "Anybody gonna do any butcherin' in this outfit, it'll be me. You draw blood and it'll set the whole mountainside wild. We ain't the only things starving this winter. Wolves and coyotes would be right pleased by a whiff of human blood." An ugly grin creased his pale face. "Heard tell boiled trapper ain't bad."

Rube swore and spat on the ground. "Damnit all, Cap'n, we ain't savages."

"Ain't you?" Kit countered in a more gentle tone. "Then you ain't killin' for meat? Way I figure it, a man draws his knife in defense or for huntin'." His attention moved from Rube to Wooten, the cause of Rube's outburst. "Your prey ain't armed. You runnin' meat on Wooten?"

"Hell, no!" Rube thrust his knife back in its sheath and stomped outside.

When the men turned their backs, Kit slumped against his makeshift backrest. His wound had been slow in healing, mostly because he had not been consuming enough food. He was lucky he had not died from the injury. Only the cold, so extreme that it had congealed his blood, had saved him. And now it was keeping the wound from festering.

"Meat don't spoil in this clime," Bridger had said to him once. Now he believed it.

But he had bigger troubles. The fight with the Blackfeet and the loss of the pack mules had delayed them too long. It was too late, now, to cross the Great Divide into the warmer valley of the Snake. They were stuck in the Rockies until the spring thaw. That was obvious.

Long before Kit had regained full command of himself, Bill Mitchell had located the cave that now housed them. Kit sighed deeply. He could not do much for his men. He wasn't even fit enough to help in the daily hunting parties.

The cave was lit by a tiny scrap-wood fire. Looking around at the gaunt, sallow-skinned complexions told Kit that most of his men would not likely make it through an entire winter unless they found game. So far, it had eluded them. In fact, the day before, he had ordered the first bleeding of the mules.

The two remaining animals were kept tethered outside during the day with a pile of peeled bark for their fodder. But at night they were brought in to keep from freezing. Their rank breaths and droppings added discomfort to the men. Even the bleeding hadn't been that successful. The mules were sickly—too much blood loss and they would die.

Mule meat, stringy and gamy, was a last-ditch attempt at keeping alive. Two of the five animals had died before they had even reached shelter. One had died since then and been consumed. If forced to eat the last two, the men, once again, would have to leave their traps and saddles behind. That option Kit refused to consider.

"Cap'n Carson! Cap'n! We found meat!"

Kit eased himself into a sitting position just as Amos and Tom Hill burst into the cave. Each waved a parfleche sack.

"We found pemmican! Enough to last a couple of weeks!" Amos' thin cheeks glowed with color. "I tasted a bit. It's dried buffalo mixed with wild blackberries."

Cries of delight roared through the tiny space as the other men rushed closer.

"Whoa! Hold to!" Kit struggled to his feet as the men turned to him. Using his rifle as a cane, he forced himself upright, fighting the giddiness that washed over him. "Where'd you get pemmican? Didn't think gophers went in for that sort of thing."

"Weren't gophers," Amos returned in a merry voice. "Me and Tom was scoutin' along that ridge back of the cave when we saw somethin' dark against the slope of the next hill." Amos' eyes went to the Delaware Indian, then back to Carson. "First thing we thought it was a deer. Tom took a bead on it before we seen it was a man."

"You shot a man?" Kit's voice was cold.

"No, Cap'n. Not a thing like it," Amos vowed readily. "Tom held his shot and we took off after the fella. Well, sir, there wasn't even enough breath in him to tell us who he was. Cold must have killed him." Once more Amos held his prize aloft. "His bad luck was our good fortune!"

"Well?" It was Rube who spoke. "You gonna dole out the vittles, Cap'n?"

"Let Amos do it. He won't cheat anybody for fear you'll hang him." Kit lowered himself to his robes and waited for his portion to be passed. The effort to stand had cost him healing time.

Part of Amos' tale didn't sit well in his thoughts. A seasoned trapper with enough supplies would have taken refuge in a cave. Still, the man had gotten this far without having lost his possibles. He must have had some sense. Why, then, hadn't he taken shelter? That was the question that haunted Kit as he sat and chewed the dead man's pemmican.

Though a few days later Kit felt well enough to go out with a hunting party, he and his men returned empty-handed. "Don't look so glum, Amos. You done fine work a few days back." Kit prodded the moping boy with his elbow. "You'll get your chance to bring down fresh game."

Amos nodded weakly. Looking more closely at the boy, Kit noticed the flush that covered his cheeks. "How long you been feverish?" Kit whispered after a quick check to make certain they weren't being overheard.

Amos shrugged off Kit's touch. "Been feelin' a mite peaked since this mornin'. Nothin' that won't pass."

But Kit was not convinced. "You feel any worse, you come to me direct. Don't tell nobody else. We just settled this crowd down with the promise of vittles for a while. No need stirrin' them up again with talk of sickness."

Kit watched Amos covertly for the rest of the evening. By nightfall the boy's cheeks were flaming red and he had taken to rubbing his neck and throat. When Amos put away his food pouch after only taking a couple of swallows, it was all Kit could do not to pry the boy's mouth open and take a look. Fevers of all kinds ranged the prairie, but it was rare when a man became ill during the middle of a mountain winter. Unless . . .

Kit munched in silence. Unless a man had been

exposed to another sick man, he thought. Rapidly he reviewed what he knew about smallpox. While in Bridger's brigade, he had heard of the havoc the disease was causing with the Indian population in the territory. Surely, he told himself, Tom and Amos would have recognized the marks of the disease on the man they'd come across if the signs had been there. But this was no time to ask.

Kit made certain that his robes were spread next to Amos' that night. When everyone else was asleep, he would ask about the dead trapper.

"No marks . . . I swear it," Amos croaked out in answer to Kit's question hours later. "I'd have known it. Had smallpox as a child."

Kit put a hand under Amos' shirt and felt the quick pounding of his heart. "You're sick, son. Something must have killed that trapper. Think what it could have been." Kit heard the sudden intake of the boy's breath and realized his tactlessness. "Listen up right smart, Amos. I ain't expectin' you to die. I learned a powerful lot about cures and such growin' up on the edge of the frontier in Franklin. Wasn't nothin' we didn't hear tell of. You think real hard so we'll know what to do."

Amos was silent for a moment. "Wasn't no signs of illness, honest. Man just couldn't talk, that's all. Swallowed his tongue, sounded like. Only he didn't. I checked."

Kit did not answer. Amos had touched a sick man. Whatever the man had, Amos had caught.

"Pray goodness it ain't serious," Kit murmured to himself after young Tuttle had fallen asleep.

*   *   *

"Course he's sick!" Rube thundered the next morning. "Any blind man could see it. The boy's got to go!" For emphasis, he hammered the cave floor with the butt of his Hawken.

Kit looked up from his squatting position near Amos. "Boy's sick, ain't no denyin' it. But you'll have to take him out of here over my dead body."

The threat was softly spoken so it wouldn't wake Amos, but that did not blunt its power. Rube shifted restlessly from foot to foot. "Don't see how you can expect a body to keep company with sickness."

Kit studied the ring of worried faces staring up at him. They were still half-starved and the weeks of forced confinement had taken their toll on the men's nerves. "Ain't asking you to stay," he said gently. "I expect every man here to move out immediately."

Rube's eyes fell to Amos. The loud hiss and rumble of the boy's breathing were what had given away his illness.

"What's he got?"

"Putrid fever," Kit shot back promptly as, almost in unison, the circle of men took a step back toward the entrance. "It'll run its course in a few days. Most men don't die from it. Had it myself as a youngster. I'm still here. Any of you worried, pack up and find a new cave. I'm stayin' with the boy."

He turned his head away and did not look back until the last of the footfalls had died away. "Phew! You've cost me a lot of worryin' before this, Tuttle, but now you've outdone yourself this turn." Gently he brushed back the damp strands of hair that had glued themselves to Amos' sweaty brow. Putrid fever had to run its own course. If the fever didn't kill Amos, all he had to worry about was keeping the boy's throat open. At least he didn't have smallpox.

The day dragged on, measured in the darkness of the cave by the painful shallow gasps of Amos' breath. Once he awakened, his eyes brightening feverishly. "Can't talk," he breathed. "Hurts somethin' awful."

Kit put his hand against Amos' cheek. "Know it does, Amos. You got to fight it. Make yourself breathe easy. No talkin'. Wastes your strength."

Amos' mouth opened and closed without sound, his lips pale and trembling. "Need a drink, son?" Kit volunteered with forced cheerfulness as he reached for a pouch filled with melted snow. "I ain't gonna leave you. Now don't go cloudin' up like you was a little city gal. Mountain men got to stick together. It's in the code."

By dawn of the third day, Kit knew that each breath Amos took was costing him too much of his strength. The inflamed throat was gradually cutting off his supply of air. As a last resort, Kit bent down and dragged Amos to the cave's entrance. There, with the sunlight to see by, he pried open the clenched jaws and took a good look at Amos' throat.

He shook his head. The whole throat was lined with a tough grey membrane. After bringing Amos back into the cave, Kit staggered to the opening again, this time for fresh air.

After a couple of gulps, his brain began to work. He must remove the membrane that was covering the boy's throat. That was obviously the only thing to do. He remembered how once he had watched a Navaho medicine man break open a cyst in a trapper's throat by inserting a thorned sandbur on a string.

"How the hell am I suppose to find those savin' devices in the middle of a Rocky Mountain winter?" Kit hollered in frustration.

He stared a long time at the brilliant white day. Even the clouds looked like snowdrifts. A sick feeling of helplessness made him churn inside. Kit thought of all the things that Amos would never see or know if he died. All because there were no worthless sandburs to stick down his throat . . . that most squaws wouldn't even favor as ornaments on their . . .

Kit wheeled around and ran to the spot in the cave where Wooten's gear was stashed. Wooten was a miser by nature. It was certain he would buy cheap Indian trinkets. When none turned up, Kit methodically emptied all of the remaining gear in the cave. He came to Amos' last, realizing that by this time his desperation had made him half-crazy.

When he dumped out Amos' possibles, the little object fell out. Whooping with joy, Kit picked it up. The object was what the Indians called a love charm, a little beaded leather bag that trappers tied around their necks to hold their lead balls. The bags were always decorated, sometimes with expensive beads and quills, and sometimes, as in the case of Amos', with fancy seeds, nuts and other dried brush that the squaw who'd made them had dyed. There, hanging on a sinew thread from Amos' pouch were five sandburs.

Taking a small portion of the pemmican he had left, Kit coated the sharp spines so that they would go down easily. Next he found a notched stick. Then, ready for the operation he pulled Amos back near the entrance to the cave to make use of the sunlight.

"If this don't work," he told the semiconscious young man, "you got to know I tried."

Forcing Amos' mouth open, Kit began ramming the burs down his throat. He worked quickly, holding the struggling Amos down by sitting on his chest with a knee pinning each arm. When all the burs had been inserted, Kit pulled the string, popping out one ball at a time. To his great relief, bits of the grey membrane had begun to tear away from the throat lining and were coming up attached to the sandburs. After the last bur was out, Kit turned Amos over so that he could begin coughing up the remaining matter.

"Here. Drink, son," Kit urged as he helped Amos lie back. "Know I hurt you but I didn't have much choice. Drink so I'll know what I did worked." Amos took the first swallow of water fearfully. But when the liquid slid down his throat without choking him, he attempted several more gulps.

"I'll be damned," Kit murmured with a weary grin. "I could be a sawbones, I had a mind. The worst is over, boy. You get yourself some peaceful sleep now." Then, before Amos could see the tears of relief that were flooding his eyes, Kit turned away.

The spring of 1834 was more beautiful than any spring Kit could remember. South of the Platte River, the air had a softness peculiar to the season. The new green of the willows trailed in the breezes. Overhead, majestic white clouds rode like galleons in the vast blue sea of the sky. The western mountains were touched red-gold where the sun had rolled back the snow. Wild plums, grapes and berries threw the first of their new runners as poppies, sunflowers and yellow tickseed carpeted the valleys.

Kit rode alone as he looked upon the emerging spring growth. He was healed and whole again. Amos, too, was alive to see the change of season. The past year had been the most difficult of Kit's life. Yet, at this particular time, he knew he would not have traded a moment of it for the safety and comfort of a life as a saddler in Franklin, Missouri.

The trapping was better than ever. The secret stream had not been stumbled upon in the intervening season. Everything was perfect. Yet each night, though he went to bed physically exhausted, he lay there for hours—wide awake.

"The sap's risin', that's all," Bill Mitchell had said with a wink when he noticed that Kit's moodiness often kept him sitting near the campfire till dawn.

Kit had shrugged off the notion. The familiar urge for a woman was somehow more pressing this year. The spring season was nearing its end. The year long celibacy was nearing its end. That was all it was, he told himself, nothing more.

There were decisions to be made. Perhaps he would sell his full year's cache of pelts to William Bent after all. Kit knew he had proved he was as good a trapper as any man in the Rockies. Hadn't he met the Blackfeet head-on in their own territory and lived to tell about it? Now, the money to be earned from the sale of his catch would be enough to buy a fair-sized ranch near Taos.

Why was he thinking such things now? He had always believed he wasn't cut out for a tame existence, and he had never given serious thought to settling down before. Royce came by his farming inclinations naturally. But Kit could not imagine a worse fate. It would be like throwing away all that had ever spurred him into the territory. Why, first thing he knew, he would be thinking of getting himself a wife and raising a parcel of kids.

Suddenly he remembered Blackfoot Smith's advice. "Get yourself an Indian gal, Kit," he recited, smiling. Maybe the old-timer was right. Maybe he was ready to start packing a squaw. It would take the starch out of him regularly. That was for certain. It would keep his mind on real business.

The memory of Grass Singing increased his desire. Pack a squaw. He liked the sound of that, and might just try it out for size.

Summer would be time enough to decide, Kit thought. At the moment he was preoccupied with digging up his party's fall cache down on Sandy Creek. It wouldn't be long before his men would be catching up to him and wanting their share.

Even before he reached the plain's floor leading to Sandy Creek, a vague uneasiness settled in. Kit knew it was not fear of riding alone. He had done that on too many occasions to feel threatened. And the feeling was more than a trapper's knowledge that late spring was the favored time of year for Indian war parties. It was more like the unsettling feeling his mother used to describe in the expression, "someone's just stepped on my grave."

Kit had been in the wilderness long enough to trust his instincts and premonitions. So, when the first flat squiggle of Sandy Creek came into view, Kit pulled in rein for several minutes and sat perfectly still. On the plain in front of him, nothing moved. Nothing much could hide in the narrow belt of cottonwoods that had sprung up along the banks of the creek. But Kit knew, even before he headed down into the valley, that something was wrong.

"The cache," he whispered to himself, sensing suddenly that his cache was the source of his discomfort. The cache, twenty miles ahead, had been found, perhaps already plundered. The thought inflamed him. Once before he had lost his pelts. Not this time. Kicking his horse into a gallop, he streaked down the grassy slope onto the flatland that lay ahead.

"Don't like this. Digging up another man's cache ain't right."

Kit heard the voice and drew closer. Three men sat hunched over a campfire, their bodies silhouetted against the night.

Kit had left his horse tethered a half mile downriver. He had crawled toward the fire through the tall, grassy underbrush of the creek bank. The time was an hour past sunset. Kit's eyes stung. His skin itched from the dozens of insect bites he had collected in the brush, but his compensation was knowing that the men he stalked had not seen him.

Lifting himself silently to his knees, Kit lay one of the two rifles he had brought with him on the ground. The other—his own Hawken—he hung over his left arm. His course was clear. He had heard the men admit that they were thieves. This situation had to be changed. It was as simple as that. Kit eased his Hawken to his shoulder. He'd squeeze off one shot, and in the second or two it would take the two remaining men to spot his location, he would get off a second round. He would have to meet the third man in hand-to-hand combat. Kit steadied his rifle and took aim.

"*Sacré!*" The deep bass voice boomed through the clearing. "Miserable coward. I do this myself. Jules St. Nair fears nothing!"

Kit checked his shot. Could it really be St. Nair?

The huge man rose to his feet, shadowing the grass with his bulk to within a foot of Kit's hiding place. "All *poltrons, les Américains.*" The Frenchman's laughter spurred one of the men to his feet.

"Watch what you call Americans, St. Nair. You figurin' to forget I'm American myself?"

The Frenchman made an insulting gesture. "We wait one hour more," he continued. "Then we dig. In the morning nothing will be left of the cache but an empty pit."

"What if the trappers come back?"

St. Nair smiled, looking down at his gun. "*Eh bien!* They would fill the pit nicely, *n'est-ce pas?*"

Kit's shot cracked through the calm night, propelling the seated man forward into the campfire. He quickly reached for his second weapon. In an instant, the second shot had plowed squarely through the second American's chest, and he too had been decommissioned without having fired his weapon.

Kit dropped flat on his belly as the Frenchman's shot sped harmlessly past, then scrambled away as fast as he could from the place where he'd been stationed. Three men meant three loaded rifles. St. Nair had two shots left.

A second ball sped past, tearing at the brush just a foot above his left shoulder. Kit sank to the ground, hissing a curse. The Frenchman must have eyes like a mountain cougar to have found him that quickly, Kit thought. He jerked his Green River free. There was little hope that the sting of the blade would have much effect on the Goliath unless it was slipped into a strategic spot. Kit knew that meant getting close to the Frenchman, and getting close meant trouble!

St. Nair's voice broke the stillness with a bellow of anger. "You come and face St. Nair, *lâcheur*. I will make a fine target. But you will pay!"

Silently, Kit tracked the Frenchman as he made his way back to the dying fire. "You see?" St. Nair taunted. "This man is not afraid. Come to talk with St. Nair, *poltron*. We make peace."

"Ain't lackin' for courage, St. Nair!" Kit roared from his hiding place. "But you're lackin'—in common sense!"

Even before the last word was out, Kit began moving, cutting a quick diagonal path that kept the trunks of several slim cottonwoods between him and the Frenchman. Much to his irritation, his taunt did not draw St. Nair's last shot.

Kit had grabbed up his own rifle while the Frenchman spoke. Now, running in the underbrush, he poured powder and dropped a lead ball into the barrel. If St. Nair came after him, he would be ready.

Sweat ran freely along Kit's face and neck, drawing the added nuisance of stinging gnats. Crickets chirped loudly in the damp river grasses as he squatted in the cottonwood grove and waited. Above him, nighthawks cried.

What was St. Nair doing? Kit wondered suspiciously. Then he heard it, the soft rhythmic tattoo of a horse's hooves on the grass. St. Nair was escaping, riding away from a fight.

Kit bolted toward the clearing, caution making him pause at the edge. St. Nair was a wilderness man, capable of the most cunning sort of underhanded trick. Perhaps the horse was riderless, a decoy to draw him into the open. But when the animal reached the ridge, a huge silhouette was visible on its back. St. Nair had truly turned tail and run.

"If that don't beat all," Kit muttered, halfway between amusement and exasperation. The big bully was a coward. When the odds were not to his liking he simply ran. Kit walked over to the two men he had killed. He didn't know them. Even if he had, it would have made no difference. They were thieves. A man turned thief took his chances of ending up dead.

After he'd piled new logs on the campfire and was sitting with a steaming cup of coffee in his hands, Kit thought some more about the incident with St. Nair. The trouble with that man, Kit sensed, was not over. He was gut-sure that St. Nair had led that bogus Indian attack on Fitzpatrick's brigade over three years ago. Now the Frenchman had tried to rob him of his pelts. True, he couldn't have known whose cache he had stumbled upon. But Kit knew, and that was enough. He would be riding into Bent's Fort within the month and would settle with St. Nair then.

Almost as an afterthought, Kit wondered if Grass Singing had been able to keep clear of the Frenchman. After all, St. Nair worked for Bent, and Grass Singing was at the fort a lot of the time. Then he remembered Bent's warning about the whipping post. The tight feeling of concern he felt for the girl eased. William might be a storekeeper, but he ran his business like a seasoned bourgeois. Grass Singing was safe. He would lay his cache on it.

Chapter 15

"Gentlemen, I give you the finest bunch of trappers this side of the Sweet Water." William Bent, his broad smile wreathed in silky black whiskers, raised his glass in salute to Kit Carson and his men. "A fine year's cache, boys. And I should know!"

Kit hoisted the silver tumbler he had been offered by one of the fort's two black servants and took a sip of the concoction Bent called "hailstorm." The fiery liquid left a pleasant icy slick in his throat. He eyed the crushed ice in his glass suspiciously. "What's in this here stuff?"

Bent looked amused. "It's my own mix, Kit. A secret, of course." He winked. "But I will say it contains some of the wild mint that grows up along the Purgatory."

"Ain't it kind of wearisome for your men, ridin'

all the way to the Rockies to fetch snow for sippin'?" Kit asked in a deadpan voice.

"We built an icehouse last year," Bent replied. "Cut blocks out of the river when it froze up last winter and stored them. A man deserves some pleasures in this sandy desert. Hear that wind howling? Never changes. Sometimes it bring a squall line hurling rain down so fast the ground runs with mud before you can make shelter. Sometimes it turns blizzard cold, chasing sleet with razor edges ahead of it. Temperature can drop fifty degrees in the time it takes a man to pull on his capote. Fiery breath of hell, or icy blasts from hell—one or the other's our lot most times. So when that sandy blast parches a man's throat, he needs a drink that'll clear the scum from his windpipe."

"Cap'n Carson's got a cure for what ails a sore throat," came a voice from the back of the room. "And don't I know it!"

Amos' comment drew guffaws of laughter from the Carson party.

"So, you see, Cap'n Carson saved all our lives," Amos said, finishing his explanation. "If it weren't for him, we'd have all caught the Putrid Fever and died."

"Of course, Amos, you know you're finished with my outfit," Kit broke in suddenly.

There was instant quiet. Kit was staring at the glass in his hand, but he knew every man's eyes were on him. "Told you before you ain't cut out for the wilderness, Tuttle. Time you went back home. Of course," he added after a deep breath, "was William Bent in need of a good man to oversee his supplyin', you might find a place right here."

Bent knew a request when he heard one, but he

also saw the stark misery in the face of the young man called Tuttle. The lad obviously worshipped his leader. To be found lacking in Carson's eyes had crushed the boy. What a mean son of a bitch that sandy-haired trapper could be, Bent thought in sympathy for Tuttle. But then, abruptly, he reconsidered that opinion.

Maybe Carson had good reason for what he'd said. This was a land where a man often was unfit for the rigors of the wilderness. Carson had saved the boy's life. Perhaps he wanted that saved life to count for something, Bent concluded.

His gaze rested on an anguished Tuttle. "Son? You come see me first thing tomorrow. I need a man who can use his eyes while his jaws are working. If you can do that, you've got a job." Without waiting for what might possibly have been a refusal, Bent turned to Carson ."You staying long?"

Kit shrugged. Bent sure looks at home here, he thought. Buckskins and a fancy dining room. What a mix! Heaps of cooked turnips and squash, fresh onions and melons, warm pumpkin pies and wild cherry tarts surrounded platters of buffalo rump roast, wild turkey and elk ribs on the linen-covered table. "You put on a repast the likes of this every night, I'll sit a spell at your table. Ain't seen so many vegetables since I was in short britches."

"You partial to vegetables?"

"Hate the gut-rotting stuff," Kit tossed back promptly, reaching for a slice of chilled melon.

Later, when the others had gone to bed, William offered to take Kit on a tour of the fort. When they reached the southeast tower, he offered a cigar and both men lit up.

From their post high above the walls of the fort, the two could view the entire surrounding area. Directly below them hundreds of faded buffalo-sided tepees glowed like huge lanterns. "It's the Cheyenne village of Yellow Wolf," William told him. "They live here just about permanent now. Owl Woman likes it that way. Can visit her relatives anytime. Purely loves to show off little Mary."

Kit smiled. He had seen the lovely little black-eyed baby girl—Bent's first child—earlier in the day. "Mighty pretty little gal, that daughter of yours. Gonna make hard times for her papa in a few years."

William nodded gravely. His daughter was half-Indian, half-white. There would be problems. "How do you feel about that, me being married to an Indian?" The question was an honest one, not a disguised apology.

Kit stared out over the cluster of yellow tepees. One dog's bark was quickly echoed by the packs that ran free in the camp. "Reckon a man's got a right to live his own life. Folks back East can't imagine what it's like, living year to year with only another man's ugly face to keep him from howlin' out his loneliness like a coyote. Makes sense a man needs a woman sometimes. Don't take much figurin' to see this ain't a white woman's world. Not yet, leastways. And when them women do come West, there'll be a mite of changes. Lace curtains on a tepee? Whew!"

William laughed. "Change is in the wind, you got to know it," he said after a moment. "Look down past the riverbank. You see those tepees on the Mexican side of the Arkansas? Cheyennes are camped there, too. Only it's the Mexican traders who get their robes.

Know why? They trade with whiskey." William's sigh was laden with worry. "Haven't seen an Indian yet who can hold his liquor. They take to it like it was sugared coffee—drink too fast, too much. Before they know it, the damned stuff has addled them permanently. A few of the camps will trade their tepee cloths, their women, even their children for another 'hollow-wood'—that's what they call a whiskey keg. They're not hunting. They're not tanning leather. They're going to starve the next few years."

Kit's temper flared. He didn't trust most Indians, especially when he was a stranger in their land, but he knew them to be honest. Honest meant they said and acted exactly as their customs dictated. Once a man had a handle on that, he knew what to expect. It did not mean he would not get his hair lifted for his effort, but at least he'd know what he was in for. Selling whiskey was the trick of a coward, a cheat. "What you aim to do about the drinkin'?"

Bent shrugged. "I keep my men trading for blankets, coffee, cloth and beads. The traditional stuff. When I know a tribe to be friendly, I sell a little gunpowder. Yellow Wolf, he turns his lead on the Pawnees and Kiowas. They're the Cheyennes' enemies. But that's not my business. All I know is that he keeps those tribes off my tail most times and I'm grateful.

"Another thing I've learned is that a man has to keep up with changes and not fight them. That's why I'm giving up trading for beaver. That's right," he nodded, noting Kit's surprise. "Know what the talk is in St. Louis? They say beaver hats are giving way to silk ones. It doesn't take much figuring to know what that shift is going to do to the beaver market. So I've been trading more and more with the Indians for buffalo robes. The Army wants them. Now there's a market that won't give out soon."

William looked away from Kit before continuing. "I'm looking for honest men, Indian-style honest—men whom the Cheyennes and Arapahos know they can trust. Got a few: Mexican Sol Silver, Blackfoot Smith and Lucien Maxwell. What I'm talking about isn't a job for just any sort of man. It gets lonely spending most of the winter in the Rockies with the wintering tribes. The business takes and uses the best a man's got to give.

"Whiskey's a weak man's tool. Won't abide it, except when the trading's done. Then I let my men leave a keg or two on the prairie so the Indians can drink to their health and safe return."

Kit listened without interrupting. He was being offered a job, a tough one. But it was no secret that the prices his furs would bring were dropping. A year earlier they would have brought six dollars apiece on the St. Louis market. Talk was that now they were worth less than four dollars apiece.

Somehow Kit did not mind that so much as he did the realization that the trade he had fought so hard to perfect was dying. But it would be foolish to hang on to the bitter end.

Kit thought of Fitzpatrick and Bridger. They would hang on. For himself, he would change trades when the time came. It hadn't come yet.

"That's a real entertaining yarn, Mr. Bent. But do you reckon, now, you can point out which is the Arapaho camp?"

William's shoulders sagged. So Carson was not

ready to turn trader. Well, at least he had planted the seed of an idea. "The Arapahos are east of here about five miles. Of course, if you can wait till morning, they'll be up here at the camp. It's Trading Fair day. You boys coming in is cause for a celebration that might rival a Taos fandango."

Grass Singing entered through the huge iron-studded gates of the adobe fort with twenty other women of her tribe. On her back, strapped to his cradle board, was her youngest brother, Nighthawk. Upon entering the gates, the pleasure Grass Singing felt could not be completely contained, and she smiled at the gatekeeper who winked at her. She had dressed very carefully, choosing a sleeveless deerskin shirt that reached to her knees. It was closed by leather whangs from armpit to midthigh, permitting a flash of her slim brown legs as she moved. Around her neck she wore the turquoise necklace for which she had traded her whole year's worth of buffalo robes. It matched the bracelet that flashed becomingly against the tan skin of her upper arm. Two sections of her hair were plaited on either side of her face, and bound with rawhide. The rest cascaded down her back to her waist.

As she walked, many men regarded her with admiration. The looks increased her confidence, but she did not join in the giggling of the other women. There was only one man's eyes she wished to see widening with desire at the sight of her: Turquoise Eyes. He had come to the white man's fort again. She had heard her father mention his Cheyenne name, Little Chief.

Little Chief was a name well-known among those of her own tribe. His exploits against their enemies, the

Comanches, had made him famous. While she could not yet publicly proclaim her pride in the brave coups of her beloved, she held the prasie in her heart and was comforted by it. For four summers she had waited. This summer Turquoise Eyes would be hers. The little deer's tail in her hair swung in rhythm to her step as she raised her eyes away from the lustful smile of still another trapper.

As sunset's light flooded the walls of the fort, the white traders and trappers climbed onto the roofs of the fort's buildings to watch the assembly below. It was not customary for Indians—at least this many—to be allowed inside the fort after dusk, but this time the unusual occasion demanded their presence. William Bent had doubled the number of guards and taken his chances.

The spectacle had been arranged in honor of the trappers and traders who had gathered within the fort's walls to do their seasonal buying and selling. There was to be a stiff watch over the whiskey sold in the cantina. Only trappers would be served, and only by the cup. It would not do to have an overly friendly trapper offering generous swigs of Taos Lightning to his fellow redskin revelers.

"This better work," William muttered to himself as he studied the colorful array below him. He had opened the fort almost against his better judgment. But he needed Kit Carson, needed him badly if he hoped to maintain his trade with the Plains tribes. That trading was being siphoned from him too quickly by the lure of Spanish brandy. And he was willing to bet, after his cozy chat with Soaring Vulture, that he would win Kit into service with the promise of marriage to Soaring Vulture's daughter, Grass Singing.

Kit, too, surveyed the Arapahos parading into the courtyard. There were warriors in full regalia. Feathers and silver ornamented their hair. Their hand-painted war shirts had been embroidered with beads and seams braided in with the scalp hair of their defeated enemies. Howling and crying to the accompaniment of their tom-toms, they moved past. Behind them came the women, singing in higher, softer voices, their faces painted with vermilion and delicate symbols recalling the exploits of their fathers, brothers, or husbands.

Kit turned away quickly when a young girl walked provocatively by. She reminded him of Renata, and he thought of setting out for Taos. He had not seen Royce in a year.

"Gonna do it!" Kit promised himself and set out to find William Bent.

"You what?" Bent's mustache quivered in agitation. "You can't be serious? Just look around you, Carson. There's whiskey and song, plus good rowdy company. What more could you want?"

Kit did not look at Bent directly. He could have left without saying anything to the man, but he felt he owed an explanation. After all, Bent had offered him a job. "Don't see as how my time is your business. Just wanted you to know I'm hieing out."

"But . . . Jehoshaphat!" William exclaimed as he stood staring at Kit's retreating figure. He swung around. Where had that little gal gotten to? She was supposed to wait for him to call her. "Oh, there you are, child." William spied Grass Singing at the edge of the women's line. She smiled up at him as he approached her and his spirits rose a trifle. Now how was he going to get those two together before that hot-headed fool galloped over the next ridge?

Inspiration struck him. He reached into his pocket for his coin purse. "Grass Singing, will you do me a great favor? A friend of mine, the one the Cheyennes and Arapahos call Little Chief, leaves us tonight." Bent found it difficult not to smile at the girl's surprised expression. "You must take this pouch to him in the traders' lodge before he goes."

Grass Singing took the pouch, then ran from Black Beard, her heart racing. Turquoise Eyes must not get away, not before she had a chance to work her magic on him.

As she ran, her moccasins whispered along in the dust. She pushed her way past the women with whom she had stood to watch her people dance, past the line of guards whom William waved out of her path. When she found herself at the entrance to the traders' lodge, she paused on the doorstep, eager to see Turquoise Eyes, yet afraid that he might already have gone.

Then she saw him. He had hoisted his Spanish saddle on one shoulder, his possibles and rifle on the other. His back was to her. Grass Singing stared admiringly at the wide shoulders and narrow waist of the man for whom she had waited so long. When he turned, she was certain it was because she had willed it.

Seeing Grass Singing, Kit seemed unsure of what to do or say. "What do you want?" he asked in a voice that reflected his confused feelings.

Grass Singing gracefully crossed the space between them, the pouch given to her by William Bent resting in her outstretched palm. "The one called Bent sends you this."

To Kit, Grass Singing's husky voice was like the whisper of a summer breeze. But a frown that had already begun deepened.

"Thanks." He took the pouch from her and their fingers met for an instant, stirring both of them. The girl backed away.

Against his better judgment, Kit's eyes remained steadily focused on her. She's a tiny thing, he thought. Not quite five feet. Why, he would be like a giant next to her. The thought made him smile first and then scowl even more seriously.

"Turquoise Eyes is ill?"

"What?" Kit's eyes widened at the sound of her voice.

Grass Singing cocked her head to one side a moment, then put a hand to her middle and rubbed. "Turquoise Eyes, he is gut-sore? Bad meat? Make him plenty goddamn gut-sore!"

The incongruence the words made coming from Grass Singing's soft lips made Kit crow with laughter. He had forgotten that she had learned her English in Bent's company. No doubt she knew enough cuss words to curl his hair. "Turquoise Eyes? Why do you call me that?"

Grass Singing looked disappointed. The man could not be as wise as her tribal council believed if he did not understand so simple a thing. She slid off the silver bracelet she wore and stepped closer to hold it up against the side of his face. With her other hand she held her fingers to his eyes. "Turquoise," she said slowly, as if to a child. Then she pointed to the blue stones in her bracelet. "Turquoise," she solemnly repeated. "Pretty, yes?"

Kit reached out to take her bracelet, capturing her hand in his at the same time. Then he put his other hand to her eyes, barely touching the fine long lashes that fluttered like butterflies against his fingertips. Touching the deer's tail in her hair, he said tenderly, "Doe Eyes." He smiled. "Doe Eyes," he repeated and ran a finger lightly from her temple to her cheek. "Pretty. Yes!"

"My name Waa-nibe. White man call me Grass Singing," the girl said as the blush rose in her cheeks. She touched her breast with two fingers. "Grass Singing."

Kit felt a rush as the lovely Indian girl brought her hand down from her full breasts. "Grass Singing," he offered, "is when the wind rides low on the prairie and the sound is like the cooing of a dove."

Quite pleased with the words, Grass Singing smiled for the first time. Kit wondered how he could have thought of running off without her. It would cause trouble, taking her from her husband and from the babe he had seen her carrying, but when she smiled at him like that he did not care if the whole Arapaho nation came after him. "You want to come with me?"

Kit saw her happy expression fade. He had said the wrong thing. Well, she had come in here alone. What was he to think? Turning away, he again began collecting his things. "Get on back to your folks before you come to harm."

Grass Singing stood motionless. "Turquoise Eyes not like?"

Kit shrugged, not looking back at her. If he told

her the truth, there would be nothing to say except that he was aching to hold her and make her his. Instead he said, "Go away before your husband comes lookin' for you. He finds you alone with me, he'll take a lodgepole to you. On second thought," he added, looking her over another time, "you're a mite too pretty for beatin'."

"Then you do like Grass Singing. Good." Grass Singing bravely stepped forward. "Grass Singing no marry. Wait for Turquoise Eyes." Her smile trembled a little. "You make her wait too long. Grass Singing grows angry. Wants to take lodgepole to *you*."

Without waiting for Kit's reaction, she threw her arms around his neck and, with great daring, she pressed her lips to his.

Kit and the girl had not been joined two seconds before he realized she knew nothing about kissing. But her nearness filled him with passion all the way down to his toes. Dropping everything to embrace her, he pulled her body hard against his. She smelled like a valley in springtime. The second kiss, which *he* initiated, lasted longer. He was quite pleased when, shuddering with pleasure, Grass Singing backed away.

"Turquoise Eyes different. Grass Singing likes pressing lips with him. No liked it with Great Bear Face!"

Kit, too, remembered the night of the Soup Dance four years ago when St. Nair had grabbed Grass Singing and stolen her kisses. "That Great Bear Face fella been botherin' you?"

"Give him plenty to worry about, he hug Grass Singing," she answered, giggling and lifting her shirt to pull a long skinning knife from the top of her leggings.

Kit was not so much interested in the weapon she wanted to show him as in what she had exposed, a firm, rounded thigh around which was bound the Arapaho chastity belt. "So, you really ain't married?"

Grass Singing casually dropped her shirttail. "Grass Singing no marry any man but Turquoise Eyes."

"But the papoose—I saw you today," Kit insisted.

"Little brother, Nighthawk, plenty good child. I carry. You marry me, we have plenty good babies. Strong like father. Muscles taut like bowstring. Swift like elk. Small and dangerous as the wolverine."

Kit folded his arms across his chest. No woman had ever proposed marriage to him before. He kind of liked the idea. "You expect me to marry you? Why you so sure I will?"

For the first time Grass Singing was afraid. If she told Turquoise Eyes of the charm she had purchased to capture him, he might become angry with her. "You do not wish to marry Grass Singing?" she asked, trying to avoid his question.

Now it was Kit's turn to wrestle with indecision. He had just about convinced himself that packing a squaw the next season was a good idea. But marriage, that meant standing up in front of the whole Arapaho village and declaring that he wanted this girl for all time. Trapped, that's what he felt, like a beaver in one of his traps. Still, looking at the curves of this lovely girl, thinking of her laughter, it was impossible to say no.

Kit didn't know what would happen. He was just as determined as ever to keep his freedom. But he would give it a try, this marrying business.

"Your father, Soaring Vulture, you reckon he'll agree?"

Grass Singing's answer was the warm embrace she gave before running joyously from the room.

"Of course the idea sounds good to you. It's me that's got to do the marryin'." Kit winced, hearing William Bent's chuckle. "You don't quit that coyote barkin', you can just go back to your mud hut."

William looked at the man riding beside him. They were leading the three horses Kit had purchased as a wedding present. The trapper had also bought and worn a red calico shirt with his buckskin trousers— even trimmed his hair and beard.

Things were looking better all the time, Bent concluded. If just the thought of marriage had Kit sprucing up in a more civilized manner, he was certain marriage would complete the transformation. At least, enough so that Kit would take the job he'd been offered.

With Grass Singing's village camped near the fort, Bent realized how convenient it would be if Kit worked for him. Besides, a much healthier tie to the Indians than selling them alcohol was marriage with one of their women. Kit would have an edge with the Arapahos now, just as he had with the Cheyennes. A sound business relationship, Bent congratulated himself silently. He made as good a marriage broker as any Spanish *dueña*. Fortunately, he knew better than to press the advantage. There was plenty of time once the young people were married.

Kit had not been idle since his meeting with Grass Singing the night before. He was in a hurry. If he was going to get married, he wanted it over and done with. From Bent he learned that Soaring Vulture was the leader of the Crazy Lime Society, the fifth order of the Arapaho lodge divisions. That meant he was a power to be reckoned with, a man who had lived through the most dangerous years of his life as a member of the fourth lodge, the *Betahanan* or Staff Society.

Soaring Vulture's lodge was easy to find among the many that ringed the crescent bend in the northern bank of the Arkansas border. It was one of the larger tepees, and near the center of the village—a place of respect. The weathered buffalo-hide outer covering displayed a large Thunderbird. The symbol was a powerful one among the Plains nations, for it represented the most precious commodity on the prairie: rain.

The two men dismounted to the jabber of the dozens of children who had followed them into the village. Dogs yapped and snapped at the heels of the two visitors but both men ignored them.

"It appears that the whole damn village knows why we're here," Kit muttered as they approached Soaring Vulture's lodge.

The tepee flap was raised and the guests were summoned by one of the sentries standing guard inside.

"Here goes nothin'," Kit murmured. Yanking his hat down firmly, he entered.

There was a full assembly of twelve warriors inside the tent, and as Kit directed his attention from one member of the Arapaho nation to the next, what he experienced was sheer terror. He had faced down a grizzly with nothing more than a twig. He had fought hand-to-hand with the Blackfeet. He had challenged three men who dared to steal his cache. But he had never before faced a father and asked him for his daughter's hand in marriage. All in all, Kit thought as sweat gathered in the folds of his neck and brow, he would rather take on the grizzly again.

William began the introductions and the Indians shook hands solemnly as they had learned the Americans liked to do. Sweat was dripping freely from Kit's chin by the time he was seated, but no one seemed to notice. He eyed his future father-in-law curiously.

The middle-aged warrior was wearing his war bonnet, a full headdress of eagle feathers decorated with silver spangles and beaded headband. It spoke well of Kit's hopes that he was being received as an honored guest.

The older man's hawk nose sat imperiously between two dark piercing eyes. Strength, Kit read in them, as well as courage and generosity. Soaring Vulture would make a good ally, and likely be an equally dangerous enemy.

After the customary offering of food, which was readily accepted, the peace pipe was brought forth— the ceremonial one upon which hung a "medicine" bag and two scalps. Kit took the smoke into his mouth when it was his turn to do so. Then he released it in the form of tiny puffs which he hoped would please the Great Spirit.

Watching Carson, Bent was impressed by the young man's obvious respect for Indian customs. He had misjudged Carson the boy; he would not misjudge Carson the man.

Kit glanced briefly at Bent when the pipe was put aside. Receiving an encouraging nod, he reached into the possible sack he had with him and pulled out one pouch containing powder and one containing lead balls. "For the great warrior Soaring Vulture. May his shots fly straight and deadly swift to strike the breast of his enemy."

Soaring Vulture nodded, the murmur of approval around him confirming the pleasure he felt in receiving Kit's gift.

"You are welcome in the village of our people," Soaring Vulture stated when the gifts were laid aside. "Little Chief's coups are many and our people speak of them with pleasure. How may we show our hospitality?"

Now it was time. As Kit looked at Grass Singing's father, he decided that his knowledge of the Arapaho tongue was not ingrained enough in him to use it for what he wished to say. Instead he chose sign language. Soaring Vulture stared attentively as Kit's hand motioned swiftly. Once Kit even saw a smile break through when he complimented the old warrior's expertise as hunter and soldier.

When Kit came to the reason for his visit he decided to say it plainly, without the fancy phrases. "I come to ask for your daughter, Grass Singing, in marriage. In her honor I offer three horses as a gift to you, her father."

Soaring Vulture's eyes widened. He grunted, and Kit thought he must have insulted the man. But then he noticed that the warrior's attention was focused not on him, but on Bent.

"What's the matter?" Kit whispered under his breath. "Offer not big enough?"

Bent shrugged before nodding and smiling at the leader of the Crazy Lime Society.

Kit made another sign, one that indicated that he would be willing to pay five horses for the girl. This met with a collective intake of breath around the Indian circle.

"Bent?" Kit began, his expression darkening. "You done something behind my back? I can smell an ambush a mile off."

Bent had no chance to reply. Soaring Vulture spoke. "Our people are gratified that you wish to take as your wife one of our daughters. We ask you, Little Chief, if it is only one wife you desire? So many horses, you may wish to take Grass Singing's two sisters as well."

Kit heard the faint intake of breath and glanced behind him. He did not know how long Grass Singing had been standing just inside the doorway, but however long it had been, she had heard enough to be very displeased.

"I will not be bought!" she exclaimed, her lips pursed in disapproval. Then she turned and ducked out of the tent.

"What did I do?" Kit demanded, swinging back to Bent.

"Don't know," William admitted as he stroked his beard thoughtfully. "Soaring Vulture, how is it that the offer of Little Chief is refused?"

"Not refused," Soaring Vulture countered with a shake of his feathered head. "It is the will of Grass Singing's father that she marry Little Chief. Grass Singing may say what is in her heart but it is our custom that Detenin will have the final word."

"Detenin?" Kit looked at Bent. "Who's that?"

"Detenin—Short Man—is Grass Singing's brother," Bent said.

"Short Man? If this is some kind of joke, Bent . . ."

"Don't worry, son," Bent interjected. "Detenin is real enough. A mite short in stature maybe, but a fighter, boy, a regular scrapper."

Slightly mollified, Kit turned to Soaring Vulture. "You will accept my horses?"

"That is for Detenin to decide. He is in the south with a war party who seek revenge on the Kiowas. Maybe he returns before the new moon."

The new moon was about two weeks off, Bent mused. Too damned long, as far as he was concerned. Kit might change his mind or give up in disgust. "You will hold the horses until Detenin returns if it is the wish of your daughter?" he asked encouragingly.

Soaring Vulture shook his head. "Grass Singing does not want Little Chief's horses. She says so just now for all the tribe to hear."

"What if I can make her change her mind?" Kit gave the father his most determined look. Suddenly, there was no doubt he wanted very much for her to do that.

"You talk to stupid girl," Soaring Vulture replied after giving Kit's request due consideration. "She listens to no voice. Gives her father great pain and costs him eleven fine horses."

"Eleven?" Kit's gaze swung to Bent, who was staring at the ceiling of the tepee. "Who said anything about eleven horses?"

"One summer ago," Soaring Vulture explained, "our friend Bent came to my lodge and offered me six horses for Grass Singing to marry Little Chief. We wait. You come, offer five horses more. Eleven horses." He nodded. It made perfect sense to him.

"You tried to buy me a wife?" Kit hissed at Bent, so furious he did not care that his temper was a breach of etiquette.

"Simmer down, Kit, before you get us in bad trouble," Bent cautioned, as at the same moment he smiled, placatingly, at the chief. "You picked her out yourself, didn't you? Did I suggest you come out here? Did I make you propose?"

"No, but damnit all, Bent! 1 knowed you was in on this some way. I ever get it straight in my mind, you're in for a sorry time." .

"That's fine by me, son. First you better set matters right with your little gal. She took a hard dislike to something you said a minute ago."

"We give sundown dance tomorrow night," Soaring Vulture said. "Little Chief is welcome to come and join us. Grass Singing may speak to you if it is her desire. Maybe yes, maybe no."

"Agreed."

Chapter 16

Grass Singing moved away from the rhythmic lure of the drums, winding a path, instead, behind her village toward the river. She did not want the pleasure the music of her people always gave her. Her heart was filled with unhappy thoughts.

"Turquoise Eyes is a liar," she whispered to the prairie plover who dipped low in the cottonwoods on his homeward flight.

She hacked dispiritedly at the tall grasses with a stick she had picked up. It was not often she was brave enough to walk alone at night. Usually, she heeded her mother's warning against the white trappers who would not care that she was a maiden. But tonight it did not matter, she told herself. The waiting for Little Chief had been in vain. He was like all the other white men, eager and impatient, not seeing her as a woman, but as a thing to be bought and sold. "Why, Turquoise Eyes, did you throw out your lure to me so many moons ago when all you would have of me you could have of any Kiowa woman?"

"Is that what you think?"

The whispered response frightened Grass Singing almost as much as the fact that someone had sneaked up without her knowing. She reached for her knife and wheeled around.

"Don't strike," Kit admonished her gently. "I ain't out to do you mischief."

"Turquoise Eyes!" She spat and stepped away. "Go away! Leave me alone!"

Ignoring her, Kit moved into the open from behind the shadow of a tree trunk. "I've been searchin' the village for you all night. Soaring Vulture gave us permission to speak."

"Only if I wish it," Grass Singing countered, lowering her weapon.

Kit shrugged and took a seat on a cottonwood stump nearby. "I ain't leavin' till you hear me out."

Grass Singing began to walk away. "Is the daughter of Soaring Vulture a coward?" she heard him call sharply, and she flung herself around to face him. "I am not a coward!"

Kit nodded. "Good. Then we can talk." He took out a rolled cigarette and lit it while Grass Singing moved slowly toward him. "I ain't the sort of man to venture where I ain't welcome," he conceded. "But you got to tell me plain why you ran away the day I came to see your father."

Grass Singing tossed her head, sending her hair flying back from her face. "You came to trade with my father. I will have no part in that."

Kit took a draw on his cigarette. Things were not getting any clearer in his mind. "I went to your father because I want to marry you. It's what you said you wanted, too."

"You did not come to do that!" Anger rushed through her as she moved threateningly toward Kit. "You came to trade with my father for a woman. You brought horses. I heard you. I am not for sale, Turquoise Eyes, not even to you." Abruptly, she turned and ran.

"Grass Singing? Damn!" Kit dropped his cigarette and took off after her. If she got back to the heart of the village before he could stop her, he would lose his only chance to speak to her before her brother returned.

She was quick, much quicker than he would have thought, but she did not head for the village. Instead, she followed the riverbank. He was beginning to wonder how much longer she would run when suddenly she dipped out of sight.

Kit stopped at the place where she had disappeared, straining to hear any sound that might lead him to her. "Grass Singing," he called. "We got to talk. I ain't gonna wait forever. Think of that."

When nothing stirred in the tall grasses, Kit swore softly and started back the way he'd come. "Didn't need no damn squaw messin' in my life anyway," he muttered halfheartedly. He didn't understand women. One minute they were all warm and soft and clinging, the next minute spitting and swiping at a man like a half-drowned mountain lion.

She caught him off guard. Kit gasped in surprise, reaching for the soft arms that encircled his neck from behind. Dropping to his knees, he flung Grass Singing over his shoulder onto the grass. She landed with a shriek, which Kit cut off by clamping his hand to her mouth. Then he dropped to his knees beside her.

"You plumb crazy Indian! You could've got yourself killed," he whispered hoarsely. Then he moved his hand away, satisfied that she would not scream again. "You're a wild one. Soaring Vulture warned me. Don't know as if we'd have hit it off anyways. Just as well you won't have me."

At first Kit did not want to believe the soft sounds he heard her making. "Didn't hurt you, did I?" He bent lower over her, putting a hand to her face and feeling the wet streaks on her cheeks. "Don't cry. Tell me what I done to you," he said tenderly and touched her face again.

"You not love Grass Singing," she answered.

"I don't love you? Hell, of course I do—I guess." Hastily, Kit looked around to make sure they were alone. When he turned back to Grass Singing, she buried her face in his chest, sobbing. His hand trembled as he ran it through her hair to stroke the wondrous softness, and he was surprised. What all of this had to do with loving he wasn't exactly certain. What he did feel acutely at that moment was that he was a man and she was a woman.

"Don't know much about this lovin' business," he said unsteadily, "but I guess that's what you wanted me to tell your father."

Grass Singing wiped away the last of her tears, ashamed at allowing Turquoise Eyes to make her cry. "I wish you to treat Grass Singing as any maiden in our village is treated," she said.

"And how is that?" Kit asked against his better judgment. He felt as though he had stepped into quicksand and each step was taking him irretrievably to a bottomless pit.

Grass Singing sat up, pulling away from the touch that had felt so warm on her skin. "I wish to be courted," she announced firmly. "In our village, when a man wishes to win the heart of the woman he loves, he will often come to the riverbank in the morning to help the woman carry water and firewood back to her tepee. He will come to her parents' tepee after dark and sit outside wrapped in his best blanket and play his willow flute for her. If she is agreeable to his courtship, she will come and sit and share his robes while he plays. Then, only then, does the man approach her father and brother to win consent for their marriage."

"Oh." For Grass Singing, Kit's response held a world of understanding. Kit was glad it was dark, or he knew she would have seen his sheepish look.

This was the wilderness. He had not thought about courtship. A man took what he could hold onto, and that still made the most sense.

"Well, I don't play no willow flute, wouldn't even if I could. As for sharin' a robe, don't take much imagination to know where that'd lead me," he admitted. "Still, I see what you're aimin' at."

He scratched his head. Franklin, Missouri never seemed so far away as when he was trying to remember how civilized folks behaved. "We done the same where I come from. Only them folks went to church socials and dances together, to church meetings, and to sing in the choir. Sometimes, when a man was bein' encouraged, he came to supper and sat in the parlor talkin' nonsense while the woman he was just about bustin' his britches over sipped tea and . . . Damned stupidest notions do take folks sometimes!"

Kit sighed. What would Wooten and Rube and Mitchell and the others think about all this? It didn't matter, he concluded. He wanted this woman. "All right," he said, giving in, "but the courtin' will have to be done my way! American-style."

"Is pressing lips American-style?" Grass Singing asked.

Kit grinned wickedly. "You bet. It's called 'spooning.' And it's definitely courtin' American-style. Now you pay close attention.

"First lesson on how to be a proper American lady, you put your little arms around me nice and hold me close. That's it. Now raise your chin. Open your mouth like you was about to taste a wild cherry. You're doin' fine. . . ."

"You got to be funnin' me," Rube declared with a chuckle.

"Seen it with these old eyes myself," Bill Mitchell insisted. "Carryin' firewood. Squaw work!"

"You seen him bring her in to supper at Will Bent's place?" Tuttle interjected.

"He didn't!"

"Did so. Saw it myself," the youngster replied. "I got a job at Mr. Bent's trader shop and he invites me to supper often. Well, I seen Cap'n Carson walkin' with his woman on his arm like they was strollin' through a city park."

"Damndest thing I ever hear tell of." Wooten rubbed his grizzled chin. "Every time, it's a woman causes a good man to turn sour. Queer as bad meat and a darn shame, too."

"Cap'n Carson's as good a man as ever rode over these plains," Amos snapped, somewhat ashamed to have armed Kit's detractors with new gossip. "If he wants to dress his woman in red satin and give her a parasol to carry, that's his business."

Bill Mitchell looked up from his squatting position. "Red satin?"

"Of course not. I'm just sayin' he could, if he was of a mind. Cap'n Carson's earned the respect of every man here, I'm thinkin'. He don't deserve no bad-mouthin' just because he decides to get hitched." Amos' face was scarlet with emotion.

"Simmer down, son." Blackfoot Smith peeled a long curl off the wood he was whittling. "If that's the way he wants to do things, Kit knows he's got my amen. Can't a body study on the freakishness of the species without a man gettin' riled?"

Amos looked sternly around the circle of smiling faces. "Just so you're through with funnin' Cap'n Carson. He's took hard with that Arapaho girl. Ain't nothin' between him and the wedding except three days."

Kit was thinking the same thing as he threaded a familiar path between the Arapaho tepees. Three days. Grass Singing's brother, Detenin, was said to have returned during the night. Today, Kit knew he would be receiving the final okay to go ahead with the marriage. After that he would set up his own tepee on the edge of the village to await the coming of his bride.

Kit found himself grinning more and more often these days. Getting himself a woman wasn't a bit pain-

ful. In fact, it was downright pleasurable. He and
Grass Singing had not been allowed to wander off
alone again, much to his exasperation, and he had
come to learn just how useful a Navaho blanket could
be when a couple stood outside a tepee with the whole
village sneaking peeks at them.

The arrangement hadn't been too comfortable,
but at least he had been able to steal a few more kisses
and feel his woman rubbing eagerly against him. He
was convinced that Grass Singing was just as eager as
he was for the courtship to end.

These thoughts were so ingrained in Kit's mind
that not until he had reached the center of the Arapaho village was he aware that something was wrong.
There were no children playing. Only a stray dog ran
out to greet him at Soaring Vulture's lodge.

"Don't go gettin' spooked," Kit muttered to himself. "It's practically your weddin' day. Your nerves are
bound to be actin' up."

Yet, when Kit entered Soaring Vulture's lodge, a
sense of trouble brewed inside him. Soaring Vulture
motioned for Kit to enter, but he did not speak. Nor
did he offer food or a pipe when Kit had seated himself.

Detenin was not present. He and Soaring Vulture
were alone. Well, no matter, Kit thought, unconvinced
of trouble. In sign language he communicated the customary greetings and praise.

Soaring Vulture's expression did not soften. During most of Kit's greetings, he had looked away.

When Kit finally made the sign that he was
through speaking, he was so angry he nearly stood up
and walked out. Grass Singing was up to some new

trick. That was it, he decided. She wanted something else from him. Well, she was not going to get it. He had already made a fool of himself over her these last ten days. His friends had teased him mercilessly behind his back and almost laughed right to his face at his strange behavior. Grass Singing would have to come to *him* now, or the wedding was off.

Soaring Vulture took his time before speaking. When he did, it was not in sign. "Little Chief honors my home," he began in the usual manner. "But the decision of marriage is not mine to make. It is Detenin's."

"Where is he?" Kit asked in Arapaho.

The older man shrugged. "He is in the village."

"Will you send for him?" Kit urged.

"He will come."

For the next hour Kit sat and stewed, turning over in his mind all the reasons he should not endure this insult. Then he pictured Grass Singing in his arms and knew that nothing short of full-scale war would keep him from her.

Finally the lodge flap was thrown back and Detenin entered. Kit knew who it was immediately. Grass Singing's brother had been described as squat—hence his name Short Man—and as having broad shoulders and a neck like a bull's. Now, as he stood in front of the two men, he wore only a breechcloth and moccasins.

Again, Kit began the extensive signs of greeting. Following that, he signed his desire to marry Grass Singing. Detenin never looked up, but Kit suspected he had seen the hand movement.

"May I speak with Grass Singing?" Kit asked in sign.

There was immediate response as Detenin growled low in his throat.

"What the hell's the matter?" Kit exploded in English.

"Grass Singing not marry any white man. Marriage no good," Detenin replied in accented English.

"What have I done?" Kit exclaimed, sounding to himself just like a whining child.

"White man bad medicine," Detenin signed in bold strokes. "Make Grass Singing cry."

Kit looked in disbelief from the angry brother to his father. "Grass Singing says I make her cry?"

Soaring Vulture shook his head. "It is not Little Chief who causes my daughter sadness. She was foolish, and now she pays for her foolishness with shame."

"What did she do?"

"We cannot speak of it," Soaring Vulture answered solemnly. "When daughter of Arapaho family knows shame, her family grieves with her. There can be no marriage. Take your horses, Little Chief."

"Who is the man?" Kit questioned coldly, triggering a startled glance from Detenin.

Seeming almost relieved that Kit had guessed, Soaring Vulture shrugged hopelessly. "We cannot find him. He lives in the great lodge of Trader Bent."

"We will kill him when he comes among us again. There will be war between the Arapahos and the whites." Detenin's voice was hot with rage.

The young fool wants war, Kit realized. Even if something hadn't happened to Grass Singing, he might have found some way to spark a confrontation.

William Bent was about to have all hell break loose on his own front porch.

"You will not kill the son of a bitch," Kit ordered, rising to his feet. "I will." He had reached the entrance before turning around.

"Who is the man?" he repeated.

"We do not know his white name," Detenin signed. "All we know is that his head scrapes the clouds, and our people call him Bear Face."

"St. Nair!" Kit clenched his fists. "I know the varmint. He don't live at Bent's Fort. But I'll find him, and after I do, I'll hand you his scalp to dance over!"

Kit was silent for a moment, then said finally, "One more thing. I want to see Grass Singing. Is she . . . ?" Kit wet his lips, his voice cracking slightly. "Is she hurt bad?"

Neither man replied.

"I'll not only kill the son of a bitch," Kit vowed to them. "I'm gonna make him sorry he was ever born!"

"Now I'm not sure," William Bent conceded to his wife as he stared out across the courtyard of the fort. "Maybe I was wrong setting Kit's sights on the Arapaho gal. Thought she was just the thing for him."

Owl Woman came to stand beside her husband at the window of their upstairs bedroom. "My husband, the fault lies not with you. Grass Singing's family has hardened their hearts against Little Chief not because of something *he* has done, but because Soaring Vulture's daughter was beaten by a white trapper."

"Grass Singing beaten? I don't believe it!"

"The rumors," Owl Woman explained, "say it was a trapper from the fort. Arapahos talk of warring against the whites. My sister Yellow Woman comes to me with additional word from my father that there will be war between the Arapahos and the Cheyennes if the Arapahos attack the fort."

"My Lord!" Bent raked his shoulder-length hair with sweating hands. "If it'd been one of my boys, I'd know. Isn't a man here ready to take on Kit, not if he hit Kit's woman first. That's asking to die. Must have been some free trapper moving through the area. Poor bastard," Bent murmured, thinking of Kit. "Wonder what he's going to do now?"

"Mr. Bent?" It was one of the sentries. "That fellow St. Nair's at the gate. Claims he's got business with you. Should I let him in?"

William groaned. Trouble with that Frenchman was the last thing he needed, especially with news of a possible Indian uprising to worry over. "No . . . well, all right. Tell him to come here directly, before he heads for the cantina."

But St. Nair had already decided what he would do. For the better part of the last year he and his two partners had roamed the foothills of the southern Rockies looking for a chance to settle his long-standing score with that damned Carson.

He spat as he rode into the fort's courtyard, barely missing the sentry who held the gate for him. "*Poltron*," he jeered as he watched the man struggling with his natural inclination to strike out. Then he smiled contemptuously when the sentry told him to go directly to William Bent's office. The American trader could wait. He had heard that a certain sandy-headed runt was at the fort—and he had business with him.

Kit scarcely looked up when St. Nair entered the

cantina, but his heart picked up its pace. Not in fear. There was no emotion in him other than an all-consuming blood lust—the emotion a predator felt that had spied its prey.

From beneath the brim of his hat he watched the Frenchman make his way to the bar and then deliberately shoulder two men aside. Kit's mouth contorted humorlessly. St. Nair was edgy, looking for trouble, looking for *him*.

Kit slumped down in his chair, not quite ready to step forward. He could see that the Frenchman needed a drink badly—so badly he could feel the tension in him from across the room. He would be generous. He would let the Frenchman drink for a while.

For more than an hour St. Nair stood at the bar doing just that. He began to laugh, making jokes at the expense of the two men he had shoved from their places at the bar. They shifted uneasily.

". . . lick 'em all, Jules St. Nair can! I lick 'em all," he roared with a rumbling belch. "Jules is pretty smart man, fine for the ladies, too. Me, I make 'em cry when old Jules drops his pants for 'em. 'Big man, this Jules,' they say. 'This Jules, he give the most experienced lady enough pleasure. And even more to the lady with no experience.' "

Kit's knuckles turned white where he was gripping the sides of his chair. St. Nair was about to tell a story about Grass Singing—he knew it. If only he could simply take the pistol stuck in his belt and blow the man's head off. But that would be the cowardly thing to do. No one would understand or accept that, even if Kit had just cause in his own mind. And to challenge St.

Nair at this close distance might mean he would lose to the Frenchman, and that he must not allow.

St. Nair's voice had dropped to a whisper. Kit tried to convince himself that the Frenchman was relating some story other than the one about Grass Singing. A searing pain streaked through him as he thought of his beautiful woman and how she must have suffered from St. Nair's brutal hands . . . No! Kit forced his thoughts back to the present. He would wait to kill St. Nair for that act. Knowing that, he would ease his torment and repay, in some part, Grass Singing's shame.

"You don't like St. Nair?" the big man called to the retreating figure of a man who had decided to end the conversation they'd been having. "You do not drink with him no longer? You insult St. Nair—make him very sad."

With surprising speed for a man his size, St. Nair launched himself from the bar and collared the man in the doorway. A yelp was the last sound the trapper made as St. Nair's meaty fist closed his mouth. Holding his victim by the collar, the huge Frenchman aimed repeated jabs at the defenseless trapper's face until his features were spattered with blood.

"*Poltron!*" St. Nair sneered, dropping the unconscious man. "He insulted me. You saw it, *non?*"

Hearing the hiss of the disapproving crowd, the Frenchman turned to face them. "Any man who does not like what Jules does, come and tell him to his face." The huge fists flexed at his side as his bloodshot stare crawled over the men at the bar. When no one moved, St. Nair threw back his head and laughed. "They are cowards, these Américains. Jules, he went to fight, and these Américains, they turn their backs. *Pol-*

trons! Women, these Américains!" St. Nair's lusty laughter exploded again.

"I tell you why Jules is here," St. Nair said, sobering. "He comes special to whip the Américain called Carson. You tell him that. Tell him I beat an Américain a day till he shows himself. Got something to tell the boy—some very special news about his squaw. He wants Jules, he find him in Cheyenne camp."

"Now, son," Blackfoot Smith cautioned when Kit rose, glaring as St. Nair reeled outside. "You ain't gonna tangle with that black bear, are you?"

"I'm going to do more than that!" he answered.

As Kit left the cantina, his gut boiled with hatred for the Frenchman. By the time he reached the door, he could see St. Nair's bulky frame already settling in the saddle. Pulling at his leather shirt, the Frenchman slipped it off, revealing a huge torso.

"It'd keep a pack of coyotes full for a month," Kit muttered to himself. He was certain he couldn't challenge St. Nair on foot. But the solution came as swiftly as all of Kit's ideas came, and he streaked toward the corral.

"Told you he wouldn't fight," Wooten announced to the crowd of men who had pushed outside behind Kit. "Ain't nothin' but a damn fool gonna tangle with that Frenchy."

"Well, he could have if he'd got some encouragement," Amos grumbled. "Cap'n Carson ain't no coward."

A big hand fell on Amos' shoulder. "No man is callin' Kit scared," Rube said softly. "Seen him in too many good fights to do that. Still, a man's a fool who sees himself a hole when a bull's charging and don't drop down it. Carson ain't no match for St. Nair, any way you fix it."

"Why you reckon the Frenchman's after Cap'n Carson?" asked another man.

Blackfoot Smith shrugged. "It's the nature of the big to hunt the small. Talkin' about Kit's woman—sure-fire way to draw him out. Only, where do you suppose that young'un got to?"

When Kit found his horse tethered to the corral fence, he swung onto its bare back, grabbed up the reins and came galloping back into the courtyard just as the fort gates were swinging open for St. Nair.

"Frenchy!"

St. Nair turned his horse awkwardly. The summer sun was heating up his beefy back. Full of whiskey, he was sweating like a pig. Before he could pull his rifle from his saddle holster, Kit pulled up right beside him, pushing his horse against St. Nair's and giving him no room to maneuver his Hawken. His eyes ice-blue and cold, he leaned his face forward to within inches of the Frenchman's.

"You lookin' for me, St. Nair? You been shootin' off your mouth a powerful lot, I hear tell. Been boastin' as to how you can take on any American that comes up the Arkansas. Well, now's your chance to prove it. I'm American, a poor bandy-legged specimen at that, and I say that *I* can take you!"

St. Nair's expression twisted as he tried to make out Kit's face through his whiskey-blurred eyes. "Carson?" he asked tentatively at first, then, "Carson! *Sacre-bleu!* I kill you today. And then," he said menacingly, "I will make love to your woman tonight!"

"Don't be too sure about that," Kit answered,

forcing a calm appearance. "Your business and mine, it's old business." Reaching into his shirt, he pulled out the worn red silk bandanna. "You ain't wearing your hanky, I see. Reckon you could've lost it up on the North Platte a few years back?"

St. Nair eyed the silk suspiciously. His dressing up like an Indian and attacking Fitzpatrick's brigade had almost been forgotten.

"I do not remember," he muttered.

"Or," suggested Kit snidely, "did you drop your britches when you was stealin' my cache?"

"It was *you* who killed my men!" St. Nair hissed.

"And it was *you*," Kit countered, "who ran out on a fight right after!" He paused, allowing time for the insult to sink in. "Are you going to run now?" he asked coldly. " 'Cause if you're not, I'm about to kill me a low, yellow-bellied skunk!"

The Frenchman roared out a Gallic oath and lurched his horse away from Kit's. When he reached for his rifle, Kit pulled a pistol. "Touch that trigger, and I'll throw you where you sit. You challenged me to a duel—the whole fort heard you. Well, I accept," Kit asserted. "We duel on horseback. Beyond the gates."

St. Nair shook his shaggy head. "We fight inside the fort where all can see. We fight with knives."

Smirking, Kit answered, "Getting cold feet, are you? Should have thought of that before you challenged me. My choice of weapons. You know the rules. If you're backin' out I'll empty my lead in your gut here and now. Makes no never mind to me."

A wild cry rumbled through St. Nair, but Kit was too deeply involved with the sport of the moment to know fear or even hesitation. What he did know was that this man had hurt the woman he loved and, because of it, would soon be dead.

"*Oui*. We fight. Any time you say."

"Now!" Kit demanded. And deliberately he turned his back on the Frenchman and rode. Once he had passed through the tunnel leading to the outside, Kit spurred his horse, reining it in when he was a short distance from the fort. He did not allow his attention to stray to the walls where trappers were scrambling to get a better view of what was happening. He did not so much as glance at the Indians who came running at the sound of the uproar. All concentration was focused on the hulk of a man he wanted to send to hell.

St. Nair came out slowly onto the grassy plain below the fort. Then, with the cry of a professional wolf hunter, he kicked his horse into a full gallop, heading straight for Kit. Jumping his mount forward to meet the Frenchman, Kit let loose with an Indian war cry of his own that echoed from the bottom of his soul.

The two men fired simultaneously. In that instant, Kit swung himself out of his upright position and hung onto the horse with a handful of mane, one heel digging into the horse's back. The trick shielded him completely. St. Nair's ball flew harmlessly past.

The Frenchman was not so fortunate. Kit heard him scream with pain as the pistol shot plowed through his gun hand at the wrist and exited through his upper arm.

Swinging upright, Kit saw that St. Nair had tumbled from his saddle. Sprawled in the dust he lay, trying frantically to stop both bleeding wounds with one hand.

"Jules, he is hurt bad," the big man pleaded as he struggled to his knees. "You no shoot him now. No rifle. You will not kill a helpless man?"

Kit looked at the man groveling at his feet and felt nothing. His first pistol was empty, so he reached for a second he had tucked beneath his shirt. Just in time he saw the shimmering knife St. Nair had pulled from his belt, and Kit yanked his pistol free, aimed and fired.

The scalp was so dirty that he was certain the Arapahos would not keep it for long. But Kit took it anyway, not even bothering to look again at the man who had haunted his life for nearly five years.

The main party of trappers fell back from him as he approached the fort, most of them muttering that Carson was a bad man to cross, a killer, and a dead shot.

Only William Bent came forward to extend his hand. "I know it cost you, taking that man's life. But you done right, son. You done right."

Kit looked squarely into Bent's face. "Only man I was ever glad I killed."

Chapter 17

Kit could not keep the smile of satisfaction from his face when the clearing ahead revealed the golden glow of his lodge. He knew that his meal would be waiting for him, warming over the tepee fire that lit up the white leather walls like a lamp shade. He knew there would also be a pan of hot water ready to warm his frostbitten toes. His pipe would be packed with fresh tobacco and his bedroll laid out, smelling of the fragrant herbs that were rolled up daily with them.

Pushing aside a low limb of an evergreen, Kit received a collarful of slush that slid down his back. It was winter on the Green River, the season for hunting, mending, and tanning new leather. This year, he had a wife for company.

Kit stomped off the snow that clung to his furlined moccasins before he threw back the flap of the tepee and entered. As always, his eyes went first to the corner where Grass Singing sat to do her sewing. She looked up as he entered, a full smile of welcome and delight on her lovely face. Kit's heart turned over in gladness.

It had not always been so good for them. There had been those first weeks after their marriage when he had thought that the pleasures of their being together were lost forever. Every time he thought of those difficult times, he wanted to kill St. Nair over and over again.

"Buffalo runnin' in the valley on the other side of the ridge," he said in greeting. "Tomorrow, if it don't snow, I'll take a ride and collect us a new carcass. You've about worn out the last robe I brought you."

Grass Singing had risen quickly, and was peeling Kit's ice-encrusted moccasins from his feet. He had never asked or expected that of her. She had always chosen to serve him.

"I will be grateful for a new robe to work in," she said.

Grass Singing's words were disturbing. She had not been "grateful" for common courtesies in several months. Something was bothering her.

"Anybody come around?" he asked. He knew they had had no visitors—he was careful not to leave her alone for long intervals—but the words made conversation.

"No one," she replied, reaching out for the bowl of warm water she had heated for her husband's feet. After he had settled into it, she handed him a plate of stew prepared from scraps left from the elk he had shot the week before.

"Good vittles," he murmured between hungry gulps.

Grass Singing was silent. When Kit finished eating, she traded the bowl in his hands for his pipe, then went to take up her work once more.

Kit watched her in silence for a long time. Six months they had been married. Six months he had been alone with her. Still, he didn't always know what she was feeling. Perhaps he never would. "You got any special desires come summertime?"

Grass Singing merely shook her head.

"Was ponderin' returnin' south, come the thaw. Could trap our way back to the Arkansas by the time the season's over." He saw her start, but then she once again lowered her head. Kit slowly put down his pipe. "Grass Singing?"

She looked up to see her husband's arms outstretched. Usually this gesture aroused her, but tonight she did not feel the urge to couple. Her lack of desire upset her since she had been taught early never to deny her husband. Reminding herself of this, she rose to come by his side.

Kit felt his wife shiver as his arms went around her, and he stiffened. He gently pressed her head to his chest as he leaned back against the backrest she had fashioned for him. "What's wrong? Tell me."

Grass Singing snuggled into the warmth of her husband's body, her tension easing a little as she smelled the familiar scents of the tobacco he smoked, and the vague, musky odor of castoreum that clung to him even when he was not carrying it. Kit shook her lightly to elicit a response, and she said in a small voice, "Must we return south?"

Not sure why she was hesitating, Kit answered cautiously. "Thought you might like to see your folks. I got to trade my pelts someplace. Might as well be at Bent's Fort. Of course, if you don't want . . ."

Grass Singing closed her eyes, her mind filled with memories. Deliberately she focused on the night six months earlier when she had gone walking along the riverbank hoping for another meeting with her beloved Turquoise Eyes.

He had done all that she asked, courting with his own brand of wooing that had made her feel both special and a little embarrassed. But more and more she longed to again feel his mouth against hers, longed to know a completion to the feelings that his touch stirred in her.

She knew what happened when a man and a woman lay together. She had lived beneath the same roof as her parents all her life. But the feelings that came with love were new to her. The experience was unlike any other in her knowledge. She had hoped to find an answer to these feelings while walking along the riverbank. Instead she had come upon St. Nair. And instead of love, she had come upon pain, bruises, and fear unlike any she had ever known.

Kit felt Grass Singing shiver again. He reached for a robe to wrap around them. "Don't worry," he soothed, in answer to what he imagined she was thinking. "We won't go if you don't want to. There's plenty of places I can trade."

Although he had spoken the words, he hadn't liked saying them. He had loved roaming the stark, golden mountains of the northern Rockies. Perhaps with time Grass Singing would overcome her aversion to returning south. Surely she wasn't concerned that she might not be welcomed by her people.

As the fire died to embers, Kit thought of the last time he had seen Soaring Vulture and Detenin . . .

He had brought St. Nair's scalp with him, and had placed it in front of the older man with respect, saying, "I bring you the scalp of the man who dared to touch your daughter."

Soaring Vulture had nodded. "Our people thank Little Chief for the revenge for Grass Singing's sake."

The compliment meant little to Kit. More important was the marriage. "I come now to ask again for the hand of Grass Singing," he'd requested, then stared pokerfaced at Detenin. "Will you accept me as your brother-in-law?"

When both men agreed, Kit sighed heavily. "Then it is only for Grass Singing to decide if she wants me. Will you send for her?"

Soaring Vulture did, and while Kit waited, he felt an unfamiliar helplessness. Grass Singing held his future in her power. Kit was frowning deeply when she finally appeared in the doorway, her expression dulled and sad as she stood between her two sisters.

Soaring Vulture spoke first. "Little Chief has brought our people the scalp of the one called Black Bear." Grass Singing looked up quickly as her father continued. "He has avenged your shame and seeks the right to have you as his wife. What is your desire, my daughter?"

As Kit watched Grass Singing, her eyes roamed over every part of him. When she spoke, her voice did not exactly make a passionate declaration, but Kit was still thrilled at the "yes" he heard. He had quickly taken his seat in front of the fire, and Soaring Vulture told his daughter to do the same.

Kit did not hear the words Soaring Vulture spoke to them. When Grass Singing seated herself next to him, he saw the firelight play over her face, showing her bruises and the swollen lip she had kept hidden. More than words ever could, Grass Singing's injuries attested to the struggle she must have made against St. Nair.

Killing had been too good for the Frenchman. He should have tortured him slowly, Kit thought, made him scream out his agony. . . .

As Soaring Vulture finished speaking, a colorful blanket was draped around their shoulders, bringing them together symbolically as man and wife. Then news of the marriage was declared in public to the villagers.

Grass Singing had not gone with Kit back to Bent's Fort. She needed to prepare herself, her family told him. So Kit went alone to the fort to collect his things.

When he returned, Kit discovered that a brand-new white-robed tepee had been erected a short distance from the main camp. The tepee, Kit learned, along with new cloths and extra robes and all that was necessary for a new bride to make a home for her warrior husband, had been a wedding present from the villagers. But Grass Singing was not inside the tepee when he arrived. He sat near the fire, but tasted none of the food prepared for him.

Finally Kit heard the soft footfalls of his wife approaching outside. Rising, he faced the door flap and waited.

Grass Singing entered quietly, her eyes lowered. Kit no longer minded that she hadn't been there to greet him. His eyes went over every inch of her, as if doing so then were his only chance to commit every line and curve to memory.

She was dressed in fine bleached elkskin. It hung in buttery folds down to her knees, ending in the heavy fringe that hid her leggings. The yoke was painted gold and decorated with blue beads and elk teeth. Iridescent sea shells shone in her hair decorations and hung from her ears. Vermilion spots had been artistically applied to her cheeks and brow, and even across the room she smelled of sweet grass and sage. On her right arm, he recognized the silver and turquoise bracelet she once told him she had bought in his honor.

Kit had taken her hand and led her to the fire. She never looked up, even when he offered her food and some of the better brandy William Bent had given them.

After eating alone, Kit could wait no longer and blurted out, "What's wrong? Don't you like me?"

Instantly he was contrite. Grass Singing could barely hold back the tears in her eyes. Lifting her head, she said, "Little Chief is angry with me. Maybe it is better I go back to my parents' lodge. Marriage is not right for us."

"The hell it ain't!" Kit had cried in alarm as she rose. Rushing to block her path, he took her gently by the arm, then guided her back to the firelight. "Look me in the eye and tell me you don't want to belong to me no more. Then I'll let you go."

Grass Singing was silent. "Tell me," Kit insisted. "I don't want a woman who don't want me. Thought

you did want me. And I sure said and done everythin'
I know how to make you want me." Suddenly he let
her go. "Go on, then. I ain't gonna stop you."

Grass Singing did not move and instead looked
into Kit's eyes. "Little Chief is a great warrior, many
coups. He can have any woman, many wives. He cannot want a ruined woman, one who can no longer have
children."

"What?" A blank look come over Kit's face.

"Atanea, my mother, and Turtle Eye the medicine
man—they say Black Bear hurt Grass Singing bad.
Maybe children, maybe not." The tears had flowed into
the corners of Grass Singing's trembling lips. "Maybe I
can give Little Chief no sons."

Kit's stomach knotted. "Damn that black-hearted
bastard!"

He had pulled her against him, apologizing when
without thinking of her bruises he had hugged her
body to his, wanting to drive all the pain out of her
and into himself. "I don't care! You understand?" he
exclaimed, almost crying. "I don't care what happens
with kids. You and me—we belong together. You
knew it before I did. You said so yourself. Grass Singing and Little Chief are one till death."

The very next morning he had packed, and they
had slipped quietly away to northern mountains to try,
alone, to mend the rift in their lives. . . .

Now, six months later, he held Grass Singing
when the nightmares threatened. He watched her keep
his lodge and make his clothes and cook his meals, but
he did not yet embrace her as his wife. At first she was
too sore. The act of holding her caused pain—though
she would not admit it until he discovered upon forced

examination that she had two badly bruised ribs. He promised then not to make her his wife until she was ready. But the days had stretched into weeks, the weeks into months, and still Grass Singing did not invite him to curl up with her. Tonight, feeling her press softly against him in her sleep, he knew he could not wait any longer.

Kit rolled back the blanket that had been covering them and gently eased Grass Singing back onto the floor. She was half-asleep, her gentle protests stirring him deeply as he bent over her and pressed her parted lips to his. Every instinct warned him to go slow. She was like a deer, easily frightened and ready to flee if startled. Her breath was warm and sweet on his tongue, and he kissed her long and deep, tangling his fingers in the luxuriant fall of her hair.

Grass Singing felt a heat rising in her, its source outside, beyond her. She yielded to it, pressing herself to the warming caresses. What was happening was unlike the melting away into sleep, because, as the moments passed, she became more aroused, then drowsy. She felt the cool night against her belly and thighs as her clothes were lifted from her. She did not open her eyes, afraid that what she was feeling would disappear. Then heat, the warmth of solid flesh, met hers, pressing and finding hidden places.

Her thighs fell open to the lure of his fingers. She began to squirm beneath their touch, seeking and retreating from the wonder she was feeling. Suddenly she was being filled, roused to a pitch she had only imagined before, then, bursting to meet it, was washed with relief.

Kit smiled into Grass Singing's face, his own

pleasure no less than hers. That moment had made all the waiting worthwhile. Afterward, when words would no longer destroy the moment, Grass Singing put a hand to her husband's cheek. "Grass Singing is truly a wife to Little Chief?"

"Yes," Kit replied simply.

"Then we may go home now. Grass Singing misses her family."

Kit sighed, torn between the new pleasures that lay before him now that the barriers were gone and the knowledge that his new Indian bride expected him to be a part of the Arapaho society. After all these years, he was about to be civilized.

"Looking older, son, but still a sight for these sore eyes!" William Bent slapped Kit on the back. "Never was happier to open the doors of this fort to anyone."

When William learned that Kit had left the Arkansas without a word the summer before, he had worried. Kit's men wanted to go off in search of him, but Bent stopped them, knowing that whatever the reasons, Kit went his own way because he had felt a need to. And now, looking at the fine, fit fellow before him, Bent knew his hunch had been right. "Just look at Grass Singing. She's prettier than ever," William complimented, giving her a fatherly hug. "Well don't just stand there, you two," he added. "Come in!"

"Missed me, did you?" Kit's cocky grin sprang to life.

William nodded, taking a seat. "That I did. Life doesn't ever get easier on the Taos Trail. Cheyennes and Pawnees have been acting up some. Shoshones shot up my brother George's caravan. Usual thing."

"Guess you could use an extra hand, then." Kit's tone was flat.

"Always can," Bent began. "Matter of fact, I just sent south for . . ." His bushy brows shot up. "Are you trying to tell me something?"

"You need a good man. I need a regular job. Leastways that's what my wife tells me."

Bent looked at Grass Singing. The beautiful Indian girl looked puzzled, but was too polite to contradict her husband in public. "Wife says so, huh? Well, okay. I need an expert hunter. Fort's getting more than a fair share of trade from the mountain boys this year. They've got big appetites and lots of money to spend. You want the job, it's yours."

"I come and go on my own time," Kit added, for clarification.

"Sure thing, Kit, sure thing. Now how about a glass of my famous 'hailstorm'?"

"You buyin'?"

William burst out laughing. "Anything you say. Got you at last, Kit Carson. Mean to keep you."

"I look another crook-horned four-legged animal in the face, I'm gonna get sick." Kit wiped his dusty face with his sleeve and took a long pull on his canteen.

He raised his eyes to the brown buzzards circling overhead like autumn leaves in a breeze. In the distance he could hear the bark of wolves whose companionship to the hunters was a constant source of irritation. Whenever a butcher turned his back, they ran up to steal unguarded cuts of meat.

Trapped. That was the word that came to Kit's

mind as he sat his horse in the midst of several slaughtered buffalo. He was smeared with so much blood and grease that his buckskins shone oily black in the sunlight.

Kit's face and beard hadn't fared much better; they were matted with a fine covering of prairie dust. The air stunk with the rank breath of buffalo and the mixture of blood and decaying meat. It had taken more than a week's ride from the fort to find this herd, and this was the third day of the hunt.

For a full year, Kit had worked as a hunter for William Bent, but the comfort of regular meals for regular pay had begun to pall months earlier.

He looked around in disgust. Where was the smell of piny turpentine and clear cold air that filled a mountain man's every breath? Where were the icy crystal streams a trapper plunged himself into to lay his traps? The stink of blood and gore had its place in a frontiersman's life, but the steady diet of dust and hard riding over flat plains was not how he meant to spend the rest of his life.

"Ain't even thirty yet," he muttered. Was a man's life to be cut off just like that—a mesa reached and settled on? If not for his wife, Kit thought guiltily, he would be back in the Shining Ones, the Rockies.

Grass Singing was happy to be living at the fort. She was near her people and visited them often. Not one complaint did Kit hear about the hard year they had spent alone on the Green River, but he knew Grass Singing had suffered. She'd developed a nasty cough that had stayed with her until the summer sun melted the last of the snow. Even now, if he did not look after her, she would tire herself with work, an effort that renewed her painful coughing spells.

Kit knew he could not ask Grass Singing to go back into the mountains with him. But if he didn't get back to the life he loved soon, he was afraid that the bitterness he'd already felt stirring would be with him permanently.

Already he was getting a reputation as a man who was hard to please. And since the day he killed St. Nair, he had noticed a mistrustful look in men's eyes when he was near. It was a look that said he was a dangerous man now, a man not to be crossed.

Grass Singing knew of her husband's discontent. When he mentioned the fact that a few of the men he knew were packing up to go north for their fall season, it was she who spoke first of his leaving with them.

"My husband, you are not happy. I feel this in my heart."

Kit looked up from his bowl of stew to where Grass Singing sat. The light was dim in the tepee. "What do you mean?" he asked.

Grass Singing laid aside her sewing and smiled at her husband with a tenderness that made him feel wrong for wanting to leave her. "You are restless, like the wind in a boxed canyon. It is not enough that we have moved out of the walls of the fort. A tepee can contain your wild spirit no better than mud walls. You long like the hawk to soar on the expanse of your wings. This you must do. My only sorrow is that I cannot follow you." She lowered her eyes quickly, before the tears that filled them could be seen.

Kit swallowed his mouthful of food. She did not

want to come with him. "Wouldn't mean I wouldn't come back first thing after the spring thaw."

Grass Singing nodded silently.

"I can make certain Bent takes real good care of you."

"No," Grass Singing protested gently. "It is better that I go to the village of my people. They need young strong backs to help with the labor."

You are not strong, Kit thought anxiously, but replied instead, "I don't aim to let nobody work my woman hard. I better stay on a while."

Grass Singing knew better than to argue. But the next morning she gathered her husband's belongings while he was out at the corral and packed his supplies the best way she knew how. When Kit returned with the news that his friends had ridden out, she pointed to his possibles and traps. "They cannot have gotten far," she told him. "A brisk ride will bring you to them."

Kit did not hesitate. He grabbed Grass Singing up in a bear hug and swung her off her feet. "Now don't work too hard, you promise? I'll come back, soon as the spring hunt is over. You need anythin', you go to Will Bent. I got pay comin' for the last hunt, enough to last you till I get back. I love you!" A hard, quick kiss and he was out the door, his metal traps clinking together as they rode his shoulder.

Grass Singing did not go to the door of their tepee. She did not want to remember her husband with his back turned toward her, riding away. She would wait for him to return and, until that time, the memory of his kiss would remain on her lips. There would be news awaiting his return, too. Gently, she slid a hand over her still-flat belly. Her mother had confirmed it only yesterday. She carried Kit Carson's child.

"Do it seem colder to you this season? My rheumatism is actin' up some, I can tell you." Gibbon hunched his massive shoulders under his buffalo robe as he sat at the campfire.

The slow, steady hiss of sleet dropping into the blazing embers was his only reply. It had been a good fall for the men. They were taking more beaver than ever before, thanks to a man they had never thought would ride with them again. Gibbon poked his neighbor with his elbow. "Do you take the right side of why Cap'n Carson left his pretty little squaw at the fort?"

Kit had drawn his robes up near the fire to sleep, so the question was whispered low. Bill Mitchell shrugged. "Any way you lay it, beaver won't come to that one. Sorry doin's, I'm thinkin'. Fine little gal. Carson's feeling queer as a gut-shot buffalo. Let it be."

Kit did not hear that particular exchange, but he knew that Mitchell, Gibbon, Wooten, and the rest had been talking behind his back. To his face, they had never dared ask the details about his grudge against St. Nair or why he and his bride had left after their marriage without a word to anyone.

"Let 'em wonder," Kit decided, and he stopped worrying about it. There was a fullness of spirit that had come to him because of the successful season. When he lay back in his robes with his feet to his own campfire and listened to the nighthawks cry, he could believe that the whole vast wilderness was his private domain. The wine-red sun of late evening would glide down behind the mountains, and if he watched long enough, he sometimes thought he saw a brief flash of brilliant green just before dusk shut down over the ridge. The air, smelling of sagebrush and woody smoke, and the mouth-watering aroma of broiled buffalo ribs made a man feel in every bone of his body that he was completely alive.

City folk could never feel it, living where they did. Civilized living did not inspire such emotion. In the wilderness, Kit knew he was part of a great, wild freedom called nature. When a man was alone there, he felt that anything could be faced.

It took a stubborn man to live this kind of life—a man who said no to failure and was likely to get madder than hell at even the slightest notion of it.

It pained Kit to realize that the only two people he had learned to care for since coming West were people for whom his kind of life was not possible. Royce was as good a *compadre* as a man could ask for. Kit smiled. Royce in city clothes and a babe on his big bony knees. It was comical. Lord! Wouldn't nobody catch him bouncing . . .

Kit rolled over suddenly and sat up. It was happening again. He had not consciously put Grass Singing out of his thoughts. He just thought it less than smart for a man to carry the image of a woman's firm breasts and soft thighs with him into Indian territory. Such thoughts might cost him his concentration and earn him an arrow in his back. But at nights it was different. He missed the warm tepee and hot food that had comforted him during his last trapping season. More than that, he missed the arms that held him even when he was too exhausted to do more than nod against them.

"Randy as a goat, that's all," Kit grouched under his breath. He knew that Grass Singing had spoiled him for the long months of denial. Well, he would just have to get used to the knot in his britches. He would wait. And ache.

"Here's for the lie! Anyway you lay it, them doin's ain't gonna shine with this crowd!" Bill Mitchell thumped the long counter of the trading post until it vibrated under his hand. As he did, an entire pile of folded pelts slid from the edge onto the floor. "One dollar a pelt! Hell's full of greenhorn cheaters. Here's for another!"

Just in time Kit reached out to deflect Bill's Hawken. The shot went wide of the clerk behind the counter, but the young man, in his first season in the wilderness, fell anyway, fainting as the shot rebounded harmlessly off the wall.

"Pull in rein, Bill!" Kit bellowed. He and the men with him had ridden in the day before from the Colorado to Antoine Robidou's trading post on the Gunnison River. Their spring season finished, they had decided to trade up north rather than tote their catch all the way back to Bent's Fort.

"What is this? You repay my hospitality by destroying my property?" Antoine Robidou, the fort's owner stood in the doorway.

Kit turned to him with a smile. He had met Robidou at Ewing Young's years ago when both men still worked the forbidden streams of New Mexico. "Sorry, Antoine. One of my boys got himself a mite worked up over the prices your clerk was offering."

Antoine was in his middle years, the relative ease

of a trader's life having bestowed on him a substantial paunch, but his black eyes were bright. "So you killed him?"

Kit looked back to where the clerk had disappeared behind the counter. "Nope. Your boy just took a sudden likin' to the floor. Be comin' around any minute now."

"Well then," Antoine suggested, "perhaps we should retire to my office. You want to discuss price, and I want to discuss the year's trapping."

They went to his office, and Kit sat down in a chair for the first time in six months.

"Silk hats!" Kit exclaimed, reacting to a comment by Antoine. "You're tellin' me my business is goin' under because some dandified city folks done up and took a shine to silk hats?"

Antoine nodded gravely. "My friend, you must have known that the bulk of the beaver trapped in these mountains went to supply the hat business. Most of the pelts are exported to Europe."

"Of course I knew it. Only . . ." Kit tossed back the last of the contents in his glass. He knew he supported a fashion industry, but that industry had never touched his life personally before. He'd never thought that one day he would have to bow to the will of a bunch of silly greenhorns who wore tall hats with their silk trousers and lace hankies.

"Damnit all, anyhow!" he shouted.

"It pains me to tell you that I can offer you no more than a dollar a pelt," Antoine responded, "and very fine pelts they are." He inspected Carson's reaction closely, and from what he saw he was convinced that the rumors about the trapper were well-founded. He was a man to be respected.

"Beaver's bound to rise," Kit added encouragingly.

Antoine shook his head vigorously. "Don't believe it. Our business was fashioned on a whim. That it survived this long surprises me. Face that first, the rest will be easy."

"What rest?" Kit questioned in bewilderment.

Antoine's smile was kind. "Why, a new career, of course."

Chapter 18

Royce and Renata Brant were troubled as they watched their houseguest. Kit had been visiting their ranch for more than a week, but he seldom spoke. And when he did it was always to remember a time when he and Royce had ridden together, a time before Renata was part of Royce's life.

When Kit wished them good night and retired to his room, Renata noticed her husband's troubled expression. "It cannot continue, Royce," she said softly. "I know that Kit Carson is your friend, and mine too, but he cannot remain here."

Royce agreed, but to make the admission seemed like stabbing his best friend in the back. "Kit needs time," he replied gruffly. "He's had a bad knock, needs a mite of comfortin'."

"Yes. And where is his wife, then?"

The Brants had heard of Kit's marriage nearly

two years before from the mountain men that occasionally called to renew their acquaintances. Every time they came, Renata held her breath until they rode off alone, without her husband. She knew the dangers of the life Royce had once led, of the seductive lure of the unknown. Once a man had tasted it, she knew the desire would never leave him entirely. What frightened her the most was that Royce could resist the others. He could wave to them as they turned toward the northern mountains and not be sorry he was staying behind. But things would be different when Kit Carson rode out.

Renata had heard the longing in Royce's voice when night after night the two men discussed their escapades with Fitzpatrick's brigade. She had seen Royce's eyes glow recalling a freedom that was now only a memory.

"Reckon Kit will tell us about his woman when he's of a mind," Royce said, lowering his voice.

Renata pouted. "You know what is wrong with him? He fears the consequence of children in his life. You have seen him watching our son Jaime so curiously." She brightened suddenly. "Look at you. You've grown thick in the middle with a wife to fill your belly."

Royce grinned at her barb. "I'm not the only one whose belly's been filled. When you reckon the babe is due? Now?"

Renata straightened her shoulders in indignation, but after a moment her mood gave way to laughter. "So, you mock my figure. I will show you. In a month *you* can carry my burden for a while and I will be slim again."

"Four years is a long time without the face of a

friend to look on," Royce realized, sobering. "Give Kit a few more days to talk to us. He listened to me bellyache often enough. Heard you out, too."

At Renata's flush of embarrassment Royce reached over and pulled her into his lap. "Don't be ashamed of your feelin's." He kissed the top of her head. "As a matter of fact, I kinda miss being alone with you, too. Not that we'd have much more to do than play a hand of euchre, seein' as how you're in the final stages of breedin'."

In spite of her halfhearted struggle, Royce caught Renata's chin and pressed his mouth firmly over hers in a kiss that at once deepened from playfulness into passion.

"Whoa there!" Royce protested as he reluctantly dragged his mouth from hers. "That ain't fair, ma'am. Especially when you're about to drag me up to the Jaramillos to dance with those pretty little daughters of his. Like as not, I'll make a jackass of myself now and carry one of them away with me right from the middle of the fandango," he teased.

"You do, señor, and Renata Brant will see to it that you never lay hands on another woman," she laughed.

Royce gave a yelp, and as Renata collapsed against him in laughter, he said, "I love you, woman." He hugged her tightly. "Now," he said, finally, "let's see if we can't get Kit to join us at the Jaramillos."

Against his better judgment Kit allowed himself to be persuaded. Because there would be a supper and dancing at the home of Don Francisco Jaramillo, he even wore a new calico shirt and bought a fancy pair of leather trousers. A tie was out, though, and he would allow Renata only to even the sun-bleached hair that brushed his shoulders.

"I'm an American, a frontiersman, and proud of it," Kit announced as she stood over him with scissors in hand.

"*Dios mio*! You look the barbarian!" Renata wailed in despair with a dark look at her husband. Then she leaned over Kit's shoulder and whispered confidentially, "This invitation, it means a great deal to Royce. He will not admit it, but to be a guest of Don Francisco Jaramillo is certain to bring him the prestige he must have to prosper in New Mexico. You will do nothing to spoil his chance."

Kit looked at the Mexican woman with mischief in his eye. "You mean I can't relieve myself in the courtyard fountain—or only when the señoritas ain't lookin'?"

Royce howled with laughter as Renata grimaced in fake desperation and left the room. "Now you done it. Renata won't speak to you for a full day, if you're lucky. When she aims her next words at you, you'll wish you were bein' dragged through cactus backwards instead."

Kit dusted the few hairs off his shoulders and turned to Royce. "She loves you. That's why she's troublin' herself over me."

"Who are you troublin' yourself over these days?" Royce returned, the humor gone from his voice.

Kit gave his friend a sour look. "You always was one to pick a wound. What're folks sayin' about me?"

Royce shrugged. "Word was you got yourself a wife a while back."

"That's true."

"Won't tell me about it, huh?" Royce returned Kit's steady look till he turned his face away.

"Ain't never told nobody the whole of it." Then in a level voice Kit began to explain all about Grass Singing and St. Nair, and how and why he had killed the Frenchman. At the end he added, "You was right all those years ago."

Royce frowned. "About what?"

Kit turned back to him. "You used to tell me how a man had to live with the consequences of what he'd done. Told me I'd made a bad enemy in St. Nair. Wish you'd made me listen. Would've killed the son of a bitch sooner, saved Grass Singing a pack of pain and heartsickness."

Royce sighed. "You couldn't know what was gonna happen. As for St. Nair, it was like trailin' a grizzly. You only knew what he'd done by the tracks he left. Let that go."

A faint smile hovered on Kit's lips. "It must be all the practice you're getting in with Jaime. You sound just like my pa. Well, here's your pound of flesh, I done fell in love. But it's such a change from the old days. You remember them days, don't you, Royce?"

"That why you came here instead of going home?"

"Don't push, Royce."

"Sorry," he answered, backing off. "Let's go. Renata's bound to be ready. We gave her an hour to pretty up."

Don Francisco Jaramillo did not live in the manner of the average Taos rancher. Kit discovered that as soon as the Brant buggy pulled through the great gates of the fortlike adobe walls surrounding the main house.

The inner courtyard was a tropical paradise of huge ferns and palms and riotous baskets of red and yellow blossoms. The trees that shaded the courtyard supported tiny lanterns. Music drifted through the thresholds of the open doorways.

Kit glimpsed satin and silk and taffeta skirts as the female company floated past on the arms of their partners. "Foofaraw," he muttered to Royce.

Once inside, Kit was amused by the stares directed his way. His was the only leather and calico outfit in the entire place. The most popular attire for the men consisted of black pants striped with satin down the outside of each leg, and also white, ruffled shirts and short-waisted jackets trimmed in braid. Aristocrats, nearly every one of them. But with emotions stirred by the music and beauty of the night, they accepted the stranger into their midst.

Within minutes Kit found himself surrounded by a half dozen anxious caballeros ready to pick his brains over the Comanche situation.

"Looks to me you'd fit right in, you had a mind to settle in Taos," Royce commented when finally he had extracted his friend from the people pressing in on him.

"Might settle in Taos one day, maybe," Kit conceded.

Royce raised an eyebrow. "That what you think? Me and a few of the other ranchers are startin' to domesticate the buffalo. Take in a few calves every season and mix them with our regular stock. They're hardier, got double the strength of the ox, and fatten up quicker on the prairie than our cows. Might set a few to the plow next year, just to see how it goes."

Kit stayed longer than he had meant to, mostly

because he did not have a way back to the Brant ranch. But quickly he retired to a corner, so as not to be drawn into the dancing. The same Taos orchestra that played for weddings and funerals and any other occasion they were invited to had not changed a number since his last visit.

"Señor Carson?"

Kit was leaning against the wall with his eyes closed when he heard his name whispered in a soft feminine voice. He put up a hand and pushed his hat back, almost expecting to see Señora Veldez, her ample physique swathed in black silk, asking him for the third time to join the others to dance. The vision that greeted him instead brought him straight up to his full five and half feet.

The girl could not have been more than fifteen, but her beauty was dark and provocative. The aquiline nose was counterbalanced by full lips set in a permanent pout. Black curls cascaded down and over slender shoulders that were encased in golden silk.

Only when the girl inclined her head slightly did Kit realize that she was a full inch taller than he. "Señor Carson, do not think me too forward," she said huskily, "but I could not forgo the opportunity to meet the Americano of whom my people speak so highly." She blushed a becoming shade of red. "You see, I know no Americanos, except the Brants."

For the first time, Kit was grateful for his reputation. It had brought him a vision of beauty. "Señorita," he replied in fluent Spanish, "it is my pleasure."

"The señor would care to dance?" the girl ventured boldly in English.

Kit did not remember what he had replied or if he

had said anything at all. But suddenly he simply walked away from the girl.

"Royce, I got to talk to you," Kit said as he rushed up to his old friend.

"Somethin' wrong?"

Kit shook his head sadly. "It's me, Royce. Guess I've had my head in the clouds, or out on the prairie, you might say. I've been thinkin' pretty hard these past few months. And seein' that señorita back there just brought me back to the real world."

"What are you talkin' about, Kit?" Royce queried, a look of confusion flooding his face.

"Trapper days!" he exclaimed. "Them bygone days are so much a part of me, I plumb can't forget 'em. That señorita looks just like Grass Singing, and seein' her made me realize how important the woman I married is to me."

Royce broke out in a huge grin. "Kit," he laughed, "I knew you'd say that someday. It was just a matter of time."

"Just a matter of time," Kit repeated, beaming. "I guess our trapper days together are over. But we'll stay friends, won't we, Royce? Well, I got to be gettin' back to the fort—and my woman."

"Guess you better," Royce returned. "Good-bye, Kit."

"Good-bye, Royce."

Royce smiled as he watched the quickly-retreating figure of Kit Carson. For once, he was not sorry to see the trapper king depart hastily.

It took almost a week of hard, snow-laden mountain riding before Kit reached the plains of the Arkansas River. His journey had been made more difficult because he had left Taos with few supplies. Even his traps were still at Royce's.

Leaving town, he had followed a winding northern trail that led him into the Sangre de Cristo Mountains. There, it had taken all his concentration and skill just to stay alive. But soon he reached the relative safety of the plains.

Kit sank into deep thought as he rode along. He had been running when he left Bent's Fort months ago. He had allowed Grass Singing to pack him off as if he were a boy on his first day of school. And he had gone. He had flown from his wife as fast as his horse could carry him. It was freedom he'd been grabbing for. Not the freedom of the wilderness. Grass Singing had not cost him that. What he had lost was the freedom to forget about the future, to worry only about himself. He had become a man concerned every hour of every day about the welfare of someone who was more precious to him than himself. Before, he had never wanted that kind of responsibility. The same way he hadn't wanted Royce's friendship or Amos Tuttle's adoration.

What drew men to other men? he wondered. What made them see in one man something they thought was lacking in themselves and could be borrowed from him? Royce and Grass Singing had made him slow down long enough to see them and grow to need them.

Perhaps this was what had saved him after all, this aching need he felt when he thought of Grass Singing. It was not just the ache of a man for a woman. That, too, but more. There was the fear that one day he would lose her.

That concern followed Kit up the Purgatory River to the banks of the Arkansas. If Grass Singing was still waiting for him, he told himself, he would make it up to her for running away, for letting the fear that he might lose her keep him out of her loving arms.

"You could've sent a man after me!" Kit complained as he paced the floor of William Bent's saloon.

William sat in his favorite chair stroking his beard. "Would you have come back, son?"

Kit spun about as another low-pitched groan sounded through the door of the Bents' bedroom. "She gonna die?" he whispered.

William chuckled. "A fine thing. The father rides all over the country for months during his wife's breeding, and now he's worried about how she's doing." The joke fell flat as William saw the blood drain from Kit's face. "Haven't you ever been at a birthing before?"

"No."

William swore. "Sit down, son," he said, more gently. "You're shredding my new carpets. Have another glass of brandy. Your woman's doing just fine. She's got Owl Woman and her mother and my new cook Charlotte. Every one of them has birthed at least two children. They know their business."

Small comfort, Kit had thought, seeing how small Grass Singing looked the first time he saw her. She was thinner than when he'd left her, with a belly so big he hardly recognized her. He had thanked Bent at least a dozen times since his arrival the day before for taking Grass Singing into his home, but since he rode in he hadn't had much time alone with her.

She had begun labor that first day, right in the courtyard of the fort. Her hair was hanging in two long plaits, one on either side of her face, and a clean elk-skin dress covered her from neck to mid-calf. Filled with adoration by her loveliness, Kit wondered why he had ever left this woman for so long.

Grass Singing had run to him, throwing her arms wide in greeting, noting his own thinness, chiding him gently for his lack of attention to himself. Kit knew he would have sobbed with joy to see her had her first pain of labor not interrupted. He had lifted her into his arms and carried her back to Bent's home.

It had been nearly twelve hours since that moment. Though the pains had steadily worsened, Grass Singing seldom cried out.

"C'mon, fella," William said buoyantly, trying to get Kit's mind off what was happening behind the door. "Sit down. Ease up. Have you heard the news about the price of beaver?"

"Yeah. Hell's full of silk hats, I hear," Kit kidded glumly. "You want to hire me to hunt silkworms?"

"Now that you mention it, I could use a good man, a trader. The price of pelts is low, but trading buffalo robes is good business. Indians are trickier than ever. What with the Blackfeet dying like flies up north on account of smallpox, most of our tribes will be staying south this year. A canny trader could make good money among them. They like you. You interested?"

A deep groan from the next room brought both men to their feet. "Wait up, son," William cautioned as Kit went for the door. "You don't want to do anything wrong."

Kit turned back to the man. "If she dies, I'll . . .

I'll . . . Should have told me, sent word, Bent." The agony that was written on Kit's features plainly answered William's question. The boy cared for his little squaw. He would not leave her again.

The door opened as the two men stood facing one another and Owl Woman entered the room.

"Grass Singing . . . ?" Kit nearly choked on his words. "She's . . . ?"

"Grass Singing's fine."

"I have to see for myself," Kit announced, pushing past Owl Woman into the bedroom. For a moment Kit's heart stopped, seeing his wife—so small and pale—in the Bent's four-poster bed. Then her lids fluttered and he covered the distance between them in two strides.

Grass Singing raised a hand and placed it on her husband's head; he had gently bowed over her. "I am sorry, my husband," she said weakly.

Kit's head snapped up. "Sorry? Why?"

"I am not very brave. The Great Spirit is not pleased with me. Our first child is a girl."

"First? Girl?" Kit looked at her with such a bewildered expression that she smiled questioningly.

"Aren't you interested in the looks of your firstborn?" William called from the doorway.

Briefly, Kit touched Grass Singing's damp face, then he hurried back into the parlor to where Owl Woman was standing. The bundle of blankets she was holding moved.

"Well? Look!" William urged, pushing Kit a little closer when he hesitated. Before Kit knew it, he was peering down at a tiny wrinkled face the color of copper. Tufts of red-gold hairs poked from the tiny head, and two miniature fists were balled and waving.

Kit swallowed uneasily. "She ain't much to look at," he said slowly. "I mean, is they all that ugly?"

William failed to hold back a roar of laughter.

The summer months were filled with joy for Kit and his family. He was riding scout for Bent's caravans along the Arkansas and occasionally as far east as the Cimarron cutoff. The nights Kit spent away from his wife and child were measured carefully, never exceeding a week unless absolute necessity demanded it.

Kit felt the richness of his life intensely. He had a job that earned him more than he had ever made before—even at the peak of his trapping career. He had a permanent home—well, as permanent as he could stand. The white tepee still stood at the edge of the Arapaho village, a beacon to light his way home. And, of course, there was little Adeline.

She grew lovelier each day, a fact that made her father thrust out his chest with pride when Grass Singing strapped her to her back in deerskin wrappings. The copper cheeks filled in and her hair grew into ringlets that bobbled when she laughed. She was a beauty.

But too often, when Kit came home early to surprise Grass Singing, he found her seated against her willow backrest, her head down and her eyes closed. Though fear gripped him every time, Owl Woman reassured him that it took time for a woman to recover from birthing a child. Kit watched over Grass Singing anyway, helping out whenever he could.

"The women of my village say you spoil me," she

scolded one morning when Kit insisted on fetching water from the river.

Kit winked. "Don't care what they say. Just jealous, that's what they are. None of them have someone like me to keep them from complainin'."

Grass Singing laughed easily. Only the night before, they had resumed their relationship as man and wife. And it had been good, a coming home for him and a renewal of devotion and passion for both of them.

"What will Adeline think?" Grass Singing screwed up her face as she spoke the name her husband had chosen. Although she knew it was important to Kit since it was the name of a favorite relative, she persisted in calling the baby Sage Blossom when he was not around. "What will your daughter think if she sees her father doing woman's work?"

"Adeline will think her mother is one very cunning woman," Kit said, chuckling, and shot out of the tepee before Grass Singing could say another word.

There was a slight chill in the morning air, and an intermittant whip of cold as the first drafts blew in from the north. Trapping season. But the thought did not stir Kit as it once had. As he walked toward the riverbank he stopped to watch two ground squirrels engaged in a lively discussion of the merits of a nut they had found. He would remember to bring Adeline this way next spring. She would be toddling then.

As Kit dipped his pails into the clear and smooth-flowing river, he pondered how to answer William Bent's request that he ride as caravan leader for his supply train. It would mean going back to Independence in a week's time. And that would mean a long separation. On the other side of it, the job meant good money and time on the trail.

Kit stood up, his thoughts once again on the feel of Grass Singing in his arms. Her waist was slender again, so narrow he could span it with his hands. Her lovely breasts were fuller and firmer, filled with life-giving nourishment for their child. He grinned cockily. There was no wondering why Adeline was so eager to be placed there.

No, Kit decided. He would not travel far this year. Maybe next season when Grass Singing and the child were stronger. Bent would understand.

Kit knew something was wrong even before he threw back the tent flap. It was the lack of any sound that had sent him flying across the last few yards to his lodge. Inside, Grass Singing lay face down in the dirt.

In panic, Kit bent over her. His eyes searched every part of her body for sign of a wound. There was nothing to indicate an attack or an accident, but Grass Singing was damp with perspiration. Her pulse was rapid, too, like a bird's.

Scooping Grass Singing up carefully, Kit eased her down to the robe-covered mats they slept on. Adeline was fine—propped up in her cradle board and happily eating a piece of quail meat.

Kit dipped a handful of water from the pail to wet Grass Singing's cheeks.

"Please. What's wrong? Talk to me!" he urged frantically.

Grass Singing opened her eyes. "I am sorry, my husband," she answered, squinting at the light. "Dizzy."

"Then don't strain yourself," Kit ordered gently. He unlaced Grass Singing's leggings and pulled off her moccasins. She was burning to his touch.

"Don't worry," he repeated several times to ease his concern as well as hers. "I'm gonna go get us a little help in a minute. You lie still. Don't move, gonna take Adeline with me. Owl Woman will feed her—she's got a baby still at the breast."

Oh God, Kit thought as he covered his wife and ran a hand over her face to brush away the stray hairs that had been dampened there. Don't let it be small-pox!

Hours later he learned that it was not. It was a fever—a bad one.

William Bent came with Owl Woman and they helped out, taking turns bathing Grass Singing's flushed skin and feeding her small sips of broth and water. But the fever did not abate, and her pulse rate did not slow.

Kit's gaze was riveted on his wife for hours at a time. The first day passed. And then the second and third. Still, Grass Singing did not improve.

"Her heart can't take much more of this high fever," William told his wife on the fourth evening when Kit went to fetch the medicine man from the Arapaho village. He shook his head, tears starting. "Don't know what it's going to do to Kit if his woman dies."

Owl Woman said nothing. She had seen the ghost spirits hovering above the Carson lodge before she had entered that day. Grass Singing would not live till morning.

When Kit came back, he brought Turtle Eye and Grass Singing's mother and sisters. A long vigil began that lasted far into the night. The sound of incantations and the odor of burning herbs filled the tepee. Tom-toms beat in slow steady rhythms to calm the gallop of the sick girl's pulse.

An hour before daybreak, Grass Singing's eyes opened and Kit forced his way past the medicine man to reach her. His hand trembled as he took hers, feeling every bone in her wrist. Yet her grasp strengthened when she recognized his face inches above her own.

"My husband?" Grass Singing's voice was faint.

"Oh God!" Kit's voice cracked as he bent over and pulled Grass Singing against him. "You ain't gonna leave me, not like I done you. Promise me. I know I done you wrong. Only don't punish me this way!" Now they watched as Kit Carson, brave trader and cunning fighter, wept and rocked his dead wife in his arms.

The winter winds whipped the Arkansas River Valley, tearing at the buffalo robes that wrapped the bundle carried on the travois. The platform had been prepared earlier, at first light, after a fearful hour when the prairie had been rent by wailings of grief. The wails had been picked up and added to until the whole night screamed with the sounds of mourning.

In the Arapaho village near the fort, there was much tearing of clothing and hair. Anguished relatives slashed their arms and chests.

The mourners kept a respectful distance from the lone, sandy-haired white man who came and stood apart from them as his wife's body was laid on the fun-deral pyre. He watched silently as her wedding tepee and all her possessions were laid in neat piles beneath the platform and then set aflame. Not a muscle moved in his face as the fire, fed by wood and wind, climbed rapidly to embrace the body. And when it was done, when there were only ashes, he turned away without a sound.

William Bent stood nearby as Kit packed his belongings and then mounted his horse. There were no words of comfort he could say. Owl Woman would watch and nourish his child till he returned. "Where are you going, son?" he asked when his friend was ready.

Kit looked down at Bent. "Lighting out for the territory. Never could abide civilization!"

Chapter 19

He spent weeks of solitude on the prairie, but soon grew tired of this and decided to return to the Brant ranch in Taos. He could no longer stand the memory of his beautiful wife, which kept coming back to haunt him again and again. He needed support from a friend, and Royce was the best one he had.

And so he stayed there and learned the ranching business. With Royce's support, he even learned to like it.

Then one day, not too long after he'd joined the Royces, he decided to ride back to Bent's Fort. There was something he wanted—and had—to do.

It did not take long. He rode out of the fort as quickly as he had ridden in. Only this time, he carried his daughter, Adeline, in his arms.

When he returned to the ranch, Royce and Renata openly accepted his child into their home to live with them and their growing family. The Royces now had another child of their own in addition to Jaime. Her name was Juanita.

A year later, during a festive evening at the house of Royce's friends, the Jaramillos, Kit finally wrenched himself from past memories and allowed himself to have a good time. He was sipping tequila and telling Royce for the hundredth time about the day he had been forced up a tree by two grizzlies when he saw her—the striking señorita he had met so long ago who had so closely resembled Grass Singing.

When their eyes met, she immediately approached him.

"Señor Carson?"

Kit smiled. "You have a good memory, señorita. But the last time we met, I was a mite rude. Walked off before we'd been properly introduced."

"I am Josepha Jaramillo, daughter of Don Francisco Jaramillo." She blushed. "I was named after an uncle."

As Kit regarded her appraisingly, her eyes lit up. He took her hand and gently kissed it.

"You're very beautiful," he said. "What's more, you remind me very much of someone I used to care for a great deal." Now he couldn't help but think of his old love.

"You are too kind," she replied. "It is not often a woman receives a compliment like that."

"I wouldn't have said it if I didn't mean it."

Josepha Jaramillo surveyed the brightly-costumed crowd. The hanging lanterns lit up the courtyard where many of the townsfolk danced to the lively orchestra.

"Señor Carson, the orchestra is very good," she hinted.

"Sure is," Kit agreed. His brow wrinkled in thought for a moment, and then he broke into a grin. "Reckon you'd care to dance, Señorita Jaramillo?"

"I would like that very much, Señor Carson," she answered, taking his arm.

Book #2 in the
WOMEN AT WAR series
by Rebecca Drury

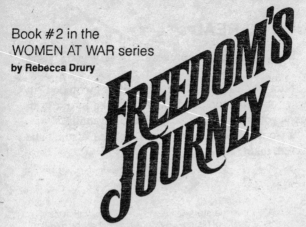

Freedom's Journey is the extraordinary story of two remarkable women and the vital role each played in the American Revolution. Carol Flemming, a beautiful and headstrong young woman from Massachusetts, struggles and fights, suffers and rejoices alongside one of America's greatest heroes: John Glover. From Bunker Hill to Long Island, from the icy waters of the Delaware to the siege of Yorktown, these unlikely patriots and lovers help forge a nation.

And Amy Schuyler, heroine of *Mourning & Triumph*, comes of age in *Freedom's Journey.* Married to a West-Indian-born innkeeper and tavern owner, the famous "Black Sam" Fraunces, she is among the most important spies of the American Revolution. Her charm, skill and courage save an army and bring a nation into being.

━━━━━━━━━━━━━━━━━━━━━━━━━━━━━━━━━━━━

First in the Powerful New Series

A Candle in the Wind

by Gene Lancour

A Candle in the Wind is the epic story of a rebellious and passionate American family. Harold Carlisle, a nautical design genius, is the founder of this tempestuous family whose fortune rides the seas from China to Africa. It follows his struggles in a growing nation and traces the disintegration of his family under the pressures of greed and politics. The marriage of a black woman to a proper New England Carlisle, the ruthlessness of the Boston underworld, a captain's secret Chinese wife and the revenge of a desperate woman are all woven into this stirring historical saga of the high seas.

Second in THE CARLISLE SAGA

by Gene Lancour

Jonathan Carlisle returns from his tormented, secret life in Macao to the family shipyard in Nequonset only to discover that bribery and blackmail have corrupted the family empire. His revelations spark an ensuing battle between him and his beautiful, spirited sister, Ellen. In a desperate attempt to reclaim his fortune, and save his son, Jonathan fights against murderers and arsonists. In victory, he realizes that his own sister is a traitor to the family cause. And Ellen Carlisle learns the bitter cost of that betrayal.